Praise for *Julius and the Watchmaker*

'An exciting romp through time, full of wonderful characters and sinister possibilities.' Lian Tanner

'Alternate worlds, time travel, mechanical horror, the demi monde of Victorian England and evil trickery all come together to make this novel a compelling read...a winner for those who love good fantasy.' *Reading Time*

'The ideas about time and time travel are intricate…they have been created, sorted and ingeniously assembled…Teen readers will also particularly enjoy the fight scenes, sly ironic humour and steampunked flights of fantasy.' *Australian*

'The alternate parallels into which Julius is hurled are rich and scary and strange…A compelling read…a classic in the making for ages twelve and up.' *Readings*

'A thoroughly absorbing read for twelve-year-olds, who can engage as much or as little as they like with the historical detail and lessons in time, while getting swept along in the adventures and fates of Julius, our likeable hero, and his slowly evolving band of friends.' *Big Issue*

THE WATCHMAKER NOVELS

Book 1 *Julius and the Watchmaker*
Book 2 *Julius and the Soulcatcher*

Tim Hehir lives in Melbourne and writes
short stories and plays. *Julius and the Soulcatcher*
is his second novel.

Julius & the soulcatcher

Tim Hehir

t

Text Publishing
Melbourne Australia

The Text Publishing Company
Swann House
22 William Street
Melbourne Victoria 3000
Australia
textpublishing.com.au

First published by The Text Publishing Company, 2016

Cover & papercut art by W.H. Chong
Page design by Imogen Stubbs & W.H. Chong
Typeset by J & M Typesetting

Printed in Australia by Griffin Press, an accredited ISO/NZS 14001:2004 Environmental Management System printer.

National Library of Australia Cataloguing-in-Publication entry

Author: Hehir, Tim.

Title: Julius and the soulcatcher / by Tim Hehir.

ISBN: 9781925240177 (paperback)

ISBN: 9781925095975 (ebook)

Target Audience: For young adults.

Subjects: Time travel—Fiction.

Dewey Number: A823.4

For Joanna
and Joey

CHAPTER 1

LONDON

Thursday 18th January 1838

5:56 PM

Julius Higgins heard the rattle and creak of a hansom cab. But there was nothing to see, only darkness.

'What is it?' said Crimper McCready.

The clatter of horses hooves grew louder.

Julius hunched his shoulders against the bone-shattering cold as he strained to see down the alleyway.

There's nothing there, Higgins.

The sound grew to a torrent.

'Move, move,' he called out to Crimper. 'Run, damn you.'

Julius pushed Crimper out of the alleyway into Lawrence Lane and jumped aside. The deafening rumble cascaded over him like a storm wave.

The hansom cab shot past them, its wheels skidding as it lurched hard to the right. The cabbie, high on his perch at the back, flicked his whip.

'Oi, mate,' called out Crimper. 'Light your lamp so folk can see you. You're a bleeding menace. I'll have the law on you.'

The cabbie pulled back on the reins and the cab halted. He twisted around to look at the two boys. His spine was bent in a half moon and his head and chin were thrust forward from his domed shoulders. He put Julius in mind of a heron wearing a billycock hat.

Uh-oh, thought Julius.

He heard a whimper from low in Crimper McCready's throat.

Julius swallowed.

Make a run for it, Higgins.

'Sorry,' said Crimper. The sound was too weak to make it far from his face.

The cabbie's eyes were unreadable in the shadow of his hat's rim as he looked down on them from his perch. The breath from his nose misted with each exhalation.

'What is it? Do you see her?' called out a voice from inside the cab. 'Do you? Do you?'

'No, sir,' said the cabbie. He snapped the whip. The horse whinnied and the cab clattered down the street and out of sight.

Julius felt as if his body was turning to liquid and

forming a puddle where he stood.

'Good job he took off,' said Crimper. 'Else I'd have shown him.'

'Yes,' said Julius. 'Lucky for him.'

After a few hurried twists and turns through the London streets Julius and Crimper arrived at the top of Ironmonger Lane.

Nearly home, Higgins. A hot meal and a warm fire await.

Lamps burned over doorways along each side of the narrow street. They didn't give much light, but they showed the way. A few more paces and Julius saw the sign for his grandfather's bookshop. *Higgins' Booksellers: Rare and Difficult to Find Books a Specialty.*

At the window, Julius stopped and looked inside. A smartly dressed girl reached across the counter accepting a coin from his grandfather. She curtsied a little stiffly, as if she were still learning how to do it. Then she dropped the coin into her purse, pulled a veil over the front of her bonnet and turned towards the door.

Julius remained at the window, watching.

The shop bell tinkled as the girl stepped out onto the footpath. She stopped, startled to see the two boys. The veil over her face moved like a ripple on water as she breathed.

Julius estimated her to be twelve or thirteen from her height, and well-to-do from her polished ankle boots and fur-lined cape. He could not see her eyes but he knew she was staring at him.

Julius marked the seconds by his heartbeats, as regular as the ticking of a clock.

He knew who she was.

She had changed in every way since the last time he had seen her, but it was still her. She was taller now, certainly better dressed, and she carried herself, if not like a lady, at least like a well-trained lady's maid.

Despite the cold, Julius felt a warmth within. He opened his mouth to say her name, but she turned and ran.

'Who was that?' asked Crimper.

'Someone I used to know,' said Julius.

But she didn't want to know you, Higgins.

'Who? Higgins, I'm talking to you.'

'It doesn't matter.'

'Higgins?' said Crimper.

'Hmm…what?' said Julius.

'The book?'

'Book?'

'Latin, remember?'

Julius felt the warmth drain away.

They went into the shop and stood near the crackling fire unwinding their scarves. Mr Higgins looked up from the book he was reading as the two boys unbuttoned their coats.

'What is the meaning of this, young Caesar?' said Mr Higgins.

'Of what, Grandfather?' replied Julius.

'The lateness of the hour. Where have you been?'

'At the extra history class, Grandfather. I told you about it.'

'Ah, yes, I recall. And is Master McCready a history scholar, too?' said Mr Higgins, studying the large, pudding-faced boy for any sign of a budding historian.

'Me? No fear, Mr Higgins, I'm here to borrow a Latin grammar book,' said Crimper.

'Borrow? *Borrow?* Books are made to be bought and sold, my boy, not *borrowed*,' said Mr Higgins. 'Where is the profit in that? Whatever next? Will you be *borrowing* a cup of tea, perchance? Would you like to *borrow* some candlelight?'

'Er…'

'Take no notice, Crimper,' said Julius. 'Grandfather's only joking.' He tossed the book to Crimper, who mumbled a thanks and hurried out the door.

'Grandfather?' said Julius.

'Yes, young Caesar?'

'The girl who was here just now?'

'Which girl?'

One of the many things that Julius found irritating about his grandfather was his strategic coyness.

'The one with the veil.'

'Veil? Oh, that one. A very well-spoken child, very

polite. Very pretty too. I bought this odd fish from her,' said Mr Higgins.

He lifted a book from the counter. The cover was worn. Its title looked like it had been cut into the leather with a sharp knife. Julius held it up to the candle to make out the letters. *A Diary of My Voyage on H.M.S. Beagle—C. R. Darwin.*

'Did she leave her name or…or her address, Grandfather?'

'No, neither. Why do you ask?'

'Oh, no reason. Is it interesting?' said Julius, leafing through the pages.

'*Odd* is the word I would use. I thought one of my more eccentric collectors might be interested; it contains some exquisite paintings of orchids. I might get two pounds for it from an orchid maniac.'

'Did the girl say where she got it?'

'She said she chanced upon it lying in a gutter and, as she loved books above all things, she hoped I might find a home for it with a book-lover who would appreciate its unique qualities,' said Mr Higgins.

Ha-ha. It's her, Higgins. It's definitely her. She nicked it.

'And you believed her?' Julius said, with a smile he couldn't contain.

'Of course not. Do I resemble a new-born infant? It is obviously stolen. It will be an "under-the-counter" sale, you can be sure of that.'

Julius stopped at one of the pages. It was a

watercolour painting of a tortoise—but not any ordinary tortoise. Comparing its size to the sailor standing beside it, Julius reckoned the creature to be as large as a tin bath.

'This Darwin fellow is obviously a fantasist,' said Mr Higgins. 'But a talented painter, nonetheless.'

'Hmm,' said Julius. He continued turning the pages. On one was a line of finely painted birds in profile, each with a slightly different beak. 'He says "The Islands of Galapagos are like a continent in miniature, with their own unique variety of creatures."'

Julius turned more pages. 'And he says here, "The variation occurring among the fauna of these islands is the clearest I have seen on my voyage thus far. Each new observation strengthens my theory. But is the world ready to hear that Nature selects, sculpts and forms her own garden?"'

'A lunatic, no doubt,' said Mr Higgins.

'What's this?' Julius stopped at a portrait of a man caught in the zenith of a scream of unimaginable agony.

'Good Heavens,' said Mr Higgins. 'I didn't notice that one.'

Plants grew from the man's mouth and nostrils and the corners of his eyes. Flame-red flowers at the ends of the stems surrounded the man's head. On the opposite page C. R. Darwin had written:

June 13th 1832. Brazil.
Village of the Soulcatchers.

Mr Skinner and I navigated up thinner and thinner tributaries for eight days until we came to the Village of the Soulcatchers. We camped on the far bank for safety and paddled to the jetty to see if the famed Reverend Merrisham would greet us and, if so, how we would be received. Having heard such strange stories of this place of the Damned I am not ashamed to say that I experienced some trepidation.

Hearing that there is a remote village on an island in the river where the souls of its people have been stolen by a race of orchids is one thing; to meet the Englishman who has lived as a missionary among them is another. How would he have adapted to this curious environment? What of the state of his soul?

We waited for almost an hour, all the while aware that we were being watched by many eyes, until a man came along the riverbank. By his black coat and breeches and white stockings we knew him to the missionary we were seeking. When Merrisham lifted his hat to greet us and the sun shone on his cheeks, Mr Skinner gripped my shoulder and cried out.

'God help us,' he said. 'It is true.'

The horror I felt when I looked at the missionary's face will stay with me until I die.

The door burst open. Crimper McCready ran in. His gaping mouth reminded Julius of the picture—that same screaming rictus of terror.

'What the—' said Mr Higgins.

'The girl's been took,' said Crimper.

'Emily?' said Julius.

'Who?' said his grandfather.

'Down the road. It was that hansom cab without the lamp. There was two bruisers and a little geezer. They threw her in the cab. She was fighting like a good 'un but—'

Julius clutched Crimper's arm. 'Where did they go?'

'I don't know. I ran here. We should send for a constable. It's kidnappers or—' Crimper stopped. He looked through the window. 'Did you hear that?'

'What?'

It was the same galloping clatter they had heard in the alleyway.

'That,' said Crimper.

Julius felt his chest tighten as if gripped by an icy claw.

They've got Emily.

'Quick, bolt the door,' said Mr Higgins. He slipped the diary under the sales ledger.

CHAPTER 2

Thursday 18th January 1838

6:14 PM

Crimper was only two steps from the door, but he was rooted to the spot in terror.

'Here it comes,' he said.

The black horse pulled up outside the shop window. The cabbie was too high in his seat to be seen, but the reins tightened on the horse's neck. It snorted once, blowing out a cloud of steam. The cab lamp was still unlit, but the lamp above the shop doorway showed the outline of the cab and the gossamer mist of sweat rising from the horse's back.

Julius lunged for the door, but Crimper retreated at the same moment, knocking him away. A man climbed out of the front of the cab with the girl slung over his shoulder. The cabbie climbed down too.

Julius pushed Crimper aside and rushed forward. He clasped the door knob.

'Bolt the door,' shouted his grandfather.

Julius hesitated. Both men looked at them through the display window. The cabbie was as thin as a workhouse dog, and a full head, chest and shoulders taller than the other man. The girl squirmed and fought in the shorter man's grasp.

'Bolt the door, damn you,' said his grandfather again.

You can't lock her out, Higgins. You can't.

In two steps the cabbie was at the door. He jiggled the handle. Julius grasped the other side, holding it fast. The cabbie's eyes looked at him through the letter H of *Higgins' Booksellers* in the frosted glass.

'Bolt the blasted door,' ordered his grandfather.

What would Mr Flynn do, Higgins? he asked himself.

Julius let go of the door knob and stepped back.

The shop bell rang as the cabbie swung the door open.

'Very wise, young man,' he said. His voice had a rasping yet oddly gentle quality to it. The cabbie remained outside on the step, his eyes flicking left and right as if in search of danger, or prey. His face was so long and thin it looked like a stalactite hanging from his billycock hat. His cheekbones were so pronounced that his pock-marked skin strained to contain them.

The other man—as squat and solid as a

bulldog—entered the shop carrying the girl over his shoulder. His faded brown, triple-caped overcoat reached almost to the ground, giving the impression that he floated, rather than walked across the floor.

He dropped the girl. She landed with a thud and a stifled yelp.

'Got a delivery for you,' he said, through a tilted slit of a mouth. He sniffed home a stream of silvery snot into his misshapen nose.

A third man barged into the shop bearing the eager expression of a spoilt child let loose in a sweet shop. He was small, shorter than Julius, and the strangest-looking person Julius had ever seen.

'What a lovely evening it is,' said the man, in a singsong voice.

That's the voice from the cab, Higgins.

The little man's smile revealed two rows of disconcertingly small teeth. They reminded Julius of old-fashioned, porcelain dentures.

Mr Higgins opened his mouth to speak but then changed his mind.

The man raised his purple, wide-brimmed hat to reveal wiry, red hair parted along the middle. His skin as dry as ancient parchment and in his small hands he held a plant pot.

Julius did not know if it was his imagination or the blood going cold in his veins, but he felt the temperature in the bookshop drop.

Crimper's flesh wobbled as he stepped back and bumped into the display table. He caught the candle before it fell, but several books spilled onto the floor.

Mr Higgins used the distraction to regain his composure and prepare himself for business.

'Have I come to the right place? Have I? Have I?' said the short red-headed man. He unbuttoned his purple frock coat to reveal a yellow-and-purple-striped waistcoat.

He's not dressed for the cold, Higgins.

'Well, I'm not sure, sir. What was it you required?' asked Mr Higgins.

Julius clenched his fists to stop them trembling.

'Require? Can you guess?' said the man. 'Can you? Can you?'

The innocently expectant tone of his enquiry froze Julius's blood solid—he could almost feel his veins cracking and splintering.

'Er?' said Mr Higgins.

'A diary, bound in leather, written by my good friend, Mr Darwin.'

'Hmm, let me think,' said Mr Higgins, as his eyes ran along the shelves.

'Shall I give you a hint?' said the man. 'Shall I? Shall I? This little thief told me she sold it to you not five minutes ago.' The man stopped smiling. 'And I want it back.'

'Oh, I see. Well, if it is stolen property perhaps

we ought to alert the constabulary,' said Mr Higgins, rather feebly.

'Or,' said the man, 'my friend here could chop her hand off.'

The stocky man pulled a meat cleaver from inside his coat. The veiled girl flinched and fought to get free.

'All right, all right, take the book,' said Julius. He snatched it from under the sales ledger.

The man's pale skin creaked like shoe leather as he stretched out a smile. His blue eyes seemed to glow faintly around the black dots of his pupils.

Julius's hand trembled as he held out the book.

'Thank you, so much, young sir,' said the man. His fingers wrapped themselves around the diary.

The stocky man tucked the meat cleaver away and slunk out of the shop with a grunt of disappointment.

'Such a pleasure to meet you,' said the small man. 'I do so enjoy acquiring new friends. I do, I do.'

He placed the flowerpot on the counter. 'Do accept this gift? I grew it myself,' he said. 'It is a little chilled at present but water and warmth is all it needs, and a little affection. Who knows? One day, it may surprise you.'

The little man left. The cabbie closed the door, and the cab groaned as he climbed up to his seat. He snapped the whip and the horse moved slowly past the window and out of sight.

Crimper's whole body sagged. Mr Higgins patted his chest gently to calm his heart.

'Are you all right?' said Julius to the veiled girl on the floor. She was breathing deeply like a disgruntled tomcat.

'I'm ace,' she said. 'Takes more than a mob of tupenny-'apenny villains to put the wind up me.'

Oh, yes, it's definitely her, Higgins.

'I beg your pardon, miss,' said Mr Higgins.

'You wot?' said the girl.

'You seem to have changed your accent. The shock has made you speak like a guttersnipe.'

'I ain't shocked. Talking posh for too long makes me jaw ache, don't it,' said the girl.

She stood up and lifted the veil from her face.

'Hello, Emily,' said Julius.

She was indeed very pretty, just as his grandfather had said. But Julius already knew that. He also knew that in a few years she would be the prettiest young lady in the whole of London. He had travelled through time and seen it for himself.

'Er…'ello, 'iggins,' said Emily, uneasily. 'How's fings?'

'Fine,' said Julius.

'Do you know this person, young Caesar?' asked Mr Higgins.

'Yes, Grandfather. We met last year when I was delivering books to Jack Springheel.'

Julius winced at the memory of Emily and her gang of street urchins surrounding him with coshes raised and negotiating a payment *not* to do him down. Luckily, Professor Fox had leapt up through the cobblestones to rescue him.

Mr Higgins knew nothing of this. Julius doubted he would believe it anyway.

'Well, little miss, I'll have my sovereign back, thank you,' said Mr Higgins.

'Wot? You bought it fair and square, Mr 'iggins. It ain't my fault wot 'appens to it after that.'

'I bought that diary in good faith, young lady. If I had known it was stolen I would have called for a constable and had you arrested,' said Mr Higgins, with the gravity of a headmaster at a school for feral children.

To Julius's surprise, Emily's lower lip jutted out in a pout and she blushed with contrition.

'Come on, now. Hand it over,' said Mr Higgins.

Emily rummaged through her purse and slapped the coin on the counter. 'Can I 'ave the flower, then?' she said.

'Why?'

'I want to see what it does. The little geeza said it might surprise you. I like surprises.'

Julius looked at the flower for the first time. It was red with four petals: one growing upwards and curving over the others like a protective hood, then two very long and thin petals—one on each side, like arms reaching out around the fourth petal, which resembled a tongue sticking out. The petals were withered along the edges and a number of tendrils hung from the base of the flower and lay on the soil like badly coiled ropes.

'I think he was joking,' said Julius. He could not decide if it was the most beautiful or the most ugly flower he had ever seen. Emily clearly liked it though.

Crimper McCready leaned over Julius and Emily to get a better look.

Mr Higgins polished his spectacles in preparation for a thorough examination. 'Hmm, it's an orchid, if I am not mistaken,' he said.

'A what?' said Crimper.

'An orchid, Master McCready. The strangest of flowers. Their mysterious ways baffle the finest minds in botany. The Greeks thought they were the spawn of animals. Surely you have noticed the orchid mania running riot in London?'

'I 'ave,' said Emily. 'There's fortunes been won and lost on those fings and there's coves wot sail around the world searching for 'em in jungles and up mountains and 'eaven knows where, and bringing 'em back and selling 'em for a sack full of sovereigns. There's murders and worse done over 'em.'

'Murders?' said Crimper.

'Yeah, and worse. Least that's wot they say. And

there's a blooming great glasshouse full of 'em at Kew Gardens.'

'How do you know all this?' said Mr Higgins.

'I'm educated, I am. I knows lots of fings,' said Emily. 'I was at Kew Gardens and I seen it for myself, didn't I? That's when I nicked the diary.'

'From Mr Darwin?' said Julius.

'I don't know 'is name, do I. It was in the glass 'ouse. We was there on our outing wiv Mrs Trevelyan. The geeza wiv the diary was 'aving a barny wiv that little geeza who was just 'ere.'

'The one with the red hair?' said Crimper.

'Yeah, that's the one. Anyway, the geeza wiv the diary waves it in the air at the little geeza. Then the geeza pushes past us—'

'Mr Darwin?' said Julius.

'Yeah, and he's saying, "You'll never get your 'ands on this, Tock." To the little geeza—'

'So he's called, Tock?'

'Yeah, try and keep up, 'iggins,' said Emily. 'Anyway, then Darwin puts the diary in 'is pocket. That's when I accidently bumped into 'im and nicked it. If they was arguing over it, I knew it was worth a few shillings. No one saw me.'

'Oh, I think they did, little miss. They tracked you here, did they not?' said Mr Higgins.

'They were roaming the streets looking for you,' said Julius. 'Crimper and I ran into them earlier.'

'Can I 'ave the flower then?' said Emily, changing the subject.

'No. It was given to *me* by way of compensation,' said Mr Higgins.

Emily pouted again.

'Oh, go on, Grandfather, give it to her,' said Julius. 'You know we'll forget to water it, and it looks as if it's about to die anyway. If it was worth anything they wouldn't have given it to us.'

Mr Higgins looked at the half-dead aspidistra on the mantelpiece. 'Go on then, take it. But you are banished from this bookshop, forthwith.'

'You wot?' said Emily.

'Grandfather means don't come back,' said Julius.

'I know wot 'e means.'

Julius was surprised to see genuine hurt on Emily's face.

'Now be off with you, and you too Master McCready. I need an old brandy and a large book—or is it the other way round?—in front of the fire, to steady my nerves,' said Mr Higgins.

'You want to walk me 'ome, 'iggins?' said Emily. 'In case anyone else tries to kidnap me?'

Crimper stifled a snigger.

'Er, yes, of course. Where do you live?'

'At Mrs Trevelyan's Academy for Young Ladies, in Newington.'

Crimper sniggered, louder this time. Emily glared

at him. He stopped immediately.

At the end of the street Julius, Emily and Crimper listened for the sounds of creaking hansom cabs. There was only the occasional ship's bell down on the Thames.

'They've gone,' said Emily. 'They got what they wanted.'

'Goodnight, then, Crimper,' said Julius.

'Yeah, goodnight,' said Crimper, but he lingered, fussing with his scarf.

Julius glanced quickly at Emily. She smiled.

'You can come wiv us,' she said. 'If you're afraid to walk 'ome on your own.'

Crimper's eyebrows tensed like a fist, concealing his currant-bun eyes. He clenched his meaty hands.

Emily blinked innocently, as he struggled to find something cutting to say.

In the end, he turned and marched away into the night.

'See you tomorrow,' called out Julius.

'Toffy-nosed git,' came the reply from further down the street.

Julius and Emily walked towards Blackfriars Bridge. ''e a friend of yours?' said Emily.

'Sort of. I help him with his schoolwork. He's

eighteen and still hasn't passed any exams so Mr Flynn suggested I help him.'

'Proper little philanthropist, ain't you, 'iggins?'

On Blackfriars Bridge a line of new gas lamps on poles rose up along the railings like iron trees. Although it was still early in the evening the streets were almost deserted. The few remaining people, wrapped in layers of coats and shawls and scarves, hurried home.

Emily stopped and rested the flowerpot on the railing. She leaned over and sniffed the black waters below. The winter cold kept the stench of the Thames at bay.

'So, you seen Mr Flynn, lately?' she said, casually.

'Yes.' Julius leaned on the railing too and listened to the rhythmic lapping of the waves.

'When?' she said.

'Umm. On Saturday.'

'Oh.'

'I see quite a lot of him. He and Grandfather are friends again, after their night in the police cells for illegal bell ringing. He comes to the shop for tea quite often. And there's the bare-knuckle bouts. I go to them with Crimper sometimes.'

'So you and Mr Flynn are mates? In the same gang?'

'I suppose so. Why do you ask?'

'Oh, no reason, just wondering.'

Julius and Emily listened to the water again.

'Do you like the school Mr Flynn arranged for you?' said Julius.

Mr Flynn had offered to find schools for Emily and her gang of street urchins as a reward for their help in the Springheel case.

'Chartwell Ladies College? I got sent packing from there for starting a riot.'

'Why did you do that?'

'I was bored.'

'Oh,' said Julius.

'So anyway, Mr Flynn sent me to Mrs Trevelyan's gaff. He 'ad to pay extra to make 'er take me. Told me to behave myself or 'e'd send me to be a lighthouse keeper's apprentice at Muckle Flugga.'

'Where's that?'

'I don't want to find out.'

Julius and Emily walked along the wide thoroughfare of Great Surrey Street.

'Mr Flynn ain't been to visit me since 'e came before Christmas to give me a present.'

'What was it?'

'A book.'

'What was it about?'

'I don't know, I didn't read it, did I. Reading's boring.'

'I see.'

'You been on any more adventures since we

nabbed Springheel?' she said.

'No,' said Julius. 'Just school, the shop and the odd book to read.'

'Sounds 'orrible.'

Julius smiled to himself.

'It *was* ace though, weren't it,' said Emily, and her face ignited with nostalgic glee. 'And when the Watchmakers came. It was like magic when the professor did that fing with the pocketwatch. It was ever so…so…exciting.'

'Yes, it was,' said Julius.

'Do you still 'ave it?'

Julius felt a heavy feeling in his chest. It was like grief and loneliness entwined inside him. It was the same whenever the pocketwatch came to his mind.

'The pocketwatch? No, it's hidden away,' he said.

'Well, if anyfing comes up, you will tell me, won't you?' said Emily.

Julius forced himself to smile. 'Yes,' he said.

'The fing is, it's all right being a lady and getting educated, and being warm and fed and all that, but…'

'But what?'

'It's boring.'

'I see.'

'So, if anyfing comes up?'

'Yes, I'll let you know.'

When they arrived at the obelisk outside the Blind School, Julius spoke again. 'Is that why you tried to sell stolen goods at Grandfather's shop? Did…did you want to see me again?'

'I didn't know you lived there, did I? Why would I know that?'

Of course, Higgins. It's the future Emily who stood outside the bookshop with you. This Emily barely knows anything about you.

'I wasn't planning on nicking naffing when we went to Kew Gardens, but the geeza was waving it about and, what could I do? And everyone knows Mr 'iggins is as bent as a Peckham peddler. No offence. So I knew 'e'd buy it off me.'

'So you were surprised to see me?'

Emily did not reply.

They walked on for a time. 'Anyway,' she said, eventually. 'If you see Mr Flynn, tell 'im I'm available. But don't tell 'im about the diary, I'm not supposed to be thieving no more.'

'I won't,' said Julius. 'But you shouldn't really be—'

'This is it,' said Emily, stopping outside large house on Elliot's Row.

A brass plaque at the gate read *Mrs Trevelyan's Academy for Young Ladies.*

'Well, it was nice to see you again,' said Julius. 'I hope you weren't too frightened earlier.'

'Me? Naaaa.'

'Well, er…goodnight then.'

''ang on. I 'ave to show you where to come and get me if anyfing comes up.'

'Yes, of course, I—'

'It's round the back,' said Emily, leading Julius along the side of the house. 'Knock on the scullery door and tell Clara you want to see me. Got it?'

At the back was a stairway leading down to the servants' entrance. Julius followed Emily down the steps. She untied the ribbon under her chin and removed her bonnet and her hair fell down across her fur-lined cape. As she looked at the candle flame in the scullery window, the faint yellow light played across her face.

'Why did you run away, earlier?' asked Julius. 'You knew it was me. I was just about to call out to you.'

Emily shrugged her shoulders. 'Don't know,' she said. 'Just did.'

'Did something frighten you?'

'No. I just wanted to go, that's all. Don't go trying to make somefing out of naffing.' She twirled the bonnet ribbon around her finger.

Julius lowered his eyes. The sudden happy shock he had felt at seeing her again had taken him by surprise. It saddened him to realise that she had not felt the same. Then he remembered again—this Emily barely knew him.

Often, in the six months since the Springheel case, he had allowed his mind to wander back to the *other*

Emily—the future, fourteen-year-old, Emily he had met in the parallel timeline.

He had fallen a little bit in love with her, and he liked to think that she had fallen a little bit in love with him. She had kissed him before he sailed on the *Bountiful*. That must have meant something. He wanted this younger Emily to be a little bit in love with him too. But she wasn't, why would she be? She was just on the lookout for an adventure.

She wanted to check up on Mr Flynn, not you, Higgins.

'I wasn't trying to make anything out of it, Emily. I was just—'

'Yeah, well don't.'

'Is that you out there, Emily?' came a voice from inside.

A face appeared at the window.

'That's Clara,' Emily said, in a friendlier tone. 'She's the one you send to get me if anyfing comes up.'

'Who's—'

'She's the assistant cook, and she's ace. She does everyfing round 'ere. She lets me in on the quiet. If Mrs Trevelyan knew I was out and about she'd send me packing.'

A key turned in the lock and the door opened to reveal a short, plump woman with wide, smiling eyes.

'Come in, come in,' she whispered.

Emily stepped inside. 'Good night then, 'iggins,'

she said. 'And don't forget, *Emily's available.*'

'Gracious me,' exclaimed Clara, staring at Julius.

'It's all right?' said Emily. ''iggins is sort of a kind of friend of mine. He was just seeing me 'ome.'

Julius lifted the peak of his cap. 'How do you do?' he said.

'Look, 'e gave me this.' Emily held up the orchid. 'If 'e calls again, send Nell up to get me, it don't matter when it is or wot I'm doing.'

'Er, very well,' said Clara, looking at the orchid in confusion, then back at Julius. 'Higgins? From Higgins' Booksellers?' she said.

'Yes, do you know it?' said Julius.

Clara's eyes widened. 'Well, I—'

'Bye then,' said Emily. 'Can't stop 'ere nattering all night. Remember, 'iggins, *Emily's available.*'

She closed the door in his face.

CHAPTER 3

Friday 19th January 1838

8:51 AM

The next morning, freezing drizzle fell over London. Julius dragged his feet along Milk Street on his way to the City of London School.

At the age of fifteen, he was in his final year and he hoped to go to Cambridge University to study history while he waited for the call from the Guild of Watchmakers to begin his time traveller apprenticeship. This morning, however, his mind was not on his studies.

He stopped at the school gate, stamping his feet and deliberating.

He had slept fitfully—dreaming of Emily and the Springheel case, of the Guild of Watchmakers lifting their top hats to him in St Paul's Cathedral, of travelling through time with the giant pocketwatch.

The idea of sitting on the hard school bench until the bell rang at half past three was already calcifying his brain. He thought of the ancient ink stains on his desk, of Mr Crowley's cane thwacking the black-board, of Crimper McCready jabbing at his shoulder, asking for all the answers.

Then he thought of the events of the previous night—of the strange man in the wide-brimmed hat, the creaking hansom cab, of the diary, and Emily. It was frightening but it had been exciting too, and it left the faint flavour in the air of an adventure about to begin.

'Got home safe, then?' said Crimper McCready, slapping Julius's back so hard that his teeth nearly shot out of his mouth.

'Oi! Careful,' said Julius.

'Sorry,' said Crimper.

'Halfwit,' replied Julius. 'Look, I'm having a sick day, Crimper. Tell Mr Crowley I won't be in.'

'Wot? But I hardly touched you. It was just a pat on the back.'

'Not because of that, pea-brain. I've got a few things to do. I'm going to see Mr Flynn.'

'Oh? About those bruisers last night?'

'Yes.'

'Tell Mr Flynn, I'd have steamed in there if they'd started anything,' said Crimper.

'Yes,' said Julius. 'I'll tell him.' He turned back the way he'd come.

'I'll see you at the bare-knuckle bout tonight, Higgins?' called out Crimper.

'Yes, maybe.'

It was a long, damp walk to Mr Flynn's lodgings in Mincing Lane, but Julius didn't mind. He always enjoyed his time with Danny Flynn, time traveller and champion bare-knuckle boxer of all London.

'Oh, Master 'iggins, come in, come in,' exclaimed Mrs Mottle, Mr Flynn's landlady, as she opened the door. 'This is indeed h'an h'unexpected h'onour.'

'Hello, Mrs Mottle. Is Mr Flynn in?' said Julius.

'Yes, 'e is. 'es up in 'is rooms h'inspecting the morning newspapers. Go on up.'

Julius bounded up the stairs.

'Would you care for some tea and 'ot crumpets, Master 'iggins?' Mrs Mottle shouted after him. 'I can 'ave Kitty toast 'em up, can't I Kitty?'

'You can, Mrs M,' came a reply from the scullery at the end of the hall.

'Crumpets would be very nice, thank you,' said Julius.

'You 'ear that, Kitty? Crumpets and tea for h'upstairs,' called out Mrs Mottle, as she bustled towards the scullery door.

'Right you are, Mrs M,' came the reply.

Julius raised his hand to knock on Mr Flynn's door, but it opened before his knuckles struck the wood.

'Julius? I thought I heard your voice,' said Mr Flynn. His large frame and broad shoulders filled the doorway. He held a slice of toast in one hand and a newspaper folded under his arm. 'Come in. Warm yourself by the fire.'

'Thank you,' said Julius.

Mr Flynn settled himself in his chair and stretched his stockinged feet towards the fire.

Julius took off his coat and scarf and sat opposite. 'Mrs Mottle's bringing up tea and crumpets,' he said.

'Good, good, I could do with a refill.' Mr Flynn drained the last of the tea from the bone-china cup.

The fire crackled and the clock on the mantel ticked resoundingly in the finely furnished room. Mr Flynn flicked his newspaper back into reading shape.

Julius picked up a slice of butter-laden toast from Mr Flynn's plate and bit into it.

'Not at school today, Julius? Did it burn down or something?' said Mr Flynn.

'Er, no. I've taken the day off. Something interesting happened at the shop last night, Mr Flynn,' said Julius.

Mr Flynn lowered the newspaper. 'Oh, yes?'

'Someone came to the shop to sell a diary. That

someone left. And not five minutes later that *someone* was brought back to the shop by a very odd fellow and two bruisers. The odd fellow said the diary was his and he wanted it back. They threatened to cut off the thief's hand unless we returned it.'

'And did you?'

'Yes, of course. Then they left with the diary.'

'Hmm. What did these fellas look like.'

'The odd fellow carrying the orchid was about five feet tall, he had red hair and badly fitted false teeth. The bruiser with the meat cleaver, was about five foot six, maybe, but powerfully built. The other man was as tall as you.'

'Did you say "orchid"?'

'Yes. They were both dressed in brown. Both with billycock hats. There was something very strange about them. It's hard to describe, it was like…like—'

'Rapple and Baines,' said Mr Flynn.'

'Who?'

'Edward Rapple and Benjamin Baines. Merchants of skullduggery. If empty graves could get up and walk they'd look like that pair. They give everyone the collywobbles and not just because of the concealed weapons they carry.'

'You know them, Mr Flynn?'

'Our paths have crossed once or twice. They call themselves Resurrectionists.'

'Resurrectionists?'

'Yes, a fancy name for body-snatchers. Although, I believe they've retired from that line of work now.'

'Er, I don't follow.'

'Since the law changed in '29 medical students can dissect executed criminals and deceased paupers from the workhouse, so they don't have to pay the likes of Rapple and Baines to steal fresh corpses from graveyards.'

'Urgh.'

'Exactly. Now they rent themselves out for villainous purposes at reasonable rates. But they still exude the stench of the grave. I think their years of manhandling cadavers have turned their minds a little. They think of the likes of you and me as the "not yet dead".'

A knock at the door made Julius jump. It was Mrs Mottle with a large tray of tea and crumpets.

''ere we are, gentlemen,' she said. 'Will you be requiring h'anything else, Mr Flynn? Kitty could do you some peppered kippers, perhaps, or a nice cheese h'omlette?'

'No, thank you, Mrs Mottle, this will see us through to elevenses,' said Mr Flynn.

When Mrs Mottle had gone, he continued. 'Rapple and Baines have been dealing with death and the dead for so long that I think they feel like visitors here—in the land of the living.'

Julius bit into a crumpet. Butter slithered down his chin.

'You mentioned an orchid?' said Mr Flynn.

'Yes. The odd fellow left an orchid in a pot, as a gift.'

'Very obliging,' said Mr Flynn. 'Listen to this report in *The Times*. I was reading it when you came:

ORCHIDMANIA: THE CAUSE OF MENTAL COLLAPSE?

In the borough of Lambeth, on Wednesday evening, cries of alarm were heard from the lodgings of a gentleman by the name of Mr Charles Darwin. The landlady of the establishment found the gentleman in a state of confusion, declaring that an orchid from his collection had climbed from its pot and chased him about the room. When the gentleman could not be calmed or reasoned with, Constable Abberline from the local constabulary was sent for to take the man to nearby New Bethlem Hospital, or Bedlam as it is more commonly called.

'Are you all right, Julius?' said Mr Flynn. 'You look like you've seen a ghost.'

'The name on the diary,' said Julius. 'It was *Darwin*.'

Mr Flynn raised an eyebrow. 'And now he's lost his mind.'

'From what I saw in the diary, I don't think his mind was that clear to begin with. Do you think there's a connection, Mr Flynn?'

'Certainly—on Thursday evening a strange fella leaves a gift of an orchid in exchange for Darwin's diary, when only the night before, this Mr Darwin fella loses his mind and accuses one of his orchids of *chasing* him round his room.'

'Could it be Watchmaker business?' said Julius.

'Possibly. But this Constable Abberline, he's the one to talk to first. I know him, he's a good man. And I'd also like to examine that orchid of yours.'

'Ah…'

'What do you mean, "Ah"?'

'That might not be possible,' said Julius.

Mr Flynn let the newspaper fall to his lap. 'How so?'

'The thief who pickpocketed the diary from Mr Darwin…The thing is, I think you might know her. I promised not to tell, so—'

Mr Flynn scrunched the newspaper into a ball. 'It was Emily, wasn't it.'

'I didn't tell you, Mr Flynn. You guessed.'

Mr Flynn let out a long, anguished sigh and looked pleadingly at the ceiling.

Julius waited until he had composed himself.

'And the orchid?' said Mr Flynn.

'I think I might have given it to her.'

CHAPTER 4

Friday 19th January 1838

10:37 AM

'That girl will be the death of me,' said Mr Flynn, as he strode across Blackfriars Bridge. A cold wind blew across their path, flapping the tails of Mr Flynn's winter coat. He pushed his top hat low over his brow to keep it on.

'You won't tell Emily I told you, will you?' said Julius, running along beside him.

Mr Flynn did not reply.

'Grandfather gave her a good telling off,' said Julius.

Mr Flynn still did not reply.

By the time they reached Paradise Row, Julius felt as empty as the streets they had travelled.

'She was sorry for stealing the diary,' said Julius.

'She won't do it again.'

'She'd better not,' said Mr Flynn. 'We'll wait, here. Abberline's beat passes this way.' He dug his hands into his pockets and sheltered in a doorway.

The minutes ticked by. Mr Flynn stared at the wall across the street. Julius shivered.

'Here he is,' said Julius, when he spied a figure in a police uniform, top hat and cape coming towards them. The man walked with that relaxed, swinging stride adopted by the peelers walking long beats in heavy boots.

Mr Flynn stepped out from the doorway and tipped his hat.

The constable's face broke into a wide smile. 'Strike me down,' he said, with a touch of a West Country accent. 'It's Mr Flynn.' He tapped the rim of his top hat with his forefinger by way of salute.

'Constable Abberline, the very man,' said Mr Flynn. 'You're well, I trust?' He extended his hand to the constable, who shook it vigorously.

'Very well, thank you, Mr Flynn,' said Abberline. 'I've been practising those moves you showed me.'

'Glad to hear it, Constable,' said Mr Flynn.

'Watch out.' The constable ducked into a boxing stance and jabbed a lightning fast punch towards Mr Flynn's chin and then twisted at the hip to aim a punch at his solar plexus.

Mr Flynn was too quick, though. He blocked the

punch with his left elbow and swung his right arm to tap the constable's top hat just enough to dislodge it without knocking it off.

The constable laughed as he straightened his hat.

'Not bad,' said Mr Flynn.

Constable Abberline raised his eyebrows in good-natured disbelief. 'Who's this young man,' he said, nodding towards Julius.

'Allow me to introduce Julius Caesar Higgins,' said Mr Flynn.

The constable eagerly shook Julius's hand. 'Hello, my lad,' he said. 'Any friend of Mr Flynn, and all that. Mr Flynn's all right with me and that means you are too.'

'Yes…er, thank you, sir,' said Julius.

'We're not meeting by chance, Constable Abberline,' said Mr Flynn.

Abberline's smile remained on his face. 'I surmised as much, Mr Flynn. People don't loiter in cold doorways for no reason. Something's come up has it?'

'You could say that,' said Mr Flynn. He took *The Times* from his coat pocket. It was folded with the orchid report to the outside. 'It's about this,' said Mr Flynn.

Abberline glanced at the newspaper. 'Yes, the lads at the station have been giving me a good old ribbing about it.'

'The thing is…' said Mr Flynn.

'Go on,' said Abberline.

'Julius's grandfather received a visit at his bookshop last night,' said Mr Flynn. 'From an odd fella named Tock.'

Abberline's eyes narrowed as he looked down at Julius. 'Tock, you say? Where have I heard that name before?'

'He was looking for a diary written by a Mr Darwin,' said Mr Flynn.

'Now there's a coincidence,' said Abberline.

'And the fella had Rapple and Baines with him.'

'That pair? Go on.'

'When they took the diary they left an orchid as a parting gift.'

'Odd.'

'Very.'

'And you think it's connected with what happened at Mr Darwin's lodgings?' said Abberline.

Mr Flynn shrugged. 'Perhaps. In any case, friends of mine have been threatened and, well, let's just say I'd like to know what's going on.'

'I suppose you'd like a look around Mr Darwin's lodgings, then?' said Abberline.

'If it wouldn't be too much trouble, Constable,' said Mr Flynn.

☞

It was a short distance to Walnut Tree Walk.

'Here it is,' said Abberline. He, Julius and Mr Flynn stood outside a respectable-looking house. A handwritten sign at the window advertised rooms for rent, at reasonable rates to single professional gentlemen.

'Bedlam's just round the corner, so when he couldn't be reasoned with I took him there,' said Abberline. 'He was still raving when I left him.'

'What was he saying, Constable?' said Julius.

'All sorts of nonsense. He was clearly mad. About an orchid climbing out of its pot. About his soul being stolen by someone called…what was it? Mr Dock? Or was he saying Tock? That's it. It must have been Tock.'

'So there is a connection,' said Julius.

The front door opened a crack, then more fully, to reveal a woman in a woollen bonnet.

'Constable Abberline, I thought I heard your voice,' she said. 'Come about poor Mr Darwin, have you?'

'Yes, indeed, Mrs Clitherow. I have a couple of independent investigators with me. They're keen to look at Mr Darwin's rooms.

The woman looked the large bare-knuckle boxer and the schoolboy up and down. Mr Flynn doffed his top hat, and Julius blew into his mittened hands and stamped his feet.

'Well, if you're sure, Constable. I…um, I suppose it'd be all right,' she said.

Constable Abberline, Julius and Mr Flynn followed the landlady up two flights of stairs.

'How long had Mr Darwin been lodging with you?' said Mr Flynn.

'Not long, sir. A few months. A very respectable young man, he was. He'd recently returned from a long voyage. He saw some things an Englishman shouldn't see, if you ask me. That's what made him like he is. Oh, don't get me wrong, sir, I never had any nonsense from him. Not like some of my other gentlemen. No, he's just a bit highly strung that's all. The nervous type, you might say, on account of being among foreigners for too long.'

'I see. Did he have any visitors?'

'Oh, no. He kept to himself. Always in his room scribbling in his notebooks, mumbling to himself about Heaven knows what. You'll see when we get there—not natural it's not.'

'Did he have a profession?' asked Julius.

'He had private means, which in my book is better than a profession. He didn't keep regular hours, but he always paid his rent in advance and was never any trouble.'

They came to a door with a sheet of paper pasted over the lock. It bore Abberline's signature.

'I thought it best to seal the room so that any clues

41

wouldn't be disturbed,' said the constable. He tore the paper off the door and unlocked it with a key provided by Mrs Clitherow.

'Thank you, we'll manage by ourselves from here,' he said.

Julius stopped as soon as he entered the room. Papers, books and clothes were strewn everywhere. 'It's like a whirlwind been through here,' he said.

'It certainly does,' said Abberline. 'Mr Darwin turned everything upside down when he was battling the imaginary orchid.'

Julius looked at the walls. They were covered with page after page of drawings of flowers and strange animals Julius had never seen before. Intricate diagrams of petals and leaves, and eyes, beaks and hooves as well as watercolour paintings of strange landscapes and native people.

In the far corner was a bed and on the bedside table was a plate, bearing the greasy remains of a half-eaten pie.

'That's where he was lying when it happened. He said he fell asleep and was woken by the thing creeping towards him,' said Abberline.

Julius moved the tangled blankets aside. There was only a creased bed sheet and pie crumbs beneath.

'Mr Darwin was rather a distracted and driven young gentleman. Nobody knew anything about him except that he'd been abroad for some years. I'll be speaking to him in a day or two, when he's calmed down,' said Abberline.

Mr Flynn shuffled through the detritus on the writing desk.

'Yes, apparently he was one of those orchid-maniacs you hear about,' said Abberline. He pointed to a row of orchids in pots on a narrow table set against one of the windows.

Julius studied them. The orchids were different colours and forms but all had the same four-petal structure. 'Did you notice this?' he said to Abberline.

'What?' said the constable.

'There's an orchid missing.'

'Well I'll be…?'

Mr Flynn closed the desk drawer he was shuffling through and came to the table.

'There.' Julius pointed to an empty pot.

'Blow me down,' said Abberline. 'I never thought to check, not with all the commotion. I feel a complete fool.'

'Look at this,' continued Julius. 'There's an indentation in the soil, as if the plant was pulled out, and there's soil scattered around the pot.'

'Our Mr Darwin might have been telling the truth,' said Mr Flynn.

'Not necessarily. He might have pulled it out of the pot himself in his mania,' said Julius.

'So, where is it now?' said Mr Flynn.

They searched the room until Abberline found a squashed orchid hidden under some papers.

'Looks like he stamped it to death,' he said.

Julius poked it with the tip of a pencil. 'It's the same as the one Tock gave us,' he said.

'Are you sure?' said Mr Flynn.

Julius looked at the other orchids then back at the petal hanging from the end of his pencil. 'Yes,' he said. 'It's the same, I'm sure.' He looked up at Mr Flynn. 'Tock said it might surprise us one day. That's why Emily wanted it.'

'Is it, now?' said Mr Flynn. He took the pencil and examined the battered petal. 'Moving or not, it's only a flower,' he said. 'What harm could it do?' He tossed it onto the desk. 'All the same, I think we'll pay her a visit.'

Mrs Clitherow was waiting at the bottom of the stairs polishing the already shiny banister when Julius, Mr Flynn and Constable Abberline came down.

'Find any clues, Constable?' she said.

'One or two,' said Abberline.

'Mrs Clitherow,' said Julius. 'Did anything out of the ordinary happen *before* Mr Darwin had his unfortunate turn? Anything in the previous few days? Anything at all?'

'No, nothing that I can think of.'

Mr Flynn tipped his top hat and turned to leave.

'Except the orchid that was left on the doorstep,'

said Mrs Clitherow.

Julius, Mr Flynn and the constable stopped. They turned back to the landlady.

'Orchid?' said Abberline. Mrs Clitherow started polishing again. 'Yes, it was sitting on the doorstep on Wednesday evening. I found it when I put Napoleon out.'

'Napoleon?' said Abberline.

'The cat. I know it's unpatriotic, but the cat's a wrong 'un so I thought it would be all right.'

'You found an orchid?' said Mr Flynn.

'Yes, in a pot.'

'Was it red?' said Julius.

'Let me think. Yes, it was. And there was a little note tied to it with a piece of cotton thread.'

'What did it say?' said Julius.

'It said, *Mr C. D., a gift from a secret admirer.*'

'And do you still have it?' asked Julius.

'The note?'

'No, the orchid,' said Mr Flynn.

'No, sir. I imagined "Mr C. D." was my Mr Darwin so I knocked and left it outside his door.'

'Why didn't you tell me on the night of the disturbance, Mrs Clitherow?' said Abberline.

'Well, you didn't ask me, did you?'

'It must have been Tock,' said Julius.

'Emily,' said Mr Flynn, to no one in particular.

CHAPTER 5

Friday 19th January 1838

3:16 PM

Julius and Mr Flynn hurried toward Mrs Trevelyan's Academy for Young Ladies, leaving Abberline to go back to his beat. Mr Flynn's face was like stone. He ignored the sleet darting at his cheeks. Julius could almost hear the thoughts grinding against each other under Mr Flynn's top hat.

'I don't like this, Julius,' said Mr Flynn.

'The orchid, you mean?'

'The odd little fellow, Rapple and Baines. Everything. Come on, hurry.'

'Mr Flynn?' said Julius, as he trotted to keep up.

'What is it?'

'Er…about Emily…'

'What about her?'

'You're not going to…to…'

'To what?'

'To send her away?'

Mr Flynn looked down at Julius, as if trying to peer through the surface of a murky pond.

'Of course not. What gave you that idea?'

'She mentioned something about lighthouse keeping.'

'Oh, that,' said Mr Flynn. 'It was an idle threat, made in a moment of desperation, and obviously to no effect.'

'You won't send her away, then?' Julius could see the ladies' academy ahead.

'No, I wouldn't do that,' said Mr Flynn. They stopped at the gate. 'I couldn't if I wanted to, Julius. You see, Emily's my ward.'

Julius flinched. He stared at the steps leading up to the front door, pretending not to have heard, or at least not to have been struck by the words. It was as if a bee had stung him and he was impatient for the pain to come so he would know how strong the venom was.

He swayed—as if the toxin was sliding into his veins. He recalled the time outside the bookshop six months earlier, when he found out that Mr Flynn was not his father. Never had been. Never would be. The disappointment had stung all the more because he had been so certain it was true. But it wasn't, and the fact that it wasn't left an ache where the certainty once was.

And now Mr Flynn had made Emily his legal daughter, just like that—and had not even thought to tell him. The venom took hold of Julius—leaching into his organs. He gripped the bar of the gate.

'I try to visit as often as I can,' said Mr Flynn. 'She's a handful though. Mrs Trevelyan's is the second establishment she's been at in six months. Whenever I visit I have to listen to reports of all the shenanigans she's been up to.' Mr Flynn paused and looked at the steps as if they were a mountain he was reluctant to climb.

'I'm sorry, Julius,' he said. 'I should have told you. I didn't think.'

'That's all right,' said Julius.

'It's a legal requirement, so I can make decisions about her education and the legacy the Watchmakers donated to her.'

'We'd best ring the bell, Mr Flynn.'

'Yes. Let's get it over with.'

Mr Flynn took the steps three at a time and tapped the brass doorknocker. Julius climbed slowly after him. Mr Flynn removed his top hat and smoothed his hair.

The door was opened by a maid, whose face lit up in welcome. 'Mr Flynn,' she said, 'We haven't seen you in more than an age. Mrs Trevelyan was starting to fret.'

Julius watched, stunned, as Mr Flynn's cheeks bloomed like a red rosebud opening its petals.

'Well, I'm here now,' said Mr Flynn. 'Is everything all right?'

'Why, yes. Why shouldn't it be?' said the maid, with a wide-eyed look in anticipation of calamity.

'Oh, no reason.'

The maid noticed Julius and ran her eyes over him as if she were wrapping him in ribbons. 'And who's the young gentleman?'

'Julius Higgins, a friend of Miss Emily. We've come to call.'

'You'd better come in, kind sirs,' she said. 'I'll fetch Mrs Trevelyan.' She scampered away across the hall, with her skirts gathered up in front to give her feet full rein.

Mr Flynn cleared his throat awkwardly and studied the tiles at his feet. Julius pulled off his mittens.

There were two stairways curving up around the walls of the grand entrance hall. Julius looked up the three or four storeys to see girls' faces staring at him over the banisters. He unbuttoned his coat and removed his hat. The faces began animated discussions with one another. More faces appeared. Soon, most of the banister space on the third landing and some of the fourth was lined with faces of young ladies, all looking down at Julius as he looked up at them.

'Mr Flynn, it is indeed an honour,' Julius heard

someone say in a Scottish Highland accent. Suddenly, all the faces disappeared and the babble ceased.

Julius turned to see a tall, strikingly handsome woman of about forty. Her jet-black hair was pulled into a bun at the back of her head. She was advancing towards Mr Flynn with an outstretched hand of welcome, but she stopped when she saw Julius.

Her spectacles fell from her nose and hung on their gold chain across her large bosom as she stared in horror.

Julius stared back in confusion.

What the bloody hell have you done, Higgins?

'Mr Flynn,' said the woman, her face pretending to smile. 'If you would be so kind as to come into my study, and bring the…*ahem*…young gentleman with you.'

She marched away, with her head held as high as her neck could stretch.

Julius looked to Mr Flynn for an answer, but he was still studying the tiles at his feet.

'Yes, Mrs Trevelyan,' he said, and fell into step behind her.

When Mr Flynn and Julius stepped into Mrs Trevelyan's study, she was standing to attention, holding the door and patting away an imagined irregularity in her hair. The room was an ornately decorated study and parlour. Paintings of regimental charges hung on the walls, interspersed with swords and daggers. Two statuettes of horses stood on the mantel and a bronze reproduction the Dying Gaul had pride of place on her desk. The raised knee of the naked warrior was worn shiny. Julius imagined it was from decades of schoolgirls stroking it for luck while awaiting a telling off.

'Please, take a seat, Mr Flynn,' said Mrs Trevelyan.

Mr Flynn sat obediently in one of the parlour chairs. Julius sat in another. Mrs Trevelyan lowered herself gracefully into a chair opposite them and adjusted the gold chain across her bosom until it hung just right.

'As you know, Mr Flynn,' she said, 'you are always welcome here, *always*. But I must insist—' She cast a glance towards Julius. 'I must insist that no young gentlemen of a certain age accompany you in future. It may cause—how can I put it?—undue disturbances among my young ladies.'

Mr Flynn looked at Julius. 'Mrs Trevelyan, I can assure you that Master Higgins is a gentleman to his bootlaces. The soul of decorum and conduct and would never, er—'

'I am sure you are correct, Mr Flynn. I have no doubt of your judgment in this matter. It is not the young gentleman's conduct about which I am concerned.'

'Oh, no?' said Mr Flynn.

'No,' said Mrs Trevelyan. 'It is just that, how can I

put it? My young ladies do not often leave the academy. They do not mix with young gentlemen of their own age. I have a duty to their parents and…*ahem*…guardians to see to their welfare and moral development. A well-presented young gentleman might—how shall I put it?—lead to *agitation* in my young ladies. I'm sure you understand, Mr Flynn.'

'Oh, indeed I do, Mrs Trevelyan,' said Mr Flynn. 'Forgive me, I should have considered the matter before I brought young Julius.'

'No apologies are necessary, Mr Flynn. I see that you appreciate my situation and will be guided accordingly in the future. Military men are always to be depended upon, I find.'

'Oh, I'm not a military man, Mrs Trevelyan. I never had that honour,' said Mr Flynn, in a suitably regretful tone.

'No? You do surprise me. You have such a regimental bearing. I took you to be late of the Irish Fusiliers.'

Mr Flynn's face bloomed red again.

'My late husband, as you know, Colonel Trevelyan, of the Cameron Highlanders,' said Mrs Trevelyan, pointing to a portrait in a gold-leafed oval frame, 'often said to me, "Bonnie, if you weren't my wife, I'd make you a Major."'

'Indeed,' said Mr Flynn.

'I kept the officers in line for the colonel when

we were stationed in Gibraltar. A kind heart and firm hand was what they needed. Such fine young men. Far away from home, so full of high spirits.' Mrs Trevelyan appeared to lose herself to her memories. She sighed as she looked at the pictures and trophies on the walls.

Mr Flynn pulled at his collar as if it were choking him. 'And how is Emily?' he asked.

'Emily?' said Mrs Trevelyan, coming back to the present. 'Such a dear girl. She exhibits so many possibilities. However, she does continue to be an unfortunate influence on my young ladies. They follow her in every way, Mr Flynn.'

'Oh, I see.'

'They have taken to calling out "oi" to one another, like barrow boys at a bare-knuckle bout. Oh, no offence, Mr Flynn. I'm sure your bouts are of a highly refined variety.'

'Indeed they are, Mrs Trevelyan.'

'Unfortunately, dear Emily has what can only be described as leadership qualities,' said Mrs Trevelyan.

'I see. And that is to be *dis*couraged?' said Mr Flynn.

'Indeed. It is most *un*becoming.'

'But I'm sure, Mrs Trevelyan, that you have leadership qualities yourself. Qualities sufficient to command a regiment, that the late colonel—forgive me for being so bold—did not find disagreeable,' said Mr Flynn.

It was Mrs Trevelyan's turn to blush. She smiled and twirled the arm of her spectacles between her thumb and forefinger. 'Oh, Mr Flynn. How gallant you are. Yes, indeed. I am sure you are correct. I have the highest regard for your judgment in all things, as you know. If Emily were to marry a military man her qualities might be put to good use. But, I fear, any other eligible young man might find her somewhat confronting.'

Julius felt a tickling on he cheeks. He knew he was blushing, but he wasn't sure why. He hoped Mr Flynn and Mrs Trevelyan didn't notice.

Just then a scream rang out from the hallway. Julius jumped.

'One of the young ladies, getting caned?' said Mr Flynn.

'Certainly not,' said Mrs Trevelyan, standing to attention. 'My young ladies receive lines for their transgressions.'

The scream rang out again. Mrs Trevelyan hurried to the door and opened it. Another scream— louder this time—was followed by much clattering and banging.

'Allow me,' said Mr Flynn. He hurried past before Mrs Trevelyan could object. Julius followed close behind. In four seconds they were at the foot of the stairs, where a young kitchen maid was screaming in terror.

Emily ran down the stairs behind them, followed by other schoolgirls. 'Wot's the matter, Nell?' she asked.

'There's a bleeding flower in the kitchen, miss. It's trying to kill us all.'

'What is this nonsense?' said Mrs Trevelyan.

Mr Flynn looked at Julius.

Cripes, Higgins. It's Tock's orchid.

'Emily, where's the kitchen,' said Mr Flynn, above the screaming.

'This way,' she shouted, and ran along the corridor beside the stairs.

Julius and Mr Flynn followed. The cacophony of cries and clattering pans grew louder as they ran down a flight of stairs and into the kitchen.

Julius stared at the chaos through a fog of flour.

Clara, the assistant cook who had let Emily in the night before, stood in the middle of it all. She was swinging a broom around her head while a fat woman in a cook's bonnet was wailing and throwing anything she could get hold of.

'Look, over there,' said Mr Flynn.

Something scurried along a shelf of jars. It flashed past too quickly for Julius to see clearly what it was. Clara used her broom as a lance to stab at it. Jars fell to the flagstones, shattering and sending up clouds of cinnamon and nutmeg.

Emily, who had worked her way into the middle of the mayhem, picked up a meat-tenderising mallet and held it ready as Julius and Mr Flynn ran past her.

The scurrying thing leapt from the shelf to the row of bells above the back door, then ran across them, ringing them as it went.

'What in Heaven's name is going on?' bellowed Mrs Trevelyan, from halfway down the stairs.

Everyone stopped and looked up.

'It's a wild orchid, Mrs Trevelyan,' called out Clara. 'It climbed out of its pot and went for poor Nell.'

'It's not right. It's not right,' screamed the fat cook. Her words were muffled by the large copper pot she had put over her head as a helmet.

The orchid stopped at the last bell long enough for Julius to see it properly. It was the orchid he had given to Emily. The tendrils that had hung down onto the soil now flicked around like whips.

'We need something to catch it in,' said Mr Flynn.

Julius looked around. It was impossible to find anything in the chaos. Wooden spoons were strewn across the kitchen table and a pot of soup had tipped over on the range, making it hiss and spit and sending up more steam than the chimney could hold.

'Here, catch,' shouted Emily.

Julius caught the sieve she threw at him.

Clara poked the orchid off the last bell with a broom. It fell into the corner and, running on its tendril legs, it made for the space under the dresser.

The meat-tenderising mallet flew through the air, just missing Julius's ear. It smashed into the floor in front of the orchid, stopping it for an instant. Julius leapt at it with the sieve.

'Got you!'

He lay over the sieve, holding it down while the orchid fought to escape.

'It's not right. It's not right,' shouted the cook.

The kitchen became still but for the flour and cinnamon and nutmeg settling like fairy dust around them.

Mrs Trevelyan pulled the pot off the cook's head and placed it on the table.

'Calm yourself, Cook,' she said.

'Could I trouble you for a jar, Mrs Trevelyan?' said Mr Flynn, with impeccable composure.

'Why, yes, of course, Mr Flynn,' she said.

Clara reached for a jar of bay leaves and tipped them out on the draining board.

'Thank you,' said Mr Flynn, barely looking at the assistant cook who was covered in flour. 'Julius, when I give the word, lift the sieve and I'll nab it. Stand back, ladies.'

Under the wire mesh, the orchid hissed and whipped, madly lashing its tendrils.

'Now,' said Mr Flynn.

Julius snatched up the sieve and used it as a shield while Mr Flynn slammed the open end of the jar over the orchid, severing two tendrils.

Two minutes later they all stood around the table staring at the jar into which the imprisoned orchid was squashed like a pickled cabbage. Its tendrils ran across the glass as if searching for a crack to break through. A cluster of schoolgirls stared from the kitchen doorway—their mouths forming perfect letter 'O's.

'Well…' said Mrs Trevelyan, as if the silence that followed spoke for itself.

'It was Emily what left that thing in the kitchen,' said the cook, her face wobbling with indignation.

'Me? I ain't done naffing,' said Emily. 'I didn't know it was going to be *that* sort of surprise. I didn't fink it—'

Mrs Trevelyan's head slowly turned to face Emily—the simple movement made Emily close her mouth, leaving her with an expression of angry inno-cence.

Clara wiped flour from her blinking eyes, smearing her powdery mask.

'Er, I think I can explain, Mrs Trevelyan,' said Mr Flynn. 'You see…er…'

'I gave it to Emily,' said Julius. 'But, I swear, I didn't know it would do this.'

'That was kind of you,' said Clara.

Julius smiled an embarrassed thank you to her.

Mrs Trevelyan smoothed out her skirt, and then

turned to the girls in the doorway. 'Back to your books, ladies, and send Nell down here,' she commanded. Then she turned to Clara. 'And I suggest we get this mess cleaned up. We have supper to prepare, do we not?'

Then she turned to Emily. 'And you, young lady, will help.'

'But I can't, Mrs Trevelyan. I 'ave to go wiv Mr Flynn. Mr Tock's the cove wot gave it to me. We 'ave to find 'im and sort 'im out.'

Mr Flynn put the jar in his overcoat pocket.

'You're staying here,' he said. 'And when I come back we'll be talking about diaries that don't belong to you.' He tipped his hat to Mrs Trevelyan and walked out the back door.

Emily glared disbelievingly at Julius.

'He guessed,' he said.

Emily continued to glare.

Julius hesitated under the eyes of everyone. Then he turned to go.

'Goodbye, Julius,' said Clara.

'Oh, yes, goodbye.'

He ran to catch up with Mr Flynn who was slapping flour from his sleeves.

'That girl will be the living death of me,' he said.

'I think we should put some feelers out at the bare-knuckle bout tonight,' said Julius. 'Somebody's bound to know about Tock, or Rapple and Baines, at least.

What do you think?'

Mr Flynn did not reply.

☛

Later that evening, after supper of honeyed ham,
baked potatoes and boiled beef with Mr Higgins,
Julius and Mr Flynn arrived at a vacant warehouse on
the southern bank of the Thames.

The babble of the bare-knuckle crowd rose to a
cheer—someone had landed a punch. Julius and Mr
Flynn were late, and the first bout was already in its
final blows as they entered. Julius wedged himself in
the corner of the ring to watch.

The smaller man, Giles 'the Gentleman'
Farnsworth, was hunched behind his fists. His oppo-
nent, Jimmy Knottley, reeled back, throwing up a
fin of blood and sweat. He fell against a dandy, who
dropped his opera glasses. The lord shouted something
into his ear. Knottley ignored him and rebounded into
the fight just as the Gentleman sidestepped and rolled
his left shoulder to prepare the right. The crowd saw
what was coming. Their roar instantly changed to a
shared intake of breath. The next second would be
talked about for years to come and it seemed everyone knew it. Giles Farnsworth landed an exquisite
knockout punch to the side of Jimmy Knottley's jaw.
A gob of saliva shot out of Knottley's mouth as he

crashed, unconscious, to the ground. The crowd erupted, and the warehouse walls quaked.

Julius looked through the haze of cigar smoke at the fallen boxer. After many nights like this he still could not bring himself to cheer, even though he knew the clamour was almost as much for the fallen boxer as for the victor, at least among the aficionados.

Crimper McCready was in the stands. Julius could see him cheering loudest of all, jumping up and down as if his ecstasy was too great to contain.

Knottley woke with a jolt when the smelling salts were waved under his nose. The crowd cheered again. His coach poured a tot of brandy between his bloodied lips. Gentleman Giles accepted the pats on the back and pumping handshakes from his supporters. Knottley rose to his feet, with the help of his seconds, bloody and sand-caked from where he had fallen. He took a few staggering steps toward Giles who embraced him like a long-lost brother. The crowd cheered again. The two pugilists spoke a few quiet words into each other's ears and then went out of the arena, arm in arm, to clean off the blood and celebrate the fight with tankards of ale and fat cigars.

When the noise died down Mr Flynn tapped Julius on the shoulder. 'I'll make some enquires,' he said. 'Here's a few shillings for a drink. But only one, mind.'

'Thank you, Mr Flynn. I'll meet you at the door in half an hour.'

Julius squeezed through the crowd to the makeshift bar. Everyone knew he was a friend of Danny Flynn, the champion bare-knuckle boxer of all London, so no one gave him any trouble.

'What's up?' said Crimper, slapping Julius on the back, slightly less hard than he had that morning.

'Want a drink?' asked Julius.

'Jolly decent of you, old man,' said Crimper.

Julius held up two fingers to the barman who responded with two tankards of foaming porter—Baxter's Brew, better known in the area as Badger's Piss. Julius dropped a shilling on the counter, and he and Crimper retreated to a barrel that served as a table.

'Cigar?' said Crimper.

'No, thank you,' said Julius. He had turned green and vomited the last time he tried one.

The two boys took a sip from their tankards and tried not to gag at the vile taste.

'Did you tell Mr Flynn about last night, Higgins?' said Crimper.

'Yes.'

'Did you tell him I was going to steam in if they caused any trouble?'

'No, I forgot.'

Just as Crimper was about to protest, Mr Flynn appeared. 'I hope I find you well, Master McCready,' he said.

'Yes, Mr Flynn, very well, thank you,' spluttered Crimper.

'Julius, you'll never guess who I've just met. You last saw him in St Paul's Cathedral.'

Julius looked up.

Not Jack Springheel?

'He has information about Rapple and Baines and he's eager to sell it. What do you think?' said Mr Flynn.

Jack Springheel's back. Cripes, Higgins.

Julius felt the Badger's Piss chill and shift in his stomach.

A familiar face came through the crowd.

'Julius Higgins,' said the man.

'Clements?' said Julius.

CHAPTER 6

Friday 19th January 1838

10:12 PM

'The very one,' said Clements. 'How are you, my boy? My goodness, you've grown a full three inches since I saw you last. Clements clamped his cigar between his teeth, freeing his hands to vigorously shake Julius's.

'I'm very well, thank you,' said Julius, relieved and astonished at the same time.

He noticed Clements's frayed shirt cuffs. His suit was the same one he was wearing when he stood at the doors of St Paul's Cathedral with a pistol in his hand when he was working for the time-criminal Jack Springheel. He looked as if he had been living in it ever since.

'Mr Flynn tells me you're involved in another case,'

said Clements. He appeared to be genuinely pleased to see Julius. He had changed sides and helped bring Springheel's downfall by putting a bullet in the villain's shoulder that day at St Paul's. He was one of the few people in London who knew about the realities of time-travel and the Guild of Watchmakers—the band of gentlemen sworn to protect the timeline.

'Yes, er…you're looking well, Clements,' said Julius, somewhat amazed by the exuberant greeting. His nose twitched. He sniffed, trying to identify the odour lingering malignantly amid the cheap cigar smoke.

'Well? Couldn't be better, Higgins,' said Clements. 'I see by the crinkling of your nose that you're onto the secret of my success. Ha, ha.'

'Er…'

Clements chuckled at Julius's confusion.

Mr Flynn slapped Clements on the back. 'I'm glad to see that your unfortunate acquaintance with Jack Springheel hasn't dented your spirit,' he said.

Julius took a sip from his tankard of Badger's Piss to distract his senses from the disagreeable smell that was setting up home in his nose.

'It takes more that the likes of Jack Springheel to put a good man like me down, Mr Flynn,' said Clements.

'And on the subject of putting good men down, tell young Julius here what you told me.'

'I know where Rapple and Baines are hiding, Higgins.'

'He's agreed to take us there for a small fee,' said Mr Flynn. 'Master McCready, you're welcome to join us. We're going to call on those two bruisers who came to the bookshop. Julius and I are going to sort them out.'

'Er, thank you, Mr Flynn but, er…I must get home to do some schoolwork, I'm a bit behind,' said Crimper.

'Oh well, maybe next time,' said Mr Flynn.

'Sure thing, Mr Flynn,' said Crimper with relief. He sucked on his cigar and doubled over in a coughing fit.

'Julius, it looks like it's just the two of us,' said Mr Flynn. 'Finish your pint and we'll be off.'

'It's all right,' said Julius. 'Crimper can have it, I'll need a clear head.'

❦

Outside the warehouse, the biting cold lifted Julius from his cigar-smoke torpor. 'We're not really going to sort Rapple and Baines out, are we?' he said.

Mr Flynn laughed. 'No, we'll do a bit of nosing around. See what we can see.'

Julius sniffed to try to clear the mysterious smell from his nose.

'My beat is in the area, you see—the tanning yards near the Bermondsey rookery. I see all the comings and goings at night,' explained Clements, as they walked along Bermondsey Street. A London fog had descended. It hung illuminated around the lamps like spectres.

'Your beat?' said Julius.

'Yes, I'm in the purefinding trade, my boy. I have a nose for pure. I harvest it at night when the roads are clear.'

'Pure?' asked Julius.

'That's dog poo to you and me, Julius, It's used in the tanneries to cure leather,' said Mr Flynn.

'Correct,' said Clements. 'Brown gold, littering the streets of this great metropolis. Think of it, Higgins, the leather on your next pair of boots might be tanned using the very pure that I pick up tonight. How many people can say that?'

'Not many,' said Julius.

Clements laughed. 'Don't know why I didn't go into the business years ago. Urban agriculture, I call it—the agrarian idyll among the cobblestones. But I'm just doing it to get my foot in the door, you know.'

'Foot in the door, where?' asked Julius.

'At the tanneries, of course,' said Clements. 'My name has been bandied about by those in the know: "Clements is a reliable fellow." "Clements knows pure." "Clements is a force to be reckoned with."

Those are but a selection of the many things being said of me in Bermondsey. This time next year, I'll be smoking cigars as long as your arm. Ha, ha.'

Julius, Clements and Mr Flynn walked on. A smell like festering sewage wafted through the fog. 'That's the tanning yards,' said Clements. 'You get used to it.' He led the way, appearing to navigate by scent alone.

They passed the workhouse on Great Russell Street and turned into a narrow street. It was lined by tenements, rising up and leaning out over their heads. Unseen dogs barked, and babies cried.

'Through here,' said Clements. He led them into an even narrower street. Julius held the back of Mr Flynn's coat so as not to lose him.

'Nearly there,' said Clements, as cheerful as a tour guide.

The street stopped and wasteground began. Julius, Clements and Mr Flynn stood there in a row, peering into the night. A muddy path stretched out before them through an expanse of swampy grass. After ten yards it dissolved into the fog.

'Lead on,' said Mr Flynn.

Clements hesitated. 'You can take my word for it, Mr Flynn. Their hideout is through there. Follow the path and you can't miss it.'

'I want to see it for myself before I part with a farthing,' said Mr Flynn.

'Three pounds, did we say?' said Clements.

'Two, if I remember correctly,' said Mr Flynn.

'Yes, of course, two. I remember now.'

The fog began to sink its damp claws into Julius's skin, making his head ache with the cold. He tried to stamp his feet quietly, waiting for Clements to come to a decision.

'Just a sight, then, and our deal is done?' said Clements.

'Just a sight,' said Mr Flynn.

'Very well…'

Julius thought he heard a curse under Clements's breath. 'This way,' said the purefinder and he walked into the fog.

'Stick close,' said Mr Flynn to Julius.

When they had gone a few paces Julius looked back. There was nothing but fog. He held Mr Flynn's coattail firmly as they walked on. Julius lost count of his steps.

Clements stopped. 'That's it,' he whispered.

Up ahead, the fog thinned and Julius could see a wall, slightly darker than the night. Beyond the wall the black silhouette of a house rose from the wasteland. Faint candle-lit rectangles showed the windows.

'They come and go at all times of the night,' whispered Clements. 'They stole a hansom cab a few days ago, and they use it to bring boxes and whatnot into the place. There's an odd fellow with them.'

'Odd?' said Mr Flynn.

'Short, gives everyone the collywobbles.'

'That's Tock,' whispered Julius.

'Thank you, Clements,' said Mr Flynn, handing over two sovereigns. 'The Watchmakers will remember this.'

'Goodnight, Mr Flynn, Higgins,' said Clements, and he skittered back along the path.

Julius had lost his sense of place. They could have been on a Yorkshire moor, but for the stench of the tanneries. At the stable door, he lit several Lucifers so that Mr Flynn could see to pick the lock. Finally it opened with a satisfying click and they slipped into the dark yard and made their way along the side of the stable outhouse until they came to the first window.

Julius peeped through the corner of the dusty windowpane. The interior walls of the building had been demolished, leaving only the outer walls and the roof. Birdcages and candles hung from the ceiling. The candles lit the cavernous lair as far as the second floor—above that, only hints of the roof rafters could be discerned.

Julius carefully shifted his position to see the floor. There were floorboards, with strips of plaster and brick where walls had once stood. Pale rectangles lined the walls, ghosts of pictures long gone.

To the left, in the far corner, stood a table covered with beakers, test tubes and large glass bulbs, in a complex arrangement connected by rubber tubing. Their contents bubbled and steamed over gas burners. Another table was crammed with pots of orchids of all shapes and colours. Julius strained his eyes and peered through the dirty windowpane to get a better look.

'What's that in the birdcages?' whispered Mr Flynn. 'Are they rats?

'I think so,' Julius replied. 'And there's orchids in some of them.'

'We've come to the right place, then,' said Mr Flynn.

Julius crept to the next window. He poked his head up and leaned to the side to see the left wall, where there was a basic kitchen and a sleeping area.

Julius cleaned a circle in the glass to get a clearer view.

A tall man in a brown overcoat lay on a bunk. Another man, also wearing a brown overcoat, sat reading a newspaper. Julius recognised them immediately as the men in the hansom cab.

Mr Flynn cleaned a circle for himself 'That's Rapple and Baines,' he whispered 'No doubt about it.'

Julius and Mr Flynn watched them for some minutes. There was little to see until one of the bubbling bulbs boiled over. The man reading dropped his paper and hurried to the apparatus as the hissing steam rose up to the rafters.

'Mr Rapple, Mr Rapple, wake up, it's nearly ready,' he said.

Rapple woke with a jolt. He stared at nothing for a few seconds as if he was trying to remember where he was. Then he swung around to sit on the edge of his bunk and watched Baines, who turned down the flame on the burner and adjusted the taps on the tubes.

The rats screeched and scurried around, making the birdcages sway on their chains.

Rapple stood up. 'They're getting excited,' he said.

A loud rapping made them both turn.

'Well done. You've gone and woken Abigail,' said Baines.

Julius ducked down below the windowsill. He sneaked past the back door and came up at the next window.

He cleaned an eye-sized circle in the grime on the windowpane and looked through. He saw a dining table near the far wall. A stained lace tablecloth was spread over it. Two small dots of red light glowed in the dark corner behind the table.

The rapping noise sounded again.

Rapple jumped. He looked around as if he had lost something that desperately needed to be found.

Baines backed away.

'Throw her something,' said Rapple.

'There's nothing left.'

'There must be.'

'She's had everything there is,' said Baines, searching frantically under the one of the tables.

Rapple untied one of the suspended cages. 'She can have one of these,' he said.

'Oi! We need that,' said Baines.

The rat squealed and scrambled up the bars. The other rats joined it, in a discordant chorus of high-pitched cries. The rapping behind the table started up again.

Rapple took a leather gauntlet from his pocket and slipped it over his hand. Then he opened the cage door, thrust his hand inside and grabbed the rat by its tail. It dangled upside down, arching its back and screeching, its teeth snapping, trying to bite Rapple's arm.

'Toss it over,' said Baines. 'Quick, man.'

The rapping grew lower and faster.

'Here you are, Abigail,' shouted Rapple. He threw the empty birdcage into the dark corner.

A giant, metal creature leapt out from behind the table and caught the cage with two claw-like append-ages.

Julius jumped, nearly falling backwards.

The creature looked like a cross between a giant praying mantis and a spider.

Baines held one of the candles hanging nearby and took a few cautious steps towards the creature.

73

'There you are, Abigail, my dear. That'll keep you quiet for a bit.'

'Let's get to work,' said Rapple. He stepped back and knocked his shoulder against one of the cages. Immediately, orchid tendrils stretched through the bars, reaching for his face. Rapple flinched. 'Bleeding things,' he said, as he scrambled to keep his hold on the rat.

'Watch where you're going,' said Baines.

'It nearly had me, that time,' said Rapple. He shook the rat to subdue it, then poured some of liquid from the bubbling bulb into a beaker.

The praying mantis creature turned the birdcage over and over in its claws, looking at it from every angle.

Julius wiped the clean circle a little wider. By the light of Baines's candle he could see Abigail clearly now.

She was almost twice as tall as a man and unlike any creature he had ever seen. One claw was made of kitchen forks and the other of knives. Her head was shaped like the muzzle of a dog. It was made of razors laid over each other like the scales of a fish. Her mouth was filled with razors too, forming long sharp teeth.

For eyes she had the casings of pocketwatches. Red light glowed behind the glass. Her head was fixed to a long neck of kitchen taps, washers and lengths of pipe. The creature turned the birdcage around, checking it minutely. Another claw came up from behind the table. It was topped with five small mirrors, which flicked open, like a hand stretching its fingers, and fanned themselves around the cage.

'She likes it, Mr Rapple,' said Baines with relief.

Rapple was not listening. He picked up a knife from the table.

'We might as well use this one,' he said, looking at the rat hanging from his gloved hand.

He swung it by the tail, hitting it against the edge of the table. Then he sawed its head off and held it over the bubbling beaker. Blood poured from the rat like wine from a bottle. When it stopped Rapple wrung the carcass out like a dishcloth to get a few last drops. Julius felt his stomach lurch.

'All done,' said Rapple, as he tossed the dead rat into a bucket under the table. The liquid in the beaker frothed and steamed for a few seconds then became still. Rapple held it up to the light and swirled the blood mixture inside.

'It's a good batch, Mr Baines,' he said, admiring his gruesome work.

Baines was not listening. He stepped closer to Abigail, watching her examine the birdcage. Her red eyes flicked from one mirror to the next.

With the candlelight nearer to her, the shadows on the wall showed more of her form: a long curved backbone with four long, leg-like appendages, bent at the knees and all jagged and haphazardly made of any piece of iron, tin or brass you could find in a kitchen or a tool shed.

A movement on the table brought Julius's eyes to a much smaller creature. It was scrabbling on a chain nailed to the table. It was too far away for him to be sure, but Julius thought it might have been made from carpentry nails and shards of tea tins. It made a clinking sound as it strained and squirmed on the table. This appeared to annoy Abigail. She rattled one of her claws. Her muzzle loomed close and her red eyes glowed brighter. The little creature tugged madly at its chain.

Abigail's claw of forks balled into a fist and slammed down on the creature. When she lifted her claw the creature struggled again, though not as energetically this time.

She slammed her claw down again and again, pounding the table until the creature was still.

Julius flinched with each blow.

Then Abigail stopped and watched the flattened creature, her claw held ready in case it stirred again. It dangled from the chain when she held it up for inspection. Then she began to pull bits off it as if she was plucking the wings from a moth.

Baines shuddered. 'Charming.'

'She's getting worse,' said Rapple.

'We should tell Mr Tock.'

'You tell him, I'm not.'

'Why should I, then?'

Abigail turned her attention back to the birdcages.

'At least she's stopped adding to herself. I wouldn't want to see her get any bigger,' said Rapple.

'Thought any more about where we'll go when Tock lets them loose?' said Baines.

'Yeah. I had an idea.'

Baines looked at him. 'What was it, then?'

'An island in the Pacific.'

'An island? I like that. We'd be safe on an island.'

They paused a while, as if imaging sea breezes and flower-filled hills.

'What a couple of specimens,' whispered Mr Flynn.

Before Julius could reply, the wall near the table began to bubble, like milk boiling in a saucepan. The bubbles fanned out into a circle as high as a door.

'Here he comes,' said Baines.

CHAPTER 7

Friday 19th January 1838

11:43 PM

Baines straightened his hat and faced the bubbling wall.

Rapple stood to attention, still holding the beaker.

Julius stared in disbelief. 'It's as if the wall's dissolving,' he said. 'I can see through it. How could that happen?'

'I have no idea,' said Mr Flynn.

Julius stared through his cleaned bit of glass at the bright circle on the wall.

'There's light coming through, like sunshine,' he said. 'It looks like the shape of rooftops. There's someone there.'

Mr Tock stepped through the bubbling wall. He was carrying a small wooden box, which he snapped shut and put in his inside jacket pocket. Then he raised his wide-brimmed hat and bowed. Behind him the wall resolved itself into peeling plaster.

'Gentlemen, gentlemen. Are you well? Are you? Are you?' he said.

'Very well, indeed, Mr Tock, sir,' said Baines.

'Yes, very well, sir,' said Rapple. He raised the beaker. 'Just fixed up another batch of blood-and-bone fertiliser.'

'*Excelentísimo*,' said Tock. 'Allow me.' He took the beaker and blew on it to cool it a little.

'Which of my darling soulcatchers would like to be fed first?' He appeared to be talking to the caged orchids.

'He called them soulcatchers, Mr Flynn,' whispered Julius. 'Like in Darwin's diary.'

Tock went to the lowest-hanging cage and stooped to hold his face close to the bars.

Julius started, expecting the soulcatcher's tendrils to shoot out towards him. But they remained still, as if Tock were not there.

'What a wise little soulcatcher you are,' said Tock. 'You know I have no soul for you to catch.'

'What did he...?' whispered Mr Flynn.

'He said he has no soul, and that the soulcatcher knows it,' whispered Julius.

'You like your food still warm, don't you? Don't you?' said Tock. He poured some of the liquid from the beaker into the soil around the orchid.

'Grow strong, my friend. Grow strong,' said Tock. 'And capture all those souls.'

'What did he say?' said Mr Flynn.

'He said it's going to capture souls,' said Julius.

'The man's insane,' said Mr Flynn.

What the Hell is going on, Higgins?

Tock suddenly spun around to face the dark corner.

'Abigail, my dear,' he said. 'Are you well? Are you? Are you?'

He beckoned to the metal creature, who climbed cautiously over the table and lowered her head for him to pat.

'You've been a good girl? Have you? Have you?' he said, stroking her gently.

Abigail nuzzled Mr Tock's side, making an almost-melodic metal scraping sound.

'Oh, she certainly has, Mr Tock, sir,' said Rapple. 'Never a peep from her, sir.'

'Such a beautiful creature, don't you think? Don't you? Don't you?' said Tock, as he patted her razor-blade snout.

A movement near his foot made him look down. 'What have we here?' he said, stooping to pick up a wriggling object.

Rapple cast a furtive glance at Baines. 'Oh yes, Mr Tock,' he said. 'Er, we've been meaning to tell you…'

'Tell me what?'

'It's Abigail, sir. She's been making things again,' said Baines.

Mr Tock peered at the object he held between his fingers. From where Julius stood it was just a squirming black dot.

'Abigail, my dear,' said Mr Tock, in a singsong voice. 'What did I say about making little things? What did I say? What? What?'

Abigail hung her head low. A metallic sound rattled around the interior of the house as she began to tremble. Mr Tock put the squirming thing in his pocket. Everyone was silent, even the rats. Abigail became still too.

Julius blinked.

A moment passed.

'Come closer, Abigail,' said Tock.

Abigail pulled back an inch.

'Abigail,' said Tock. 'Do I have to repeat myself? Do I? Do I?'

She raised a foot and took one step closer. Then she lifted her face towards his. Tock stroked her snout.

'There, there,' he said. 'Nothing to fear, my dear, nothing at all.'

Abigail's body loosened.

Then Tock took a hold of her head. Abigail flinched. Her knees buckled slightly.

'I am the Maker, not you,' said Tock. 'Do you understand? Do you? Do you?'

Abigail nodded her head.

'Good,' said Tock. Then he stabbed his finger through her eye.

Baines jumped. Abigail shrieked, making the glass in front of Julius's face vibrate.

Tock held her head firmly and pulled his finger out. Shards of glass fell to the floor.

'Shall I blind you? Shall I? Shall I?' he said, like a spoilt child, furious with his tin soldier. Abigail trembled as he held his finger over her other eye.

Cripes, Higgins. The man's deranged.

'I think I've seen enough,' whispered Mr Flynn. 'Let's go.'

Julius and Mr Flynn crept across the yard. Mr Flynn edged through the gate first. Julius opened it a little wider.

It creaked.

Julius froze. He and Mr Flynn listened. There were no sounds.

That was close, Higgins.

Julius turned his head to look at the house. Tock's pale face appeared at the window and smiled at him with his too-small teeth.

'Run,' said Mr Flynn.

He grabbed Julius by the shoulder, and hoisted him into the dark fog. They would have to use memory to find their way back, there was nothing else to help them.

Julius held tight to the flap of Mr Flynn's coat pocket. He concentrated on Mr Flynn's sounds and movements, as he could barely see him.

A sharp hiss cut through the darkness behind them, like a hundred Lucifers being lit at once.

Then another.

Julius looked back as they ran. Through the fog he saw two pale yellow lights rise up as if they had been thrown. They hissed over their heads and landed on the ground between them and the way out of the wasteground.

'They'll see our position if keep going that way,' whispered Mr Flynn.

The gate groaned. Another light ignited and hissed, then another. They landed to the left and right.

They're making a cordon to cut us off, Higgins.

Julius heard running feet across the boggy ground—heavy footsteps and light ones, and the sound a giant creature might make if it was made of metal.

More lights ignited and flew through the damp fog. A single red light glowed dimly, showing Abigail's position.

A dark figure ran at them. Mr Flynn jumped aside and Julius heard the crack of bare knuckles against bone, immediately followed by a grunt and the thud of a limp body hitting the ground.

'Julius,' hissed Mr Flynn.

Julius stepped three paces towards his voice. He found Mr Flynn crouched over Baines and extracting a meat cleaver from the fallen man's hand. Baines's face was splattered with blood.

'Over here,' called out Baines weakly, before Mr Flynn hit him with another bare-knuckle blow.

Julius grabbed Mr Flynn's coat and they hurried into the darkest corner of the foggy night.

'Mr Baines? Are you there,' called out Rapple's rasping voice.

'Over here,' came the muffled sound of Baines trying to speak through broken teeth.

Another light ignited almost directly in front of Julius and Mr Flynn. They froze. Mr Tock stood smiling at them, his blue eyes glowing. He held a giant Lucifer in his hand, apparently unconcerned about the meat cleaver in Mr Flynn's.

'How nice.' he said. 'Have you come to call? Have you? Have you?'

A sound behind Julius made him start.

Where's Abigail, Higgins?

Baines groaned out in the fog somewhere.

Mr Flynn held the cleaver ready.

'Why? It's our young friend from the bookshop,' said Tock. 'Mr Rapple, are you there? Are you? Are you?'

'Yes, Mr Tock, sir. I'm right here, sir,' said Rapple.

Rapple emerged from the fog, wielding a machete

in one hand and a giant Lucifer in the other. Julius heard the metallic sound of Abigail moving closer.

'Step aside and let us pass,' said Mr Flynn, in a voice that would normally have produced obedience from even the most hardened bruiser. It only made Tock smile wider.

'We can't do that,' said Tock. 'Can we, Mr Rapple?'

'No, we can't, Mr Tock, sir,' came the reply.

Julius saw the red light of Abigail's remaining eye through the fog.

Mr Flynn swung around so that he had both Tock and Rapple in his sight. Rapple was as tall as him, but Tock barely came up to his watch chain. 'I'll not say it again,' said Mr Flynn. 'Step aside or I'll be the one who's chopping limbs off.'

Tock chuckled.

Julius prepared to duck behind Mr Flynn.

'Did you like my gift? Did you? Did you?' said Tock to Julius.

'Your what?' said Julius.

'The orchid,' said Tock. 'Did you give it away? Did you? Did you?'

How does he know, Higgins?

The red spot of light was coming closer.

'Why are you spying on me?' said Tock. 'Tell me. Tell me.'

'I'm not,' said Julius. 'I just—'

'That's enough,' said Mr Flynn.

Julius tightened his grip on Mr Flynn's coat tail. He instinctively knew Mr Flynn's plan—go for Rapple, floor him, then run across the wasteground to Bermondsey.

'Kill them,' said Tock.

Rapple threw the light at Mr Flynn, and lunged at him with the machete raised.

Mr Flynn was too quick. He dodged the light and sidestepped his attacker. Julius leapt out of the way. Rapple checked himself and turned back to strike. But Mr Flynn was quicker still. He swung the meat cleaver and the blunt side caught Rapple squarely on the cheekbone. Rapple's legs buckled, and the machete fell.

Mr Flynn jumped aside as Abigail came towards them. Julius fell and rolled over, colliding with Rapple who reached out to grab him. But Julius kicked out madly, and his foot connected with Rapple's chin. The man cried in pain. Mr Flynn grabbed one of Abigail's claws and smashed the sharp edge of the meat cleaver into the side of her head, shattering what remained of her broken eye and leaving a deep gash in the razor scales.

Abigail let out a screech of metal grinding against metal and fell back.

Julius scrambled to his feet and searched for the machete.

'Come on,' said Mr Flynn, reaching past the fallen

Rapple and grabbing Julius by his shoulder.

'Do call again,' called out Tock, as they ran through the cold fog, using the faint lights still burning about the wasteground to find their way.

At the Bermondsey rookery Mr Flynn tossed the meat cleaver over a wall. Julius's body was like a blanc-mange on a merry-go-round—quivering and fragile.

'That was one frightening customer,' said Mr Flynn. 'I've never met a man I couldn't put the wind up if I put my mind to it.'

'He was completely without fear.'

'How did he know you gave the orchid away?' said Mr Flynn, leading the way through the dark alley-ways.

'I don't know,' said Julius. 'At least he doesn't know who I gave it to.'

'Aye,' said Mr Flynn. 'Let's keep that way.'

'Tock walked through the wall,' said Julius. 'One minute it was there and the next it like some sort of liquid.'

'Aye.'

'Do you think he came from a parallel realm, like the Grackacks?' said Julius.

'If he did, he's found a doorway between the realms.'

'That's not very reassuring,' said Julius. He shuddered when he recalled the Grackacks' realm and his terrifying time there. He wondered what Tock's realm would be like. Would it be full of short, frightening people with staring blue eyes?

'The soulcatcher orchid didn't go for him like it went for Rapple,' said Julius. 'What did he mean when he said he didn't have a soul?'

'Damned if I know,' said Mr Flynn.

They arrived at the bank of the Thames and stopped. Across the river Julius could see the faint silhouette of the dome of St Paul's Cathedral.

Mr Flynn took the jar containing the orchid from his pocket. He shook it lightly and held it up to catch what light there was. It wriggled and writhed behind the glass.

'It certainly wants to get at you, Mr Flynn,' said Julius. 'But the one in the birdcage didn't even know Tock was there.'

'But it made Edward Rapple flinch like a shepherdess,' said Mr Flynn. 'And what was that he said about getting away when they're let loose?'

'What if Tock's planning to release the soulcatchers in London?' said Julius. 'There was a painting in Mr Darwin's diary of a them growing out of a man's mouth and nose and eyes. It looked like he was screaming in agony. We can't let that happen here.'

'Let's hope that was just a painting,' said Mr Flynn.

'The Watchmakers will want to know about this,' said Julius. 'I think we should get the pocketwatch, Mr Flynn.'

Mr Flynn put the jar away. 'You're right, Julius,' said Mr Flynn 'It's time to get the pocketwatch.'

A spasm of new life ran through Julius, as if someone had called out his name in a crowded room. His skin tingled as if fireworks were going off inside him. He was going to hold the pocketwatch again.

'Do you think you could summon the Watchmakers with it, Julius?'

It took Julius a moment to realise he was been spoken to. 'Yes,' he said. 'I'm sure. I saw the professor do it.'

You're going to hold the pocketwatch again, Higgins.

Its porcelain face was as clear in his mind as if it was right there before him, as white as sunshine on snow. Its tick-tock was the beating of his heart.

'We should get it now,' he said.

CHAPTER 8

Saturday 20th January 1838

1:13 AM

Julius and Mr Flynn climbed the steps of St Paul's. Julius lit a Lucifer to help Mr Flynn as he sorted through a ring of keys.

'You have a key to the cathedral?' said Julius.

'Of course,' said Mr Flynn.

The city was silent, as if it was watching them open the cathedral door.

Inside, it was as black as a coalmine on a Sunday. Mr Flynn struck another Lucifer and lit a nearby candle for himself and one for Julius. The darkness receded into the corners and alcoves.

They walked across the tiled floors between the pillars and arches that lined the nave, and past the rows and rows of empty chairs. 'I've only just realised,' Julius whispered, 'that when Tock spoke—'

'Yes?' said Mr Flynn.

'His breath didn't mist.'

'Something to do with his parallel realm, perhaps,' said Mr Flynn.

Up ahead, the Grand Organ rose towards the domed ceiling. Laughing cherubs looked down at them from the polished wood panels. Six months earlier, Julius and Mr Flynn had locked the pocketwatch in a secret drawer in the stairs behind the organ. Julius felt its tick-tock in his heartbeat again. He followed Mr Flynn up the stairs. At the fourteenth step Mr Flynn sat down and took a small, golden key from his waistcoat pocket. He ran his fingers across the grain of the wood at the back of the organ, feeling for the keyhole.

'Here you are, my little beauty,' he whispered.

He slid the key in and the lock clicked open.

This is it, Higgins.

A tiny drawer sprang out from the wood panelling. There was the pocketwatch, its face like a full moon in the night.

The ticking was already pulsing through Julius's veins.

Go on, Higgins.

As soon as his fingertips touched it he felt a wave of warmth run through his body. He lifted the watch from the drawer. It fitted perfectly into his hand; its weight was just right. Julius held its face close to his. It glowed quietly, like a smile.

The hands told the correct time—half past one. The second hand swept across the Roman numerals. Tick-tock, tick-tock, tick-tock.

Mr Flynn locked the drawer.

Julius held the pocketwatch close to his candle and studied the engraved design on the back. He found the tiny letters *J. H.* among the swirls—the initials of John Harrison, the man who had made the pocketwatch that could travel through time.

The face was a plain, white film of porcelain, thinner than onion paper and webbed with tiny almost-invisible cracks where the face opened up as it prepared to jump through time.

Julius ran his finger around the side, feeling for the tiny compartment that contained a strand of his hair. It flicked open like a secret on a spring. With this hair inside the pocketwatch it was *his*, in a way the professor had not fully explained. Julius felt the belonging, but he couldn't explain it either.

The pocketwatch was growing warmer in his hand. Was he imagining it or was it glowing a little brighter? He looked up to Mr Flynn sitting on the step above him.

'Time to summon the Watchmakers, Julius,' said Mr Flynn.

They climbed down the stairs and stood under the

dome of the cathedral. It was as if they were standing inside an elaborately carved and decorated cave with a ceiling as high as the stars. Shafts of gossamer moonlight fell through the dome windows, making the space above their heads seem liquid and alive. The air crackled with the cold.

Julius thought about the last time he had held the pocketwatch in the cathedral. It was six months ago. He had managed, with the help of Emily and her gang, to outwit the time-criminal Jack Springheel and put an end to his plans to help the Grackacks invade London. When it was all over, Professor Fox tapped three times on the pocketwatch, and then once again, to summon his ten compatriots. Green light reached out and separated into ten strands, forming a circle. Ten gentleman in frockcoats, top hats and canes had appeared in flashes of light—the time travellers who called themselves the Guild of Watchmakers. They put right the mess that Jack Springheel had caused. Now, their help was needed again.

Julius spun the pocketwatch in the air just as the professor had done. But as soon as he let go, it fell back into his hand.

'Try again. Concentrate,' said Mr Flynn.

Julius stared at the pocketwatch.

What's wrong, Higgins?

He tried to make it the only thought in his mind, tried to feel the spinning cogs and wheels on the palm of his hand, tried to believe that he could make it happen. He willed the pocketwatch to understand what he needed.

He spun it again.

Nothing happened. The pocketwatch lay in the palm of his hand. He could feel its warmth, feel the ticking of the mechanism.

Mr Flynn appeared to be thinking.

Julius peered at the pocketwatch. What had he missed? What had he done wrong? Perhaps it needed a little time after it came out of the drawer?

The answer might be in Harrison's diary, Higgins.

It was still at the bookshop, on the shelf behind the counter. He was just about to tell Mr Flynn, but he remembered: Harrison's diary was his secret.

The memory ran a cold finger down his spine. At the end of the Springheel case, Julius was about to confess to Mr Flynn that he had stolen the diary from his grandfather to give to Jack Springheel. That was when Julius thought that Mr Flynn was going to confess that he was really his father. But that did not happen. Julius's face burned at the memory. Julius had misunderstood Mr Flynn's kindness as that of a father. And in his disappointment Julius had kept the diary hidden under his jacket. He had held the two secrets ever since: the secret of the diary and his secret wish that Mr Flynn could be his father.

'We should put it back,' said Mr Flynn.

'I could take it home,' said Julius. 'Practise with it.'

'It has to go back.'

Julius's fingers clasped the pocketwatch.

'No.'

The word rang around the cathedral.

'It has to stay in the drawer,' said Mr Flynn. 'The Watchmakers can't risk losing it again. And you can't jeopardise your apprenticeship.'

Mr Flynn's words were kind but firm. He handed Julius the key. 'Don't worry. We'll sort this out ourselves.'

'Yes,' said Julius. He knew Mr Flynn was right.

He took a candle and climbed the stairs behind the organ. He sat down and held the pocketwatch, not looking at it, just feeling its tick-tock whispering to his body. Tick-tock. Tick-tock. He counted the ticks, telling himself that on the twentieth tick he would put the pocketwatch back. He ran his fingertips along the wood grain and found the keyhole. The pocketwatch slid snuggly back in its place. All Julius was left with was his own heartbeat.

He sat back and stared at it. The second-hand moved around the face. Tick-tock, tick-tock, tick-tock. The sound was gentle and precise. He listened, not able to imagine being parted from it.

He felt something shift inside him. He knew what he was going to do.

He took the watch and slipped it into his pocket.

He closed the empty drawer and locked it. His hand gripped the watch as he walked down the stairs and across the tiles and handed the golden key to Mr Flynn.

'All done,' said Julius.

'Good lad,' said Mr Flynn. He held up the jar. The soulcatcher's pale tendrils pressed against the glass searching for a way out. 'We'll start on this business tomorrow. Too late for anything tonight.'

Julius looked Mr Flynn in the eye so there would be no suspicion that he had done anything wrong.

'And Emily's available,' he said.

'What?' said Mr Flynn.

'I mean, she said she'd be willing to help, if anything came up.'

'Hmm, did she now?' said Mr Flynn. 'I'll think about it.'

CHAPTER 9

Saturday 20th January 1838

3:48 AM

Julius slid his key into the door at Higgins' Bookshop.

'Good night,' said Mr Flynn. 'I'll speak to Abberline tomorrow, see if he'll introduce me to Mr Darwin. We'll ask about that painting of his.'

Julius opened the door a crack and slipped in without ringing the shop bell. The clock ticked on the mantel. He crept to the counter and rifled through a drawer until he found a candle stub. He lit it and reached for Harrison's diary on the shelves behind him. He had returned the diary to his grandfather at the end of the Springheel case with an apology and a story about having shown it to an eager potential customer.

As Julius turned to put the diary on the counter he saw two pale-blue eyes staring at him from the far corner of the bookshop. He jumped and the book fell to the floor.

'Good evening,' said Tock.

The little man emerged from the dark corner. As he drew closer to the candle flame Julius saw a cruel smile spread across his face. His eyes bore into Julius, making him step back into the bookshelf. He was trapped. Tock approached with exaggerated care, as if Julius was a frightened deer in a forest. He walked along the front of the counter to the gap near the entrance to the parlour.

Julius put his foot on Harrison's diary and very carefully slid it behind him into the corner.

Tock's smile stayed set on his face. He dropped Darwin's diary onto the counter with a thud that made Julius jump. The image of Tock stabbing Abigail's eye flashed through his mind.

Tock's smile twitched as if he was trying not to laugh. He tilted his head to one side to study Julius. He was half a head shorter than Julius, but there was something about the little man's fearlessness that was terrifying. Julius gripped the pocketwatch tight.

'You interest me,' said Tock. 'Shall I show you why?'

Julius stared until Tock spoke again.

'What are you doing in Darwin's diary?' said

Tock. He opened the book and tapped a page. 'What? What?'

Julius looked down at a fine pencil drawing of a native boy and girl. They looked exactly like Emily and him.

It can't be, Higgins. It can't.

His mind was a whirl. The girl was pretty, with a thick, dark hair. She had a cheeky smile, just like Emily. The boy wore a wary, anxious expression and could have been Julius's twin. At the bottom of the page Darwin had written. *I shall call my saviours Adam and Eve. I am forever in their debt.*

'That's not me. He just looks like me,' said Julius.

It can't be you and Emily, Higgins?

The pocketwatch grew warmer in his hand, almost burning.

But it is you, Higgins.

Tock held the page up. He looked from Julius's face to the drawing.

'Perhaps you are correct,' said Tock. 'A remarkable coincidence though, don't you think? All the same, I should like to see that pretty pickpocket's face again,' Tock smiled. 'Tell me where she is.'

'I don't know,' said Julius. 'I don't know who she is.' He stared into Tock's eyes, willing him to believe the lie.

His mind was racing, searching for answers. Had he and Emily had gone back in time? What had they done that Darwin would be forever in their debt?

Tock ran his finger over the girl on the page. 'Such a sweet smile.' He looked at Julius. 'Why did you peep through my window? Why? Why?'

Julius swallowed. He gripped the pocketwatch as if he was trying to absorb it into his hand.

'I...I was curious.'

'Why? Why?'

'Because, well, you frightened me.'

This seemed to please Tock. 'Who was that uncouth brute with you? Who was he? Who was he?'

'Charlie, I think. I don't know his second name. I paid him a ten shillings to come with me, in case there was any trouble.'

Tock's smile began to fade.

Julius tried not to break eye contact.

'Where is the orchid?' said Tock. 'Where is it? Where is it?'

Julius tried to look like he was trying to remember.

'The old fool said he gave it to a customer,' said Tock.

Does he mean Grandfather, Higgins?

'Is that true?'

'I suppose it is,' said Julius. 'He didn't say anything to me.'

Tock stared, unblinking at him. Julius wondered how much more he could take. Could you die from being stared at?

'Mr Higgins shouldn't give presents away. It's very rude,' said Tock. His petulant tone surprised Julius. He seemed hurt.

Tock reached into his pocket and pulled something out. 'Look what I have,' he said. 'Look. Look.'

A mouse-sized thing wriggled in Tock's small, pale hands. It was a many-legged, no-headed creation, made of copper wire and bent and twisted sewing needles.

Tock held it gently. 'Abigail made it,' he said. 'She trickles her consciousness into them and they begin to squirm and jiggle. They want to live you see—consciousness wants to continue. It does. It does. But she grows bored with her children.'

In one sharp movement Tock slammed the creature against the edge of the counter. Julius jumped. Tock slammed it down again, and again, until it stopped moving.

'All gone,' said Tock. He examined the mangled creature. 'Do not mourn it. It has no soul…just like me.'

Julius blinked in confusion

Tock twisted the creature until it came apart and let the pieces fall to the floor.

Julius stared into Tock's blue eyes. How long had he been standing there? It seemed like hours.

Tock's expression softened, becoming almost friendly. 'I shall have your soul,' he said. 'I shall have everyone's soul. I shall. I shall.'

Julius lip trembled. He clenched his jaw.

Tock put the diary into his coat pocket and pulled a small wooden box from his inside pocket. 'Good night,' he said, and he leaned over the candle stub and blew it out.

Julius's heart jumped in his chest. Tock's eyes glowed faintly in the darkness.

'If we meet again,' said Tock, 'you will be sorry.' He turned away and walked through the curtain into the parlour.

Where's he going, Higgins?

Julius heard the tinkle of glass breaking—it was something delicate. He tried to think what it would be. They did not have any dainty glass ornaments. He snatched Harrison's diary from the floor and hid it inside his coat. His knees trembled as he went to the curtain and pulled it open an inch.

The parlour was dark. He strained to see any movement. All was still. After a few moments' hesitation he lit the candle stub.

The parlour was empty but something caught his eye. On the wall next to the fireplace, vapour was rising from a damp patch the size of a dinner plate. Julius stepped closer. An acrid odour made his nose twitch. As he drew nearer, the damp patch diminished, until it disappeared completely. On the floor beneath it were tiny shards of broken glass.

Julius put his hand on the wall. It was warm.

Tock went through the wall, Higgins. But how? And where did he go?

Julius sat in his fireside chair and stared at the wall, half wondering if Tock would return. After a few minutes he took Harrison's diary out. Surely there would be something is in about how to summon the Watchmakers. All he saw was page after page of tiny writing, intricate diagrams, and row upon row of mathematical calculations. His eyelids became heavy and the page before him began to blur. He fought to keep his eyes open, but in a few seconds he was asleep.

☛

Julius woke to the sound of someone hammering on the shop door. He looked around the parlour trying to remember why he had fallen asleep in front of the fire. The pounding continued.

Then he remembered.

Tock came to call, Higgins.

He looked at the curtain covering the doorway to the shop. Had Tock come back? Was he angry with him for bolting the door?

The hammering continued.

Julius pulled the curtain aside. A crowd of men were peering in through the window.

What the bloody hell's happening, Higgins?

'There he is. I see him,' shouted one of the men. 'Open up, Higgins, damn you, we haven't got all day,' called another. The pounding increased in urgency.

Of course! It's Saturday morning, Higgins

For as long as Julius could remember Saturday mornings at Higgins' Booksellers involved a profitable few hours of pandemonium when his grandfather's most avid and demanding customers came to collect their orders. The shop usually opened at ten sharp. Julius looked at the clock. It was three minutes past and the door remained locked, hence the near-riot on Ironmonger Lane.

Julius let the curtain fall.

Why hasn't Grandfather opened the shop, Higgins?

'Grandfather. Grandfather,' he called up the stairs.

No reply came. Julius ran up the stairs two at a time. He knocked on his grandfather's bedroom door and opened it. The room was empty and the bed had not been slept in.

Grandfather?

'Open up, Higgins. Open up,' came the shouts from outside.

Julius ran down the stairs and into the shop. The front door was shaking under the blows of the customers. Without any time to think, he unlocked and unbolted the door. Cheers rang out in Ironmonger Lane.

Julius was going to tell everyone that the shop

would be closed for the day, but he was lifted up and carried back inside by a tidal wave of kid-gloves, walking canes and literary periodicals. He only just managed to slip behind the counter.

Three hours later the last customer had been served. Julius slid the bolt on the front door and leaned against it, enjoying the stillness of the empty shop. He closed his eyes and considered letting himself fall asleep where he stood. But then he remembered.

Where's grandfather, Higgins?

As his mind began to churn, there was a knock at the door.

'We're closed,' said Julius, without moving.

The knocking persisted.

Julius spun around and shouted through the frosted glass. 'I said, we're closed.'

'Oi, 'iggins,' came the reply. 'Let me in.'

It was Emily.

'What do you want?' he said, recalling her murderous expression in the kitchen the day before.

'To come in. It's freezing out 'ere.'

He looked at her outline through the frosted glass. A sudden rush of resentment made him want to shout at her to go away and never come back. Immediately he felt ashamed of himself.

If Mr Flynn wants a daughter why shouldn't he have one, Higgins?

He tried to push the feelings down.

'I'm busy,' he said. 'Come back later.'

'Let me in, 'iggins. You want me to get frostbite?'

Julius leaned his forehead on the frosted glass and closed his eyes. He missed liking Emily. He sighed and opened the door.

Emily stood there in her bonnet and fur-lined cap. Her purse hung from her wrist. She smiled. ''ello, 'iggins.'

'Hello.'

She walked in without being asked and stood at the counter like a customer. 'Wot's wrong? You get no sleep? You look terrible.'

'Thank you,' said Julius.

''ow did everyfing go yesterday?' she said.

Julius bolted the door. 'We found the two bruisers' hideout. Mr Flynn knows them, They're Rapple and Baines.'

'And? Wot 'appened?'

'Tock was there. There were rats in cages, and orchids. Like the one Tock gave us. They're called soul-catchers, and there was a large metal thing,' said Julius.

'Ace. Start talking,' said Emily. 'Why's it called a soulcatcher?'

'Darwin said the native people believed it trapped their souls.'

'How?'

'I don't know,' said Julius. 'I'm sorry about Mr Flynn finding out about you stealing the diary. He guessed. But I told him that you were available.'

'Ace,' said Emily. 'Wot did 'e say?'

Julius remembered the drawing of the native girl.

'Wot's wrong, 'iggins?' said Emily.

'Er, nothing,' said Julius. Tock was looking for her. She seemed so small. What if Baines had cut her hand off? What else might they do to her?

'You look like you've seen a debt collector, 'iggins.'

'No. It's nothing. I was just…' Julius shook his thoughts away. 'You're not vexed with me then?'

'Vexed? Me? No. Well, maybe a bit,' said Emily. 'Clara says it's best to be agreeable to people. She says you gets more from the world if you're civil to it than if you knock it on the 'ead wiv a pickaxe handle. So I'm giving it a try. I'm not promising naffing, mind.'

'No,' said Julius. 'Of course not.'

'Clara's ace,' said Emily, ignoring Julius's sarcasm. 'If I could pick someone to be my ma I reckon I'd pick 'er.'

Julius felt a quiver of anger arising.

You've got a brand new father, isn't that enough?

He walked into the parlour and fell into his chair. Emily followed. She looked around and sniffed.

'Not bad,' she said. 'Could do wiv a woman's touch.'

Julius considered putting a few coals on the fire, but he was too tired to move.

'You made an impression on 'er,' said Emily.

'On who?'

'On Clara. She was asking all about you. Me and 'er spent the 'ole bleeding day scrubbing that bleeding kitchen. Look at my 'ands now, red raw. That's slave labour, that is. I'm only a little girl. I've a good mind to report—Oi, 'iggins, try and stay awake when I'm talking to you.'

'Sorry, I didn't get much sleep last night. And grandfather's gone somewhere so I was working in the shop all morning.'

'Where's 'e gone?'

'I don't know.'

Julius looked at the dying fire. He clutched the pocketwatch to stem the fear rising up inside him.

Where is he, Higgins? What has Tock done?

He winced when he thought of Tock smashing Abigail's creature.

'Wot's that?' said Emily. She sat on the arm on his chair.

'What?' Julius looked at his hand. He was holding the pocketwatch.

'That's the one the professor used, ain't it, 'iggins,' she said. 'The one to get the Watchmakers.'

'Er…yes, it is,' said Julius.

He noticed Harrison's diary half hidden down the

side of the chair. He tried to recall how he came to have the pocketwatch in his hand. Then he remembered.

You stole it, Higgins.

'Wot's wrong, 'iggins? You all right?' said Emily.

'Me? Yes. I'm fine.'

How could you be so stupid?

He pictured himself handing the key back to Mr Flynn.

Emily could pick Mr Flynn's pocket. She'd do it if you asked her, Higgins. Then you could put it back.

'Wot's wrong, 'iggins?'

We could put the pocketwatch back and Mr Flynn would never know. Emily could put the key back in his pocket.

'Nothing's wrong.'

'Don't look like it to me,' said Emily. 'Are you in trouble, 'iggins?'

'Tock was here last night, in the shop.'

'Wot did 'e want?'

'He wanted to know who had the orchid.'

'You didn't tell 'im did you?'

'No. He was here earlier, too. Apparently grandfather told him he gave it to a customer.'

'Good old Mr 'iggins. I knew 'e wouldn't shop me,' said Emily. 'So where's Mr 'iggins?'

'That's just it. I don't know.'

Julius held up the pocketwatch. Its presence reassured him. It was almost like having Mr Flynn in the parlour with them. The tick-tock tickled the palm of his hand. Julius concentrated for a moment. Was the ticking growing stronger?

He picked up Harrison's diary and flicked through it, but he put it aside again and sighed.

You'll be studying that for years before you understand any-thing, Higgins.

'Anyway, 'iggins,' said Emily. 'You don't 'ave no ma, do you?'

'No. She died when I was born.'

'Cos I was finking…'

'Thinking what?'

'Wot if she wasn't, you know…dead?'

'What are you talking about?'

'Oh, 'iggins,' said Emily, with exasperation. 'It's as plain as the snot up your nose.'

'What is?'

'That Clara's your ma. She even looks like you, in the right light.'

'That's nonsense.'

'Suit yourself.'

Julius looked at the watch face. It seemed to glow slightly.

'Did you see that?' he said.

'See wot?'

'Nothing.'

Julius stared at the pocketwatch, willing it to glow again. Something shifted. He could feel cogs and wheels interlocking in his mind. For just a moment he imagined he understood the whole mechanism all at once, in a way that words could never explain.

''iggins?' said Emily.

The pocketwatch jolted and rose above his hand. It hung bobbing in the air an inch above his palm.

Emily's eyes widened. 'Did you do that, 'iggins?'

'I think so. I'm not really sure.'

'Make it do somefing else.'

Julius let all his thoughts fall away. He wanted to be aware of only the pocketwatch, nothing else.

The watch face opened into concentric circles.

'Cor,' said Emily.

Then the watch expanded into the shape of a cone and the inner workings were in plain view. The interlocking cogs and wheels were spinning smoothly, not in the usual stop-start motion of a watch. The pocketwatch rose higher above Julius's hand and the underside stretched down into a cone too. The tick-tock was replaced by a myriad of ticks and clicks that sounded like a swarm of crickets having a discussion.

Julius drew his fingers up and the pocketwatch rose up too. Without touching it he gently moved his fingertips as if to spin a top.

The pocketwatch began to spin.

'Cor. That's amazing, 'iggins,' said Emily. 'Wot else can it do?'

Emily didn't know about the time-travel capabilities of the pocketwatch. She knew it could be used to

111

summon the Guild of Watchmakers—she had seen the professor do it. But when Julius had told her he had time-travelled, Springheel was holding a blade to her throat. Had she been paying attention?

'It can travel through time,' said Julius.

'Frough wot?'

'Through time.'

'Wot do you mean, 'iggins?'

'It's difficult to explain.'

Deep inside the mechanism Julius saw a point of blue light. It grew steadily and shone out from the pocketwatch. Suddenly the cogs and wheels were spinning faster. The clicking and ticking grew louder, and turned into a polyrhythm. Soon the wheels were spinning too fast to see.

Emily grasped Julius's shoulder. 'Wot's 'appening?'

'I think it wants to take us back in time,' said Julius.

'Where?'

'I'm not sure,' said Julius, 'But Darwin wrote that he was indebted to two children.'

'So?' said Emily.

'I think the children might be us,' said Julius.' He grabbed her hand and shifted in his chair to face her. 'Whatever happens, don't panic.'

'Wot?'

'And bend your knees when you land.'

'Land where?'

'We'll know when we get there.'

Julius tapped the side of the pocketwatch and clasped Emily's other hand.

Everything went black and silent.

The next thing Julius knew he was tumbling through space.

Ha, ha. You did it, Higgins.

In front of him was the pocketwatch, as huge as London. The mechanism stretched up like a mountain. The massive wheels and cogs moved so slowly that it took hours for each second to pass. With each tick, the universe quaked silently around him.

Both Julius's arms were stretched out hundreds of miles on either side, but he could see Emily's hand in his, as clearly as if it was next to him. He couldn't see Emily, though. She was floating on the other side of the gigantic pocketwatch, which flew through the eye of a galaxy faster than it took to sneeze.

You did it, Higgins.

They careered through galaxy after galaxy for what seemed like an eternity and a minute all at once.

Then everything went black again.

CHAPTER 10

Friday June 29th 1832

1:35 PM

Julius hit the ground and rolled over. All at once he knew he wasn't in London. Strange cries like whoops and whistles filled his ears. The air against his skin was warm and moist. Dancing points of bright light shone down around him. He snapped his eyes shut but the light burned inside his eyeballs.

Someone fell through foliage and swore.

'Wot the bleeding 'ell just 'appened, 'iggins?' she said.

Well done, Higgins. All accounted for.

'It's all right, Emily,' said Julius. 'We've travelled through time.'

He blinked his eyes to accustom them to the light. Tints of brown and green swam before him. The shapes resolved into large leaves at the base of a tree. The whoops and whistles in his ears clarified too.

It's monkeys and birds, Higgins. Just like at the zoo.

An arm's length away the pocketwatch spun in the air. Julius held out his hand and it flew to him. He clasped it and put into his pocket. Then he realised he was wearing only a pair of tatty shorts and a ragged shirt with its sleeves torn off.

He looked around. He was in a forest, but not like any forest in England. The air was so warm it tickled his skin. The trees were unlike any he had seen before. They towered above him, forming a ceiling of shifting patterns. He understood the dancing light now—it was speckles of sunlight falling through the ever-changing leafy roof of the forest.

'Cor,' said a voice nearby.

Julius turned to see a very pretty native girl step out of a clump of giant leaves. She was barefooted and wore a tatty smock. Her black hair fell over her shoulders and her skin was the colour of copper.

It's the girl from the diary, Higgins.

'Oi. Who are you?' she said to Julius.

'Julius Higgins,' he said.

'No you ain't,' said the native girl. 'Wot 'ave you done wiv 'im?'

That's it, Higgins. The pocketwatch has made new forest versions of us.

'It's all right, Emily. It *is* me, I promise.'

The girl eyed him suspiciously.

'The pocketwatch did it,' said Julius.

'Did wot?'

'It sent our atoms back to the parlour at home and took our consciousnesses travelling through time and space. Then it landed us here—wherever that is—and wrapped the atoms of the forest around our minds to make local versions of us.'

The girl stared at Julius. Her eyes were darker, but the right shape, and her nose had that upturned end.

She stroked her arm. 'I've gone all brown.' She looked Julius up and down. ''ave we travelled frough time?'

Julius nodded.

'And frough space?'

Julius nodded again.

'And landed 'ere?'

'Yes. It looks that way,' said Julius.

Emily smiled. 'This is ace, 'iggins. You've done a good job.'

'You're pleased then?'

'Not 'arf. Is this what Mr Flynn and the professor do? Time-jumping about 'ere and there whenever they feel like it?'

'Something like that,' said Julius. 'They do it sparingly, I think, and it's usually in pursuit of time-criminals.'

'Yeah, yeah, wot ever,' said Emily, looking up at

the leafy forest canopy. 'Wot 'appens now?'

'The pocketwatch brought me, I mean *us*, here for a reason,' said Julius. 'I'm sure of it. We've already been here—in the past, I mean. There is a drawing of you and me looking like this in the diary. I didn't understand at the time, but I think I do now. We did something to help Darwin. Something so wonderful that he said he'd be forever in our debt.'

'So we're in the past, right now?' said Emily, 'to do somefing we did years ago?'

'Yes.'

'But, 'ow will we know what that fing was?'

'I don't know,' said Julius.

Emily patted the nearest tree and looked up. 'Big, ain't they,' she said. 'We should 'ave a look round, 'iggins. See wot's wot.'

'I think that's a path,' said Julius. He pointed along a worn strip of dirt winding along the forest floor.

'It goes that way too,' Emily said, looking in the other direction. She twitched her nose as she considered. 'This way,' she said, and set off.

'Why this way?' said Julius.

'Why not, 'iggins?'

A few hundred yards along the path the trees began to thin. Up ahead the sunshine poured down like ghostly treacle.

Emily stopped suddenly. Julius bumped into her.

'What is it?'

'Did you 'ear that, 'iggins?'

They crouched and listened. A sound emerged through the screeches and squawks. Julius strained to make it out. It seemed out of place in the forest.

The sound grew louder. There were footsteps too. Something heavy, on two legs. And it was coming towards them. Julius peeped through the foliage. A large black creature was ambling in their direction.

Julius was just about to grab Emily's hand and run for it when the sound fell into place in his ears. It was a hymn—'Abide with Me', if he was not mistaken.

Emily's eyebrows tensed as she recognised it too. The sounds of footsteps grew closer—the distinctive thud of boots on hardened earth. Julius peered through the bushes. The great black lumbering thing was whipping the bushes with a stick and coming closer.

Julius and Emily edged back into the forest greenery trying to make themselves invisible. A few yards away the thing broke out onto the path and strode towards them swinging its stick like a scythe.

Julius stared in disbelief.

It was an ageing clergyman with red orchids growing from each side of his mouth like tusks. He wore full black attire including a black felt hat. He was humming another hymn now. It sounded like 'Rock of Ages'.

Julius and Emily stayed out of sight until he lumbered by.

'Did you see 'is face, 'iggins?'

'Yes, I did. Come on,' said Julius.

Julius jumped out onto the path in time to see the clergyman step out of the forest and into the sunshine. The light was so bright it seemed to subsume him, turning him into a black-coated shimmer, that grew smaller and smaller as he walked away.

Julius stepped into the sunshine and shaded his eyes.

'Don't stop, 'iggins, we'll lose 'im,' Emily said.

Julius grabbed her arm and pulled her back. 'Wait.'

Emily twisted impatiently. 'Wot?'

Julius pointed to the ground. 'Look. Soulcatchers.'

Small red orchids were growing up through the grass all around them. Some were only inches from their feet.

'Do you notice something, Emily?'

'No. Wot?' she said, shading her eyes, too.

'They're all leaning towards us,' said Julius. 'It's like they're watching us.'

Julius held Emily to stop her from moving. 'Remember the soulcatcher in the kitchen,' he whispered.

Emily nodded. They stepped as slowly and cautiously as frightened snails into the clearing where the soulcatchers thinned out. The orchids tilted their petals, as if keeping them in sight. But none of them tried to pull itself out of the ground.

Julius breathed a little easier.

'I fink they're all right,' Emily whispered.' She gingerly approached one.

'Be careful,' said Julius. 'Don't touch it.'

'Why not?'

'I don't know,' said Julius. 'But Rapple was terrified of one of those, even when it was in a cage. So I think we should be too.'

Emily squatted down. ''ello, little fing,' she whispered. 'You wouldn't 'urt me, would you?'

Julius leaned over her shoulder. 'They're not as wild as the ones in London,' he said.

Emily held her hand out as if the soulcatcher might be a dog who wanted to sniff it.

'Careful,' said Julius.

'I know,' said Emily.

As her hand came closer the soulcatcher's tendrils slowly lifted and reached out to her. Emily drew back. 'Friendly little fella, ain't 'e.'

'We shouldn't be out in the open,' said Julius. 'They'll see us.'

'Who'll see us, 'iggins?'

'I don't know.'

Up ahead they saw a row of native huts. When they got closer they saw that they were spread along a riverbank. Some of the huts stood over the water. They were all built on stilts with ladders leading up to the doors. The clergyman was nowhere to be seen.

Nothing moved. The village was silent. But flame-red flowers grew out through the doors and windows of the huts and up through the roofs, and across the ground. They even entwined themselves around the stilts. The whole place had the feel of a giant funeral wreath.

A memory stirred in Julius's mind. Something in Darwin's diary about a damned village.

'This is the Village of the Soulcatchers,' he said. 'We're in Brazil, I think, in the jungle.'

'I ain't never been to a jungle before,' said Emily. 'Where do you fink everyone is?

'Did you see a painting in Darwin's diary?' said Julius. 'Of red flowers, growing from a man's face.'

Her eyes lit up. 'Yeah, I seen it. It's just like that cove who just walked past. But 'e ain't got so many.'

'We need to be very careful, Emily,' said Julius.

'You already said that, 'iggins.'

Before Julius could reply there was a shriek further along the shore and a man's voice called out angrily. He stepped out from the forest pulling a small boy by his arm. The boy screamed and struggled as he was dragged towards a jetty. The man shouted something, as if trying to call for assistance. Julius could not understand what he said.

Emily leapt up. Julius grabbed her and pulled her back.

'Wait,' he said.

'Oi.' Emily pushed him away. 'This could be wot we're supposed to do,' she said. 'Maybe we're supposed to save the nippa.'

'We don't know what's going on yet,' said Julius.

Emily glared at him. 'Mr Flynn would 'ave dropped that cove by now if 'e was 'ere.'

'But he's not,' said Julius. 'I am. I got us here, and I'm in charge.'

As soon as he said the words he knew he had made a mistake.

'Who says you're in char—'

'Shush,' said Julius. 'Look.'

The clergyman appeared at the doorway of one of the huts. He called out and waved his arms. Again, Julius could not understand what he said. The clergyman climbed down the ladder with difficulty and lumbered to the jetty. Julius could hear someone else's heavy boots running towards them from behind. A man ran past panting and calling out as he went.

He was struggling to carry a shoulder bag, a folding stool, a book and specimen jars. He was further weighed down by clothes better suited to an English winter than a jungle.

'That's the cove wot I nicked the diary from,' said Emily.

'That's Charles Darwin?' said Julius. 'Are you sure?'

'Course I am. I'd swear it on a Bible.'

Julius and Emily watched Darwin run to the jetty. He dropped the folding stool and the jars but kept running. He shouted something to the man who was struggling to hold the child.

'I can't understand wot they're saying,' said Emily. 'But they look as English as rickets and rain.'

'Neither can I,' said Julius. 'I'm not sure why?'

The clergyman arrived at the jetty first. The man holding the boy pointed a heavy stick to keep him back. Darwin threw his bag and diary down and strode up to the man. He pushed the stick aside and took the man by his lapels, shaking him and shouting into his face. The man swung his arm to strike and the two men spun around in an ungainly waltz.

The child pulled his arm away and sprinted back along the jetty and disappeared into the forest.

'Well done, nippa,' said Emily.

The man pushed Darwin away. They glared at each other for a moment, then both leaned on the jetty rail to catch their breath. The clergyman stood some distance away, watching.

Darwin pushed himself off the rail. He picked up his hat and sat down. The tips of his boots touched the water, making ripples on the surface. He said something in a conciliatory tone. But the other man was not to be mollified. He paced up and down, shouting and gesticulating. Darwin ignored him.

Eventually the man climbed into a canoe tied to the end of the jetty. He called out angrily to Darwin, and then sat with his arms folded, like a brat at a birthday party.

Darwin untied his neckerchief and stooped at the riverbank to swirl it through the water. He mopped his brow with it and he tied it around his neck. Then he wearily gathered his scattered belongs, exchanged a bow with the clergyman and walked to the end of the jetty. He untied the canoe from its mooring and climbed in.

Julius and Emily watched the two men paddle across the river to the far shore.

'It ain't right,' said Emily. 'Everywhere you go there's some cove wot wants to kidnap some poor little bleeder.'

Julius tried to remember the other man's name from Darwin's diary. Was it Smith or Simmons? Or Skinner?

Yes, it was Skinner, Higgins.

'Darwin wrote in his diary that he and Skinner, who must be that man, were being watched by many eyes,' said Julius. 'It could have been the village children.'

'What did Skinner want wiv the nippa, then?' said Emily.

'I'm not sure.'

The clergyman stood at the jetty watching Darwin

and his companion unpack their canoe on the far shore and potter around their campsite. Their gestures and bearing made it clear that Darwin and Skinner were not speaking to one another.

'So Darwin's the one we 'ave to 'elp,' said Emily.

CHAPTER 11

Friday June 29th 1832

8:34 PM

Julius and Emily stood on the riverbank some distance from the village. Darkness was descending and the forest sounds were gradually changing— distant whoops and squawks were being replaced by chattering insects and the occasional low growl.

Above them, stars appeared in the navy-blue sky.

'Seeing as 'ow you're in charge, gov,' said Emily. ''ave you arranged lodgings for the night? Cos I ain't sleeping out 'ere where no wild fing can eat me.'

'I think we should introduce ourselves to the clergyman,' said Julius. 'We can ask if we sleep in his hut.'

'And 'ave you ordered supper, cos I ain't 'arf starving.'

Julius stomach growled. 'We'll find something,' he said.

The light quickly faded as they made their way along the riverbank back to the village. It was almost dark when they got there. Across the river an orange glow showed where Darwin and Skinner had their camp.

A faint light shone from one of the huts built over the water.

'That's the clergyman's,' whispered Julius. 'It's the only one without any soulcatchers growing out of it.'

A stifled yell rang out.

Julius ducked.

'Over there,' said Emily. She pointed to a hut where soulcatchers were bursting through the roof.

She made to go towards it but Julius held her back. Emily twisted out of his grip and faced him.

'Look, 'iggins,' she hissed. 'If we ain't gonna 'elp no one then wot's the point of us being 'ere. You said yourself, the pocketwatch took us 'ere cos there was somefing we 'ad to do.'

'And if we get ourselves maimed or killed we won't be much good to anyone,' Julius said back.

'You fink I don't know that,' hissed Emily. 'I've survived all my bleeding life on the streets. You don't do that by being stupid.'

'I know. I'm sorry. It's just, we have to be careful.'

'Follow me, 'iggins and watch me being careful,' said Emily. 'You can take notes if you like.'

Julius sighed and followed her up the ladder. At the top Emily peeped round the open doorway.

'I can't see naffing,' she whispered.

'Here,' said Julius. He spun the pocketwatch and tapped it. Blue light shone out. Emily's eyes opened wide in horror and pity.

'What is it?' he whispered.

Emily just stared.

Julius looked through the doorway. He recoiled, almost falling over the rail around the hut's veranda. Orchids were spread everywhere like ivy—along the floor, up the walls, across the ceiling. In the far corner was a human face almost hidden by the flowers. It was caught in a scream, the skin like dried leather. Stems grew from its gaping mouth, nostrils and eye sockets and spread across the room.

'It's a soulcatcher,' said Julius. 'Like the painting in Mr Darwin's diary. So it *was* real.'

But it was not the screaming face or the orchids issuing from it that held Julius and Emily's horrified attention. It was the little girl asleep in the entwining flowers. She wore a ragged dress made from a man's shirt with the sleeves cut off. It was made to fit her with safety pins at the waist and shoulders.

Julius stepped through the doorway. The carpet of soulcatchers rippled like a field of wheat in a breeze.

It felt like a warning. Julius stepped back, bumping into Emily.

'It's got the nippa,' whispered Emily. 'It's killing 'er.'

Julius held out an arm to stop her.

Emily glared at him. 'Let go of—'

'Wait,' said Julius. 'Use your eyes. It's not killing her.'

Emily looked closer at the sleeping child. The tendrils were stroking her skin as if soothing her.

'It's the child's mother,' whispered Julius. 'She sitting on her lap. See? You can make out the woman's body beneath the orchids. See her foot there, and her hand.'

'But her ma's dead,' said Emily.

'I know. She's been mummified,' said Julius. 'It looks like the soulcatchers are growing out of her, feeding off her and sucking her dry.'

The child twitched and raised her arm as if fending something off. The flowers rippled and leaned closer to her.

'She's 'aving a nightmare,' said Emily.

One of the flowers stroked her cheek and the curve of her jaw with its petal. The girl shook her head and mumbled something. Suddenly, her eyes opened. She sat up in a flash and stared at the intruders in the blue light.

Julius stretched out a hand to reassure her, but

before he could say anything the girl leapt up and shot out the window.

'She weren't too pleased to see us,' said Emily.

Julius stared at the leather-skinned face, stuck in a scream. It was just like the face in Darwin's diary.

'Is there one of these in every hut, I wonder?' he said. 'Are they all food for the orchids?'

'And the nippa?' said Emily. 'Why is she all right?'

'I don't know. The soulcatcher knew the child. It seemed to care for her.'

'Like it was still 'er ma,' said Emily.

'What if the consciousness of the mother flowed into the orchids as they sucked her dry?' said Julius. 'What if her mind is *in* the orchids now?'

'So she ain't really dead?' said Emily.

'I don't know,' said Julius. 'Her body certainly is. Perhaps it's something different than death—something we haven't seen before.'

'Like wot?'

'I don't know,' said Julius. 'Tock said he wanted to catch everyone's soul.'

'You fink 'e meant this?' said Emily.

Julius stared at the carpet of orchids. 'I hope not,' he said.

He tapped the pocketwatch and put it away.

☛

Julius and Emily stood in the middle of the village. Above them millions of stars flickered, and in the forest millions of insects chirruped. Across the river Darwin's campfire was only a faint glow. The only other light came from the clergyman's hut.

Julius went up the ladder. Through the door he saw the clergyman lying asleep on a bed made from poles tied with twine. On a table was some kind of native lamp. Its flame lit the interior dimly, showing bare rush walls and rush mats on the floor. Some books and pieces of yellow fruit as large as penny loaves sat on a shelf in the corner. On the wall above the bed hung a cross made from two pieces of wood tied up with the same twine that held the bed together.

'He's asleep,' whispered Julius.

Emily stood over the clergyman and leaned down to study him more closely. The petals on each side of his face quivered as he breathed.

'Sleeping like a baby,' she whispered.

Slowly, so as not me make any sound, she picked up the two pieces of fruit. She sniffed one then carefully bit into it and chewed it cautiously. Then she took a larger bite and handed the other one to Julius.

'Not bad,' she whispered.

Julius was too hungry to object to eating stolen food. When he bit into his the juice ran down his chin. He tried to suck it up so he didn't lose a drop.

The flame on the lamp flickered and diminished.

Emily gently nudged the lamp but it did no good. 'It's going to go out,' she whispered.

'We can sleep over there by the wall,' whispered Julius.

Emily nodded. They sat together on the floor and watched the clergyman's belly rise and fall. Julius felt Emily's shoulder rest against his.

Gradually the lamp flame grew smaller and went out. Outside the insects chirruped, and inside the clergyman began to snore.

'I 'ope 'e don't do that all bleeding night,' whispered Emily.

Julius smiled to himself. He lifted his arm and to his surprise Emily shifted to allow him to put it around her. She laid her head on his shoulder and sighed.

'You all right, Emily?' he whispered.

'Ace,' said Emily. 'You?'

'I'm all right.'

☞

Julius woke with a start.

''iggins,' hissed Emily. She shook his shoulder.

'What?' he whispered. He was wide awake instantly.

'Did you 'ear that?' she said.

'Hear what?' Julius looked around. The forest sounds reminded him where he was.

'Shush, listen.'

Julius listened. The chirruping and chattering made a constant wall of noise. The clergyman had stopped snoring.

'I can't h—'

'Shush,' hissed Emily. She nudged his side to shut him up.

Julius strained his ears to hear. There it was—a slithering and a flickering sound. It was a whisper compared to the chirruping. But it was there. Something was moving very quietly, trying not to be heard.

Julius stared into the darkness, trying to see. His ears were becoming accustomed to the sound. It was all around. He felt Emily's arm slip around his.

'Somefing's coming,' she whispered.

Julius took the pocketwatch out, but dropped it in his haste. The slithering stopped as soon as the watch hit the floor. Julius froze. He listened. The slithering started again. He reached out, blindly searching for the watch.

Found it.

He spun it and tapped its side. Immediately blue light shone out as the pocketwatch spun above his open palm.

Emily screamed. Julius gasped.

The clergyman jolted and sprang up.

Orchids surrounded the doorway. Hundreds of them were crawling along the floor and walls.

Julius and Emily jumped to their feet. The soul-catchers were closing in on them.

The clergyman stared at Julius and Emily, his mouth agape like a surprised haddock. Emily threw one of the books at the soulcatchers, squashing one and scattering those close by.

'Out the window,' said Julius. 'Jump into the river.'

He flung the table at them, scattering more.

Emily leapt onto the windowsill.

'Stop,' cried the clergyman. 'Not the river.'

Emily grasped the sill to stop herself from falling.

'Why not?' said Julius.

'It's teeming with piranha fish,' he said.

'Wot's that?' said Emily.

The clergyman looked at her as if she was the stupidest thing he had ever seen.

'Man-eating fish. They'd strip you to the bone in ten seconds,' he said.

Julius faced the advancing soulcatchers like a goal keeper at a village football game. 'Climb onto the roof,' he shouted over his shoulder.

The nearest soulcatchers were only feet away. 'Do something,' he shouted to the clergyman.

Julius saw Emily's foot disappear at the top of the window.

'Come on, 'iggins,' she called out from the roof.

The clergyman waved his arms at the soulcatchers. 'Shoo. Shoo,' he said.

Julius tried to climb, one-handed, onto the window-sill. The clergyman threw himself into the carpet of soulcatchers, waving his arms and kicking his feet. They carried on over him as if he wasn't there.

Julius grabbed the pocketwatch and shoved it into his pocket. Suddenly it was dark again. A hand grabbed his shoulder.

''iggins, up 'ere,' said Emily.

He stood on the windowsill and scrambled onto the roof. He looked around frantically. The ceiling of stars shone above the river and the village. There was nowhere to go. Julius spun the pocketwatch again and tapped its side. The blue light illuminated the few square yards of branches and dried leaves where they would make their last stand.

The slithering was all around them now, drowning out all other sounds. The soulcatchers were climbing up to the roof on all sides. They would be overrun in seconds.

'It has to be the river,' said Julius. He grabbed Emily's hand. 'There's no other way.'

'I can't bleeding swim,' she cried.

Julius snatched the spinning watch and put it into his pocket.

'Neither can I,' he said.

CHAPTER 12

Saturday June 30th 1832

4:02 AM

Julius and Emily scrambled to the river side of the roof and leapt over the advancing soulcatchers. Julius's legs kept running through the air as if they were trying to keep him up.

Splash. He hit the water and kicked out with his arms and legs hoping to ward off the man-eating fish. Was he still holding Emily's hand? He didn't know. He only knew that he couldn't breathe.

His foot hit something. He pushed up. Something was pulling him down—was it Emily's hand? Yes, it was. He didn't know if his eyes were open or closed— all was black. Was he being eaten alive yet?

His foot touched something again. This time he used his grip on Emily's hand to pull her closer. He felt her other arm wrap around him. He pushed up with both legs as if he wanted to jump to the moon. Up they went.

Julius broke through the surface. The night sounds exploded around him. He opened his mouth to suck in the air, and the river water rushed in. Julius felt himself going down. Had the fish started eating him yet? He still couldn't tell.

He felt Emily's arm around his neck. Her grip tightened and he felt the reassuring sensation of something solid and in control. He was being pulled up to the surface. He spluttered out some water and gulped in a mouthful of air before he went under again.

He grabbed at Emily. She was steady in the water, like a warm, soft rock. Julius pulled on her shoulder and came up for air. He breathed, a whole lungful this time.

Emily was holding onto something to keep her up. Julius reached for it too and touched solid wood. He hugged it tight. He had never in his life been so pleased to meet a fallen branch. He made a mental note to be more appreciative of trees from now on.

'You all right, 'iggins?' said Emily.

He gurgled something and coughed up water. He hugged the branch while he got used to breathing again. He could hear Emily doing the same.

It still did not feel like he was being eaten alive. He moved his legs to check them. They were still there.

He hoped Emily's were too.

'Got to get on dry land, 'iggins,' she spluttered.

'I know. Man-eating fish,' said Julius. 'Are you all in one piece?'

'I fink so.'

He felt Emily's arm wrap around him from behind.

'Move,' she said.

Julius pulled himself along the branch until his feet touched the riverbed. Then he dragged himself and Emily towards the bank. He could see the dark outline of the clergyman waving them into shore.

Julius fell onto the bank with Emily still clinging to his back and lay there exhausted.

'Get up, quickly. You must leave the island now,' said the clergyman. 'The soulcatchers can sense that you're not one of us.'

Julius rolled onto his back and stared up at the stars as the clergyman looked down at him.

'I'm alive,' said Julius.

'Congratulations,' said Emily.

'Thank you.'

Then Julius remembered the pocketwatch. He patted his sodden shorts. It was still there. He wrapped his hand around it. It was wet but he could feel its tick-tock in his hand and through his body.

Safe and sound, Higgins. Safe and sound.

'Are you listening to me?' said the clergyman.

'Wot you mean, "not one of us"?' asked Emily.

'Not carrying the soulcatcher seeds in your blood,' said the clergyman. 'You must go back to you own village.'

''ow do we do that then, gov?' Emily asked.

'I have a canoe,' said the clergyman. 'Leave now, but steer clear of the men on the far shore. Darwin is a good fellow but Skinner has no scruples. He is an orchid hunter.'

'We saw 'im try to kidnap a nippa?' said Emily.

'Yes, he wanted to take the child back to England to parade before his orchid collector friends. He wanted to show the child go mad and sprout flowers from his mouth, and to watch his soul being taken by the soulcatcher. Come quickly, I'll take you to the canoe.'

'Sure fing, gov,' said Emily, getting up from the mud.

The clergyman led Julius and Emily upstream, along the riverbank.

'Hurry, now. Hurry. You must not come here again,' he said as he they went. 'This island is damned. *We* are damned. Do you understand?'

'No, I don't fink so,' said Emily.

'Our souls are taken by the soulcatchers. Never to be released. You wouldn't like that to happen to you, would you?' said the clergyman.

'No, not on your nellie, gov,' said Emily.

They walked on. Following the river's edge.

'Here we are,' said the clergyman. He set about sweeping leaves and twigs away from a canoe. Julius helped him to pull it out over the water.

'Now go, quickly,' said the clergyman. 'Ask you parents to whip you as soon as you get home. It will do you good.'

'Sure fing, gov,' said Emily.

Julius climbed into the front of the canoe and Emily behind him while the clergyman held it steady. They grabbed the paddles from under the seats.

'Off you go, and God be with you,' said the clergyman. 'Don't come back or I'll whip you myself.'

He pushed the canoe out onto the water.

It wobbled, almost capsizing. 'Steady,' said Julius. 'One paddle on each side like Darwin and Skinner did it.'

'Aye, aye, cap'n,' said Emily, dipping the paddle into the water like it was a soup ladle.

They zigzagged their way into the current.

Dawn was on its way. The forest sounds were changing again and the shades of black and charcoal were turning to dark-greens and browns.

'I fink we should get 'ome for our whipping, 'iggins, don't you?' said Emily.

Julius turned around to answer her, nearly tipping the canoe.

'Oi, careful,' said Emily. 'Don't give them fish a second go at us.'

'Sorry,' said Julius. 'We'll steer for the other side and keep watch on Darwin and Skinner.'

'Aye, aye.'

Julius and Emily pulled into the shore and crept along the riverbank to Darwin's camp. They crouched in the undergrowth and watched.

After a while Skinner stirred. He sat up and rubbed his neck. Then he glanced over at Darwin lying fast asleep on his side under a blanket. With great care Skinner laid his own blanket aside and stood up. He drank silently from a canteen. Then, in his bare feet, he crept over to a leather satchel and undid the buckles.

'Wot's 'e up to?' whispered Emily, close to Julius's ear.

Skinner took a specimen jar from the satchel and glanced at Darwin.

'Wot's in the jar?' asked Emily.

'I'm not sure,' whispered Julius.

Skinner moved towards Darwin. He knelt and carefully lifted the blanket away. Then he slowly unscrewed the lid of the jar and held it out as if he was going to pour something over Darwin.

'No,' shouted Julius. He ran from his hiding place waving his arms. Skinner turned in surprise and Darwin woke with a jolt, knocking the jar out of Skinner's hand. Skinner rolled back and the soul-catcher inside fell out and latched onto his face.

Skinner screamed and writhed on the ground clawing at the orchid. He managed to catch it and fling it at the dead campfire. Emily picked up a piece of firewood and pounded it into a green and red pulp.

'That's for your mates last night,' she said to it.

Red lines cut across Skinner's face where the soulcatcher's tendrils had cut into his skin. He said something Julius did not understand. Darwin leapt to his feet and said something back.

What strange language are they speaking, Higgins?

Skinner scrambled to his knees and covered his face with his hands. When he took them away they were smeared with blood. A look of complete incomprehension filled his face and quickly turned to rage. He glared at Julius and Emily. Then he lunged at Darwin, who jumped aside. Skinner fell into the campfire. The cold ashes rose up in a cloud, covering his face and hands. Darwin said something which, again, Julius did not understand.

Of course, that's it, Higgins. You only understand the native language.

Skinner sobbed and mumbled to himself, ignoring Darwin.

'Wot's going on, 'iggins?' said Emily. 'Why don't Darwin speak English proper?'

'He does,' said Julius. 'It's us. Remember, when we time-jumped here, the forest wrapped its atoms around our consciousnesses and made local versions of us. So that means we're speaking the local language, but it sounds like English to us because we can understand it.'

'But the clergyman,' said Emily. ''e spoke to us.'

'Yes, but in the native language,' said Julius. 'When he spoke to Darwin and Skinner it was in English.'

Skinner shouted something at Darwin, who shouted back.

'I fink they've fallen out,' said Emily. 'Must 'ave been somefing Skinner said.'

Skinner glared at Emily through his ashen mask.

'Step away, Emily,' said Julius.

Then Skinner glared at Julius. He said something that sounded like a threat.

''e's not 'appy wiv you, 'iggins,' said Emily.

'We should go now,' said Julius. 'I think we've done what we were supposed—'

Skinner roared like a wounded animal and ran at Julius. Julius stepped back and tripped.

'Oi,' shouted Emily. Skinner turned to her as she swung her piece of firewood like a cricket bat. It hit Skinner square on the side of the head. He fell like a rag doll and lay motionless on the riverbank.

Emily dropped the wood.

Darwin ran to Skinner and rolled him over.

'I didn't mean to do 'im in,' said Emily. 'Honest.'

'It's all right,' said Julius. 'He's breathing.'

Darwin sat back and slumped his shoulders. His

face was crumpled in anguish.

'Don't cry, Mr Darwin,' said Emily. ''e ain't dead or naffing.'

'He can't understand you, Emily,' said Julius.

Across the river Julius saw the clergyman watching them. A line of small children stood behind him, all staring blankly.

'We've got an audience,' said Julius. 'We should go now, Emily.'

Darwin saw them too. He stared, bereft, muttering to himself.

'We can't go till 'e draws us in 'is diary,' said Emily. She ran to Darwin's bag and rummaged through it. Darwin did not appear to notice or if he did he didn't care.

She came back with the diary and a pencil.

'Emily, stop,' said Julius. 'You can't make it happen. You can't tell him to draw our picture.'

'Why not?' said Emily. 'Darwin owes us 'is bleeding life. That's worth a poxy drawing.'

'This isn't the way time travel is supposed to work,' said Julius. 'If we give him the idea draw the pictures we'll be altering the past. He has to come up with idea for himself.'

'But we've already altered the past, 'iggins,' said Emily. 'Because of us, it was Skinner wot got seeded instead of Darwin. Now Darwin can come to London and get 'is diary stolen by me, and that's 'ow we'll know all about Tock, and all about—'

'Yes, I know, I know,' said Julius. 'Let me think.'

'While you're doing that Darwin can draw our picture,' said Emily. 'I ain't never 'ad no one draw me before,' She turned to Darwin. 'It'll 'elp you take you mind off fings,' she said.

She pointed to his diary and mimed drawing her face. Darwin looked at her as if in a daze.

'Go on,' she said coaxingly. 'It'll do you good.'

Slowly, Darwin reached out and took the diary and motioned her to sit opposite him.

His face took on an expression of earnest concentration as he drew her portrait. Julius watched over Darwin's shoulder, listening to the scratch of the pencil on the page.

Darwin was a skilled artist. He captured Emily's smile perfectly with a few deft strokes.

'That's ace,' said Emily, when she saw it. 'Your turn, 'iggins.'

Julius sat for his portrait next. When Darwin showed him the finished result Julius saw a worried looking native boy looking back at him.

'Emily,' said Julius. 'We have to go now. We can't risk altering anything else.'

They said goodbye to Darwin and waved to the children on the far bank. The children just stared back blankly.

CHAPTER 13

Saturday 20th January 1838

1:35 PM

Julius and Emily held hands around the pocket-watch as it spun through space and time. Julius tried to gather his thoughts. They had created a loop in the timeline. But had they done it correctly? The only way to find out was to go back to their own present to see if it was the same as they had left it. What if they landed in an altered present? What could they do to put it right?

It felt like only a few minutes before everything went black.

Julius was falling. He landed on a soft chair and bounced off it. He opened his eyes and looked round.

Emily landed on Mr Higgins' chair. She righted herself and slumped into it.

The pocketwatch flew into Julius's hand.

'That was…' she said. She looked around the dusty parlour, lost for words. 'You look like 'iggins again,' she said.

Julius checked the clock on the mantel.

'We've only been gone a few minutes,' he said.

'Everyfing looks the same?' she said. 'That means we did it right, don't it?'

Julius felt a shiver run through him. He had forgotten what it was like to be cold. Emily was right, everything looked the same. The same crumbs on the tablecloth. The same books stacked by his grandfather's chair.

How would you know if you've altered the timeline, Higgins?

The fire was almost out. Julius dropped a couple of coals onto it and stared at the flames licking around the fresh fuel.

What now, Higgins?

He tried to recall the Village of the Soulcatchers. It seemed so far away.

'What you finking about?' said Emily.

'The child sitting on her mother's lap.'

'Oh…'

'Do you really think Clara could be my mother?' said Julius.

'Don't see why not?'

'Do you miss your mother, Emily?'

147

'You don't miss wot you never 'ad,' she said.

'No. I suppose not.'

'Wot's this?' said Emily. She picked up a scrap of card near the fire poker. 'It looks like a calling card,' she said. She blew the coal dust off it and read it.

Tiberius Tock
Alchemist–Explorer–Orchidologist
Between the Walls

'That's it, Emily,' said Julius. 'That's where Tock's taken Grandfather.' He sprang up and went to the wall where the damp circle had been. '"Between the walls." He must have taken Grandfather through here.'

'Can we go after 'im?' said Emily.

'I think so,' said Julius. 'Professor Fox used the pocketwatch to move between realms during the Springheel case.'

'Come on then, wot we waiting for?' said Emily.

'For me to work out how to do it.'

'Well. Get on wiv it, then, 'iggins.'

Concentrate, Higgins. Concentrate. Let the pocketwatch guide you.

The professor had spun the watch and tapped it and blue light had shone out, forming a dome. Julius spun the pocketwatch and tapped it.

A sphere of blue light grew until it formed a

dome around them. Looking through it, the parlour appeared as many shades of luminous blue.

Julius tapped it again. In his mind he saw a tunnel made of light, stretching through the wall into another world. The pocketwatch opened out, the cogs and wheels whirled silently, and the blue dome stretched out, just as he had imagined. The wall dissolved and the tunnel of light stretched out beyond it.

Julius felt Emily's hand grab his forearm. He stared ahead, trying to make out the hazy shapes at the end of the tunnel of light.

Emily's fingers dug into his arm.

Here goes, Higgins.

They walked through the wall.

''iggins?' said Emily.

'Shush. I'm concentrating.'

A ghost-like image of a beach and an expanse of sea began to appear at the other end of the tunnel. Above them a wide sky opened up.

'You ain't 'arf full of surprises, 'iggins,' said Emily.

She gripped his arm tighter. Julius could smell and feel a faint salty breeze. It was a bright sunny day. In the distance he could hear a harmonium or a hurdy-gurdy. He didn't recognise the tune.

Julius looked up, shielding his eyes and blinking at the blue sky above. White shapes flew past. When his eyes grew accustomed to the brightness he realised that the shapes were seagulls.

Over the promenade's ornate railing was a beach of white sand, and beyond that a flat, turquoise sea.

'Look over there,' said Emily. 'It's like a bleeding toyshop.'

Julius looked around. All kinds of automatons were strolling along a promenade as if they were pets. They were all made of brass and copper with the most intricate workings. They were painted in colourful patterns or dressed in beautifully tailored suits and dresses. There were two-legged clockwork creatures like little elves, four-legged ones like dogs or cats, six- and eight-legged ones resembling beetles and spiders. They were all being led by people wearing brightly striped clothes. Some of the women held parasols, and the men wore hats with wide brims. Sometimes, when one automaton met another, they strained on their leads to sniff each other or shake hands or embrace.

'It's like a dream,' said Emily. 'Everyone's so beautiful. I want one of those clockwork fings.'

They came to a crowd around a shopfront. Its sign read:

Papa Putching—Toymaker
Winding—1 penker
Repairs, and alterations, trade-ins, spare parts

People sat on benches, chatting and admiring one another's automatons while they waited to have them wound. A boy sat on a stool outside the shop winding the automatons one by one with a large key

'Mr 'iggins wouldn't like this,' said Emily. 'They're all too cheerful.'

No, he wouldn't, Higgins.

Julius looked for a grumpy old man in a black frock coat. Is this where Tock had taken him?

The town rose up from the beachfront and spread out over a hill. The houses were all brightly painted. Flags waved on spires and the trees rustled in the breeze.

'I don't think were in the right place,' said Julius. 'It's too nice to be Tock's realm.'

Julius heard a sound from inside the toymaker's shop—the chink of a tea cup on a saucer perhaps? Snatches of a conversation wafted through the open door. He recognised one of the voices.

'Grandfather?'

''e' can't 'ear you,' said Emily.

Julius stared through the door at Mr Higgins. He was sitting by a woodstove with a cup and saucer in his hand and an anxious expression on his face. An old man sat on a stool at a workbench by the window— Papa Putching, he presumed.

'Yes. Well, I prefer a good book, myself,' Mr Higgins was saying.

'Ah, yes, the delights of the written word. I concur, sir,' said the man at the workbench. 'But, aah, the delights of clockworking.'

'Quite,' said Mr Higgins.

'Why, look around you, sir,' said the man, waving his hand towards the shelves of clockwork toys. 'The precision, sir. The hours of toil. The mysteries of gearing ratios. The illusion of life created from the correct combination of rods and pinions, cogs and flywheels, and then there are the gyroscopes, perhaps the greatest discovery yet? They produce independence of movement you see—unpredictability. When that is achieved, well...'

'Yes, quite,' said Mr Higgins. He folded and unfolded his handkerchief anxiously. He did not appear to be listening.

Emily tugged at Julius's sleeve. 'Told you 'e wouldn't be 'appy 'ere.'

'He looks ill,' said Julius. 'We have to get him home.'

'Wot can we do, 'iggins? 'ow can we get your grandpa back?' said Emily.

'I'm thinking. He can't see us or hear us because we're not really here.'

'At least it's nice 'ere,' said Emily. 'Maybe 'e could set up a bookshop and—'

'Grandfather's going to have an apoplexy if we don't get him home,' said Julius.

He looked at the pocketwatch. The cogs and wheels were spinning faster than his eye could see.

'Wot are you thinking, 'iggins?' said Emily.

'I was thinking that the pocketwatch could make us materialise, if I knew how to ask it.'

Julius peered closer into the spinning mechanism.

How did you put the professor in the Grackack realm?

'We have to find somewhere quiet,' said Julius. He looked around. 'Over there.' Julius and Emily ran into the shade of an alleyway and made sure no one was looking.

Intuitively, he placed the tip of his finger on the side. It immediately stopped spinning but remained bobbing in the air. Emily gripped his arm again. Vibrations from the pocketwatch ran through the tip of his finger and through his body. His skin tingled and erupted into goosebumps.

'Cor,' said Emily.

'You can feel it?'

'Yeah,' said Emily. 'It's like a mob of ants is trying to tickle me to deaf.'

'Hold still, I think we're doing the right thing. It feels right.'

Julius felt an almost imperceptible change in the vibrations coming from the pocketwatch. A slight slowing of the speed, but a shifting too, a shifting in the layers beneath. The vibration spread throughout his body, through his bones, his mind, to the tips of his eyelashes.

Suddenly, the pocketwatch closed up with a snap and fell into his palm.

Julius looked around. The blue dome was gone. He ran out of the alleyway and stood among the strollers and their pets.

The sea breeze blew stronger against his face. The sun felt warmer. The air was fresh and salty, making him almost hungry to breathe it in.

CHAPTER 14

Saturday 20th January 1838

2:43 PM

Emily held her face to the breeze and closed her eyes to feel the sun on her eyelids. She was dressed in the same style as the people they had passed— yellow and white stripes with wide skirts and white petticoats. Perched on her head was a wide-brimmed sun hat with a yellow ribbon hanging down the back. Her hair hung loose over her shoulders, and her pale skin had a light summer tan.

She looked down at her new dress and her hands smoothed out the folds as if she was trying to believe it was real.

Julius was wearing a summer suit of pale green with dark green pinstripes. Under his chin was a canary-yellow cravat.

'Don't we look a picture?' said Emily.

She noticed her refection in the workshop window and flicked her hair over her shoulder. The toymaker saw her and waved. Emily waved back.

'They can see us, 'iggins,' she said.

Julius was already at the door. He slipped inside.

'Young Caesar!' exclaimed his grandfather, spilling tea on his waistcoat. 'What in Heaven's name is going on?'

'Hello. Welcome,' said the man at the workbench.

He looked to be about the same age as Julius's grandfather. His head was completely bald but for a few wild strands of white hair sprouting from behind his ears. His blue eyes were magnified by thick lenses in silver-rimmed spectacles.

The toyshop smelled of sawdust and creosote. The walls were lined with shelves of clockwork toys. And an untidy array of clock parts, tiny pots of paint, tools and notebooks lay scattered across the workbench. A wisp of steam rose from the spout of the kettle on a stove in the middle of the room.

'Please, take your time,' said the old man. 'Only the finest automatons, all good little machines. So life-like you could almost forget to wind them. All made on the premises.'

Emily whistled her approval. Mr Higgins tried to mop up the spilt tea with his handkerchief.

'Do you 'ave any clockwork ponies, sir?' asked

156

Emily. 'I'm partial to a pony.'

The man put a finger to his lips to help him think as he ran his eyes along the shelves. 'I don't think I do,' he said.

'Well, thank you for the tea, sir. Most obliged,' said Mr Higgins.

He got up, looking for a space to put his cup and saucer down. In the end he handed them to the toy-maker.

'Do come again, sir,' said the man. 'We could talk more of cog ratios, my favourite subject.'

'Yes quite,' said Mr Higgins. He turned to Julius. 'Young Caesar, let's be off.' He strode past Emily and out of the shop as if she was not there.

'I'll be back about the pony,' said Emily.

Julius and Emily looked at each other and then ran to catch up with Mr Higgins as he hurried along the promenade. He was mumbling to himself and polishing his spectacles with his handkerchief.

'Are you all right, Grandfather?' said Julius.

'No. I'm not. And what is that child doing here? I specifically banished her from the shop.'

'We're not in your poxy—I mean, I'm not in your lovely shop,' said Emily.

Mr Higgins adjusted his spectacles on the end of his nose as he hastened along. 'I think I might have had a turn, young Caesar. It happened to your great-uncle Ned, you know.'

'What are you talking about, Grandfather? What happened?'

'Nothing happened, I imagined it all.'

'Imagined wot?' said Emily.

'All *this*,' he replied and waved his handkerchief about. 'Oh, my poor heart. It's…it's overwork, and too much butter, that's what it is.'

'How did you get here?' said Julius.

'Here? But I'm not *here*. I'm at home in front of the fire, sound asleep. Oh, wake up, wake up, you old fool.' Mr Higgins punched his sides.

'Grandfather, wait. Did Mr Tock visit you?' said Julius.

Mr Higgins stopped. He looked into Julius's eyes. 'What do you know of Tock?'

'He left a calling card.'

'I threw that in the coal bucket. The man's a scoundrel.' Mr Higgins stared out across the sea. 'He came to the shop again, all sugar and syrup, he was. He apologised for the previous "misunderstanding". Said he wanted to know how his gift was faring. Wanted to know if I'd watered it and kept it warm. I told him I gave the dratted thing away. Then I told the fellow to leave. He must have mesmerised me.'

'What happened then?' said Julius.

'I imagined we walked through the wall of the parlour. Mr Higgins stared into the distance as if reliving the experience. 'He had a box of glass vials. He broke one of them against the wall and it hissed like acid. It must have been some sort of narcotic. That's it. I've read about that sort of thing.'

'Wot happened then?' said Emily.

'The fellow took my arm and it felt as if we stepped right *through* the wall into this…this seaside dream. The fellow said that I should stay here. I told him I had a business to run…I…I had deliveries, orders to fill. But he laughed. And he disappeared through the wall and left me here.'

Mr Higgins hurried away. He removed his spectacles and polished them again. Suddenly, he stopped.

'What day is it?'

'Saturday,' said Julius.

'Good gracious, I must wake up. I should be in the shop. What will my customers think?'

'It's all right, Grandfather. I dealt with the morning rush,' said Julius.

'Did you? I knew you were a good boy, Julius. Even if it's just a dream.' Mr Higgins smiled for the first time. 'The nice gentleman in the toyshop offered me a cup of tea. Under the circumstances I accepted his offer. Tea can be very restorative when there is no brandy to be had.'

They stopped at the spot where Julius and Emily had entered the realm.

'You think that pocketwatch can get us back, then, 'iggins?' said Emily.

'What is that appalling child talking about?' said Mr Higgins.

'Don't get vexed, Mr 'iggins, I'm only trying to 'elp.'

'It's difficult to explain, Grandfather,' said Julius. He spun the pocketwatch in the air. 'You'll have to trust me.'

'Trust you?'

'Steady on, Mr 'iggins. It ain't good for a man of your years to get too excited,' said Emily, and she patted the old man's arm.

Mr Higgins glared at her. 'That's it. I'm fetching a constable.' He looked around anxiously.

Julius tapped the pocketwatch. It opened out and the cogs spun.

'Hold my hand, Grandfather. We're going back to the parlour,' said Julius.

'No we're not,' said Mr Higgins. 'What nonsense.'

He began to stride away in search of a constable. Emily jumped into his path. 'Oh. Beg pardon, Mr 'iggins,' she said.

'Get out of me way this instant,' said Mr Higgins. He ripped his spectacles from his nose and began to polish them again as if his life depended on it.

Julius placed the tip of his finger against the side of the pocketwatch and took his grandfather's hand.

'Take my 'and too, Mr 'iggins,' said Emily.

Mr Higgins did not notice her hand slipping into his as he stared, dumbfounded, at the pocketwatch bobbing in the air. Emily and Julius led him in a clumsy dance to turn back to face the wall.

Julius felt the vibrations coursing through his body.

'Good Heavens,' said Mr Higgins. 'I'm having palpitations.'

'I bleeding 'ope not,' said Emily.

'What did you say?'

'Naffing…Oh, look.'

Blue light shone out from the pocketwatch. It grew to form a dome over the three of them.

'Good gracious,' said Mr Higgins, as a ghost-like image of their parlour appeared before them.

'Time to wake up, Mr 'iggins,' said Emily and she led the old bookseller through the gossamer wall into the parlour.

When they were all inside Julius tapped the pocketwatch and the blue glow disappeared. It closed up and fell into his open palm.

The parlour was dark and cold. They were in their London clothes again.

'Great Heavens above,' said Mr Higgins, as he stumbled into his chair. He stared at the fire. It had all but gone out. The travel between realms had rendered him speechless.

'I'll see to the fire,' said Julius.

'Yes. Very good,' said Mr Higgins, as if in a trance.

Julius removed the guard and snapped some kindling. 'I'll make us some tea as well.'

'Tea, be damned,' said Mr Higgins.

He staggered to the cabinet, poured himself a large brandy and drank it down in one.

'Ahhh. That's better,' he said. He poured another and returned to his chair, cradling his glass. He took out his watch and squinted through the gloom to compare its time with the clock on the mantel.

'It's well past five o'clock, young Caesar. I must have slept all afternoon.'

'Yes, Grandfather,' said Julius. 'You probably did.'

'Did you say something about working in the shop this morning?' said Mr Higgins.

'You weren't well. You slept here by the fire.'

'Yes, of course, now I recall. I dreamt about...Oh, never mind.'

Mr Higgins settled back into his chair. Then he noticed Emily. 'Julius, what is that appalling child doing here. I told her never to set foot in the shop again.'

'She was helping me.'

Emily smiled sweetly, as if she were one of the better behaved angels in one of the more refined regions of Heaven.

Mr Higgins was not convinced. 'Did Mr Trollop come for his order?'

'Yes.'

'And that scoundrel, Thackeray?'

'Yes,' said Julius.

Mr Higgins looked at the growing fire with satisfaction. 'You're a good boy, Julius.'

He took a sip of his brandy and let out a long tired sigh. Then he noticed the tea stain on his waistcoat. Julius watched his grandfather's face as he tried to make sense of a stain appearing in the real world when the spill had occurred in his dream.

'Grandfather,' he said. 'I wanted to ask you something.'

'Yes,' said Mr Higgins, as he touched the stain with the tip of his finger.

'About my mother…'

Mr Higgins looked up. 'I beg your pardon?'

'I want to know what happened to her. What was her name?'

Mr Higgins drank the last of his brandy and went and poured another. 'Did Mr Gissing come in?' he said. 'I got his damned poetry book.'

'Did you hear what I said, Grandfather?'

Mr Higgins swirled the brandy in the glass. Julius waited.

'She's gone,' said Mr Higgins.

'Dead?'

'No. Not dead. *Gone.*'

'Was her name Clara?'

Mr Higgins winced.

It was Clara, Higgins.

'Where did she go?' said Julius.

'How the blazes should I know?'

'Why did she leave?'

'Did young Mr Dickens come in? You didn't give him credit did you?'

'Please, tell me.'

'There's nothing to tell. She was here and now she's not. She's gone.' Mr Higgins swallowed the brandy in one gulp.

'Why did she leave?'

The words made his grandfather jump and stare. Julius and his grandfather glared at each other. Then Mr Higgins spoke. His words were slow and measured, as if Julius was a disobedient dog.

'Julius. There is nothing to be gained by—'

'Please, tell me, Grandfather. I only—'

'Be quiet,' shouted Mr Higgins. 'I will not be harangued like a common criminal in my own home.' He appeared to be frightened by his own outburst. He looked at his glass, contrite, but still angry. 'Your mama was a disgrace to her family,' he said, quieter this time. 'It is best for all concerned that she is gone.'

Mr Higgins seemed to shrink, folding in on himself. 'And now,' he said, 'I would rather be alone. Perhaps you could walk that child home and see that she does not return.' The words were slow and carefully pronounced. The conversation was at an end.

Emily sat on the edge of a chair, as still as a stuffed bird.

Julius buttoned his coat and made for the door. Emily jumped up to follow. But Julius lingered, wanting a final word from his grandfather.

With exaggerated deliberation, Mr Higgins poured himself another glass, and walked back to his chair. He sniffed as if to show that he had finished with a tiresome topic. He turned away to face the fire, and let out a long sigh. Julius pulled the curtain aside and went into the cold, dark shop, fumbling for his key. Emily followed him.

On the floor in front of the door a pale rectangle caught his eye and he stooped to pick it up. It was a note, with his name written across it in pencil. It was too dark to read in the shop and, in any case, he wanted to be out of there. And he did not want to return.

He rattled the key in the lock and opened the door. At the end of Ironmonger Lane he opened the note.

Julius,
No one home when I called. I'll be at Bedlam tonight to see Mr Darwin. He has agreed to speak to me, as Abberline has told him about the orchid Tock gave you. I'll stop by tomorrow and tell you what I learned.
Yours
Danny Flynn
P.S. Abberline said Mr Darwin was raving something about an orchid-hunter called Skinner being in London. Did you come across his name in the diary?

165

Julius felt an icy shiver run through him.

Skinner? What's he doing here, Higgins?

He looked around for Emily. She was standing some distance away, waiting. He put Mr Flynn's note into his pocket.

'Who's it from, 'iggins?' she asked.

'Mr Flynn. He's going to Bedlam tonight to see Mr Darwin.'

'Ace. We'll go too. I've always wanted to meet a proper lunatic.'

'Darwin was raving about Skinner being in London,' said Julius.

'But 'e can't be,' said Emily. 'Darwin wouldn't 'ave let Skinner come back. 'e'd 'ave left 'im in the village, wiv them man-eating fish to guard 'im.'

'Maybe we didn't get it right,' said Julius. 'Maybe we're in a present where Skinner *wasn't* seeded. We'll have to see what Darwin says. Then I'll know what to say to Mr Flynn.'

'Wot you mean, 'iggins?'

'Emily.'

'Wot?'

'Promise me something.'

'Wot?'

'Don't tell Mr Flynn about our time-jump.'

'Why not?'

'Because…because I'm not supposed to have the pocketwatch.'

'You mean you nicked it, 'iggins?'

'It's difficult to explain. Do you promise?'

Emily paused. 'Yeah…all right. If that's what you want,' she said.

'I'll tell Mr Flynn everything,' said Julius, 'when I know what's going on.'

'We going to Bedlam then?'

'Yes. But we're going somewhere else first.'

'Where?'

'To see Clara.'

Julius walked across Blackfriars Bridge and down Blackfriars Road. He hunched his shoulders against the cold and fixed his eyes on the ground. The more he thought about the conversation he had just had, the more angry he became. Angry at his grandfather for his indifference. Angry at his mother. But for what? For leaving? For carrying on her life without him?

''iggins,' said Emily, 'slow down.'

He ignored her.

''iggins, slow down. My legs is shorter than yours,' she said. 'You're vexed, ain't you?'

He did not reply.

'Look, 'iggins, if she really is your ma, it don't matter what your grandpa says. 'e's just a crabby old git.'

Emily's teeth chattered in the cold. Julius found his face warming to a smile at the sound.

'And Clara's got good news,' said Emily. 'She's got a new situation. She's going up in the world.'

'What?'

'She's to be under-'ousekeeper at Walworth 'ouse. She'll be working for a Lord.'

'When?'

'Monday. But she's moving tomorrow.'

Julius wheeled around and strode off again. He turned into Elliot's Row. Mrs Trevelyan's Academy towered above the other houses on the street.

Julius stopped in the dark shadow of the wall and waited for Emily to catch up.

'You staying out here, then?' she said.

Julius dug his hands further into his pockets and looked at the path leading to the front steps.

'Did you 'ear me?' said Emily.

'She's leaving tomorrow?' said Julius.

'Yeah, I'm 'elping. Mrs Trevelyan 'ired a four-wheeler for all her fings.'

'She's going to Walworth House?'

'Yeah. It's ace. Lord Bloomingbury's as mad as a marquis. The 'ouse is e-*bleeding*-normous, and it's full wiv animals—hundreds of 'em.'

'What are you talking about?'

'He's got his own menagerie, wiv animals from all over the world.'

'And she wants to go?' said Julius.

'Course. She answered an advertisement in *The Times*. Lots applied, I shouldn't wonder. Mrs Trevelyan gave her an excellent character reference…'

Julius heard a trailing off of Emily's voice. Something was wrong.

'What is it?' he said.

'Naffing.'

'Tell me.'

'It's naffing,' said Emily. 'Well, the fing is, the advertisement was asking for 'ousekeepers wiv no 'angers-on, no families.'

Julius waited for Emily to continue.

'But that was before you came. She thought she didn't 'ave no family, not then,' said Emily

Julius thrust himself off the wall and strode into the middle of the street.

'Oi,' hissed Emily, so as not to be heard by anyone else. Come back, 'iggins.'

Anger surged through Julius's body.

No family, Higgins. No family.

''iggins. Come back,' said Emily.

'Why?'

Emily pulled at his arm, spinning him around. 'You 'ave to tell 'er.'

'Tell her what?'

'That you know. That it's all right.'

'She should be the one telling me.'

'Yeah. But what if she's afraid?'

'Of what?'

'That you won't want 'er.'

Julius turned away.

'All right, be like that,' said Emily.

Julius heard her turn on her heels and walk to the gate.

''iggins,' she said. 'If I 'ad a ma I wouldn't be sulking about it.'

'I'm not sulking.' He said it quietly, although he felt like shouting out to the whole of London.

He walked past Emily and around the side of the academy to the head of the stairs that led down to the scullery.

'Oi, manners,' she whispered and pushed past him. 'I'll go first. Don't worry, she'll be glad you've come.'

Julius listened to the scrape of Emily's soles as she skipped down the steps.

Emily waited at the scullery door, her hand poised to knock, as if checking that he was still with her. Then she knocked.

The sound boomed in Julius's ears, even though it was no more than a tap. He heard shuffling at the window and his heart began to pound.

Clara's face appeared. Julius knew she had seen him. He looked away, fighting the urge to run.

He counted Clara's steps coming to the door and

ticked off the different sounds—the key turning in the lock, the bolt turning in its bracket and drawing back with a sharp clack.

Julius stepped back into the shadows.

The door opened.

Clara held a candle. It lit up the frightened questions all over her face.

'There you are, Emily, dear,' she whispered, not looking at Julius. 'I was worried.'

She opened her arms to usher Emily inside.

Julius sank back further into the shadows.

He saw Emily and Clara's eyes meet. Emily whispered something.

Julius watched Clara's round face, watched the fear and indecision. Emily untied the ribbon of her bonnet. Clara busied herself unbuttoning Emily's cape.

Then she stopped. Something changed within her, and her body straightened as if fortified. Courage took the place of fear.

She looked into the shadows. 'Hello, Julius, dear,' she said.

CHAPTER 15

Saturday 20th January 1838

5:37 PM

Clara's words sounded perfect to Julius. The cadence of her voice stirred a hint of a memory.

'Hello,' said Julius.

'So you know?'

'Yes,' said Julius.

'I'm glad,' she said. 'Come inside, dear.'

She hesitated when Julius came close, as if she did not know what to make of his nearness. Julius pretended to be colder than he was so he could remain hunched up and brittle.

'This way,' Clara said, and led them into the kitchen. A lamp gave a soft glow, and the fire in the range warmed the room.

'Emily, my dear, why don't you warm up some

milk? You must be frozen,' said Clara. She entwined her fingers, knotting them together.

'Right-o,' said Emily.

Clara stood behind a chair by the range. A book lay open on the table nearby. She clung to the back of the chair to stop her fingers from fidgeting. Emily draped her bonnet and cape across the table. She took a copper pot from a hook and fetched a pitcher of milk from the pantry. Clara handed her a wooden spoon.

Julius unwound his scarf from around his neck and stood in the corner. He could feel every sound vibrating through him—the dull clatter of the copper pot, the lapping of the milk around the wooden spoon.

Emily had her back to him as she stirred the milk.

Julius watched Clara. She was looking at the pot, pretending to be interested in Emily stirring it correctly. He knew she was trying to find the words for what she wanted to say.

'Isn't it funny,' she said, at last, 'that you and Emily should be friends?'

Julius waited to hear what she would say next.

Emily stirred the milk.

'And Mr Flynn. He was a close friend of Papa's once. They fell out years ago, you know. It was lucky I was covered in flour, yesterday, or he'd have recognised me.' She glanced at Julius to see if he was going to speak, then continued. 'Mr Flynn comes to visit Emily, but he never comes below stairs. I'd be ashamed to meet him again.'

Clara paused, as if deciding what else she should say.

Julius waited.

At last she said it. 'I couldn't believe my eyes when I saw you,' she said. 'I knew it was you straightaway.'

Julius dug his hands deeper into his pockets. 'Were you glad?' he asked. The words came out wrong. They sounded like an awkward stranger.

'Of course I was. I know you so well. I walk along Ironmonger Lane on my half-day holiday every month. Sometimes I catch a glimpse of you. I've seen you growing up. Seen the display tables you've set up in the shop window—very artistic.'

Julius felt himself thawing. His eyes smiled.

'How is Papa?' Clara said.

Emily stopped stirring and waited for Julius's reply.

'We fell out, just now,' said Julius, and he sniffed as if it were of no concern.

'Oh…'

'I…I asked him why you left.'

'I see. And, um…what did he say?'

'Nothing.' Julius stared into the darkest corner of the kitchen. He felt as if he was going to cry. 'I have to go,' he said.

'Wait, please, Julius,' said Clara. She reached out as if to touch him, but held back.

Julius stood still, waiting.

Clara lowered her eyes, preparing her words. 'I made a mistake a long time ago,' she said quietly. She hesitated, not wanting to go on. 'I ran off with someone. It doesn't matter who.'

She studied Julius's face for a moment. 'I came back on a stormy night, like a drowned rat. I didn't have anywhere else to go. I was seventeen, unmarried and in the family way. Mama had passed away so there was only Papa left. He took me in, and you were born upstairs, three days later. You were beautiful, with your baby smell.'

Julius hung his head. He had to grit his teeth to stop himself from crying. He had never thought of himself as a baby. For some reason that he could not fathom, he felt like a big brother to his baby self.

'There was gossip up and down Ironmonger Lane,' said Clara. 'Your grandfather couldn't hold his head up in the street. He'd had such plans for me—I was going to marry well, I was so clever, so refined, I was going to bring the family back to its proper station. We both loved you, Julius. It was just… difficult.'

Clara pretended to clear her throat to stop her tears. Julius looked up, glancing quickly at her before looking away again. He clenched his jaw, fighting a battle inside himself not to cry in front of her.

'So you left,' said Julius. 'To have you own life.' He

had not meant the words to sound so harsh.

Clara looked up, startled. Julius watched closely as her face told him what he already knew—she was searching for a lie.

'It was difficult at home, Julius,' said Clara. 'Your grandfather…' Tears pooled in her eyes. 'Your grandfather brought you up, all by himself. You mustn't forget that, Julius. He could have handed you over to the parish or…or sent you to a boarding school. But he didn't.'

What's she talking about, Higgins? He looked after me because she left.

Emily turned to look at Julius. Julius could feel his face burning and tears pooling in his own eyes. He glared at her. She quickly looked away. He did not trust himself to speak.

'I'm here now,' said Clara.

'Milk's ready,' said Emily, as if bringing joyous news.

Julius sniffed and ran his hand under his nose.

'Emily said you have a new position,' said Julius. 'You're going away.' He tried to sound conversational. It came out all wrong.

'Not *away*. Not far,' said Clara. 'I…I'd like you to visit.'

'No family ties,' said Julius. 'That's what the advertisement said.'

Clara stared at Julius, stunned. 'I know, but…'

Her words died. He could see the realisation in her face. She had betrayed him a second time. The pain in her eyes pleased him.

Now she knows what it's like.

Julius began to rewind his scarf. Clara clasped her hands.

'I'm going,' said Julius. It was barely a mumble.

'But the milk?' said Emily.

Julius was already at the door. 'I have to meet Mr Flynn at Bedlam.'

''ang on, 'iggins. I'm coming wiv you.'

'I'm going by myself,' said Julius. The curtness in his voice stopped her dead.

'Oi. Don't be like that,' she said.

Julius barely heard her. He ran from the kitchen, up the steps and into the freezing night.

He was out the gate and hurrying along St George's Road when he heard footsteps running to catch up. He thrust his hands deeper into his pockets and quickened his pace.

'Go back,' said Julius.

'But you might need me, 'iggins. You might—'

'I won't need you and stop calling me "'iggins" like you were a costermonger's daughter. It's "Higgins" or "Julius". You're getting an education, use it.'

'Oi, don't speak to me like—'

Julius stopped abruptly under a gas lamp and faced her.

'Go away. Go. Away,' he shouted. 'You're not wanted.'

The gas light cast a pallor across Emily's face. Julius studied every feature, every contour and individual eyelash, waiting to see the pain fill her eyes when his words sunk in. She had a father in Mr Flynn and a mother more or less in Clara. She had got them so easily and she seemed to take them for granted.

He wanted to see her feel pain too.

But Emily was silent, her face devoid of expression. 'Suit yourself,' she said, after a few moments. 'See if I bleeding care.'

She studied his face with a contemptuous blankness. Julius's anger shrivelled and died. He swallowed. She smiled to herself and then walked back towards the gate.

'Emily…Em—' he called out.

She kept walking.

'Emily, come back.'

She went through the gate and Elliot's Row was silent again, empty.

'See if I care,' he said, his anger reigniting.

At the end of the street he stopped. The things he had said to Emily stabbed at him. He closed his eyes and cursed himself.

'She knows I didn't mean it,' he said. He clasped the pocketwatch for comfort.

You could time-jump far away, Higgins. And keep time-jumping until you find an empty land where there's no one to complicate things.

He walked on in a wretched haze until he came to iron gates guarding the grounds of the New Bethlam Hospital. All was dark, but for faint lights in many of the windows. The hospital was built of grey stone with wide columns and a dome at the centre. It reminded Julius of the dome of St Paul's. But this was not a cathedral; it was a place for lunatics. He went to the side gate and looked through.

He could keep walking until dawn, until he came to a valley with a stream running through it. He could hear the flowing water already. He could sleep on the bank.

The iron railing was cold against his cheek. He pressed against it even though it stung. Clara's face came to his mind again.

Something was wrong. He ran their conversation through his mind. What was all that about Grandfather not giving him to the parish or sending him to a boarding school? Clara was hiding something? He stared at the dark dome, as if the answer was there. The cold was forgotten. Neither she nor grandfather wanted him to know why she left. But why?

His words to Emily came back: 'Go away. You're not wanted.'

Would Emily forgive him? He doubted it. He had stung her too deeply. Her blank face said so—it was a hundred times worse than tears or anger.

Julius banged his forehead against the rails to punish himself and to stop himself from crying.

The only one you've got left is Mr Flynn, Higgins.

He walked through the gates and up the gravel path until he came to a heavy, oak door. A bell-pull hung on the right side near a brass plaque. The gas lamp above the door gave out just enough light for Julius to read the words *New Bethlem Royal Hospital— Insane Asylum.*

He pulled the handle to ring the bell. The sound frightened his anger away.

A large woman in a grey dress and a stiff white collar opened the door. Her sleeves were rolled up showing her muscular forearms. Her grey hair was pulled so tightly back into a bun that it looked as if it hurt. She ran her eyes from Julius's head to his toes and back up to his head again.

'Yes? What would you be wanting at this late hour?' she said, pronouncing each word as if carving it from ice.

Julius swallowed. 'Mr Darwin.'

The woman considered the matter. 'Are you family of Mr Darwin?' she said.

'No, a friend of Mr Flynn. Mr Flynn called to see him too. Constable Abberline arranged it,' said Julius, trying to force some confidence into himself.

The woman looked at Julius as if she had not bothered to listen. 'You are unwell?' she said. 'A little anxious, perhaps?'

'Yes. I haven't been to a place like this before. It's rather…er…'

'Intimidating?' said the woman.

'Yes. Intimidating.'

Julius's admission had a mollifying effect on the woman. Her face relaxed as if his fear satisfied her.

'Your name?' she asked.

'Julius Higgins.'

The woman considered it for a moment. 'Mr Flynn is already here,' she said. 'Come inside.'

The flames of the gas lights along the walls hissed and the odour of the burnt-off gas lingered like a taste at the back of Julius's throat. He followed the woman along the corridor. A scream rang out. The woman stopped and listened. When the scream ended she walked on.

Lunatics' faces, contorting in screams and crazed laughter, filled Julius's mind. The woman led to him to what looked like a waiting area—there were empty chairs and an oak-panelled counter. Mr Flynn was standing there.

'Is this boy known to you, Mr Flynn?' said the woman, before anyone could speak.

'Julius?' said Mr Flynn.

'I got your note,' said Julius.

Mr Flynn nodded to the woman. 'Aye, I know the lad,' he said.

This seemed to satisfy her. 'You'll be pleased to take a seat,' she said and walked away along one of the corridors.

Mr Flynn took the jar containing the soulcatcher out of his pocket. 'I brought this to show, Mr Darwin,' he said.

The soulcatcher's tendrils pressed against the glass, still looking for a way out.

Julius started. He remembered the jar Skinner held over Darwin. He clutched the pocketwatch.

'Are you all right?' said Mr Flynn, putting the jar away again.

'Yes.' Julius turned away, pretending to look around while he tried to compose himself. 'It's an odd place,' he said.

'I got here just ten minutes ago and I've got the collywobbles already,' said Mr Flynn. 'I'll be glad to see the back of the place. If you're not mad when you arrive you soon will be.'

Julius forced an unconvincingly laugh.

'Do you remember Skinner's name in Darwin's diary?' said Mr Flynn.

Julius turned to face him. 'Skinner? No, I don't think so.'

Mr Flynn tried to make a reassuring expression.

'We'll be out of here as soon as we can,' he said. 'They told me Darwin's getting ready to leave. His doctor discharged him this afternoon, but Abberline asked him to wait for me to see him home.'

Julius was barely listening. His whole mind was on the warmth of the pocketwatch. It was calming him, clearing his mind.

You should tell him everything now, Higgins.

'Mr Flynn—' he began.

A young man came towards them, pulling on his coat as he went.

Julius recognised the man immediately. It was Charles Darwin. His hair was a thinner and his face a little fuller, but it was definitely him.

Mr Flynn took his hat off.

'You are Mr Flynn, sir?' said the man. 'Constable Abberline tells me that I can trust you.'

'That is so,' said Mr Flynn. 'Allow me to introduce Julius Higgins. This is the young man who received the other orchid.'

Darwin glanced at Julius while he anxiously fiddled with the lapels of his coat.

'I'm pleased to hear that the doctor discharged you, Mr Darwin,' said Mr Flynn.

Darwin snorted. 'They know me here. I am engaged in research with one of their patients,' he said. 'They know I'm not mad.'

'I don't follow, sir,' said Mr Flynn.

He smiled at Mr Flynn's confusion. 'Do you still have the orchid?' he said. 'I should like see it.'

Mr Flynn took the jar out of his coat pocket and held it out to Darwin.

'Yes. It's a soulcatcher,' said Darwin. 'Destroy it. Burn it. Promise me you will.'

'Of course,' said Mr Flynn. 'But, why? I don't understand.'

Darwin looked hard into Mr Flynn's eyes. He appeared to be weighing him up. He ran his trembling hand through his hair.

'A man named Tock has got his hands on some soulcatcher cuttings. He means to propagate them. He sent a pickpocket to steal my diary—it is full of my botanical observations of the soulcatcher. There is vital information in it about the soulcatcher's life cycle.'

'Go on,' said Mr Flynn.

'What I have to tell you, you will not believe,' said Darwin. He looked intently at Julius and Mr Flynn, calculating how much he could trust them. Then he continued. 'Tock is a genius. But he is also a fiend.' He stopped as if to see how his words were being taken.

'I'd agree with you about the fiend part, sir,' said Mr Flynn. 'After what Julius and I have seen of him.'

This appeared to give Darwin the confidence to go on. 'I met Mr Tock at a lecture on orchids at the Horticultural Society,' said Darwin. 'He was all delight and smiles, wanting to know about my explorations in Brazil. He asked me if I knew anything of an orchid that extracts people's souls—it is the stuff of rumour among the orchid-maniacs, you see. I am sorry to say, I made a grave error in telling him a little about the Village of the Soulcatchers. One day he asked for my assistance in propagating the soulcatcher cuttings he had somehow obtained. I refused, of course. He was most displeased. Then he asked to borrow my diary. Again, I refused.'

Darwin appeared to drift off into his own thoughts.

Julius shuddered as he remembered the native child sitting on its mother's lap and the smaller soulcatchers creeping into the clergyman's hut trying to seed him and Emily.

'I have seen a village laid waste by the soulcatcher,' said Darwin. 'If Tock succeeds with his propagation plans it will be calamitous. I was at my wits end searching for him. And then a soulcatcher was left outside my door.'

Darwin stopped as if he did not want to go on.

'The life cycle of the soulcatcher is strange even for an orchid,' he said. 'When it matures, individual buds pull themselves off the mother plant and send down roots into the ground. But they pull themselves out at night and go in search animals or humans to seed with their tendrils. When I saw the orchid in the pot outside my room I knew it was such a specimen.

He had managed to propagate it from the cuttings without my help. I didn't know what to do with it. I took it in as if in a dream, a nightmare. I fell into a stupor. When I awoke I saw the orchid climbing out of its pot. It was quicker and stronger than the ones I observed in Brazil. I must have screamed the house down.'

Darwin looked from Julius to Mr Flynn. His face was contorted with terror.

'A horrifying experience, no doubt, sir,' said Mr Flynn.

'We have to stop Tock,' said Darwin. 'He intends to release the soulcatchers all over London.'

'Why would he do such a thing?' said Mr Flynn.

Darwin fiddled nervously with his lapels again. 'Tock is the strangest of men. He told me once that his Maker told him he had no soul. I told him the Bible tells us that all God's children have souls. He laughed at me.'

'Why did he laugh?' said Mr Flynn.

'He said he was not made by God,' said Darwin. 'I am sure he means to carry out some insane revenge— if he has no soul he will take everyone else's and the soulcatcher is his means of doing so.'

Mr Flynn cleared his throat. 'I see,' he said.

'I believe he has my diary, so he has the means,' said Darwin. 'He will do it, unless we can stop him. Will you help me?'

'We will,' said Mr Flynn. 'You have my word on that.' He put his hand on Julius's shoulder. 'Isn't that right, Julius,' he said.

'Yes,' said Julius, trying to sound convincing.

'Good,' said Darwin. He fussed about his coat as to fend off a growing fear. 'But, there is someone I must introduce you to, if you are to understand what we will be up against.'

'We can call in on him on the way home, if you like,' said Mr Flynn.

'There is no need,' said Darwin. 'He is here in Bedlam. The man is the subject of the research I mentioned. Skinner's his name. George Skinner. He was an orchid-hunter.'

Julius started. Skinner was here in London when he was supposed to be in Brazil. He opened his mouth to ask if Skinner was seeded but stopped himself. He was not supposed to know anything about it.

CHAPTER 16

Saturday 20th January 1838

9:12 PM

Darwin led Julius and Mr Flynn through the gas-lit corridors of Bedlam. The whole of Julius's body was shaking as he walked. He gripped the pocket-watch, trying to concentrate on its constant rhythm. He hunched his shoulders to make it look as if he was shivering from the cold.

When they came to a door Darwin selected a key from a key ring and turned it in the lock.

'Do not be alarmed,' he said. 'The lunatics cannot get out.' He locked the door after them. Another corridor stretched ahead. Julius and Mr Flynn exchanged a glance then followed Darwin past padlocked doors, each bearing a piece of card with a name inscribed on it.

Conspiratorial whispers wafted around them as they walked on. Someone cackled. Julius jumped. He felt Mr Flynn's hand on his shoulder.

'It is a lamentable place, sir,' said Mr Flynn to Darwin's back.

Darwin did not reply. At the end of the corridor he turned to them. His face had grown pale and drawn in the short journey. 'Forgive me,' he said. 'These corridors fill my nightmares. We are nearly there.'

At a large steel-plated door he fumbled with the key ring, searching for the correct key.

'Do you have your own keys, sir?' said Mr Flynn.

Darwin found the one he wanted. 'Yes,' he said. 'Bedlam's Governor, Lord Bloomingbury, is an orchid collector. His Lordship understands the danger of the soulcatcher and has given me every assistance.'

'With what, sir?' said Julius. His voice trembled a little.

Darwin unlocked the door. 'You will see,' he said.

Julius and Mr Flynn followed him through the door and Darwin locked it behind them. There were three other doors off the empty room, one on each wall. All were made of steel and each one had a rectangular hatch at head height.

'This is where Bedlam keeps its most dangerous inmates,' said Darwin.

Darwin turned down the gas lights a little, and then went to the closest door. He fidgeted with his lapel again as if trying to compose himself.

'There's no name on the door,' said Julius.

'Skinner's presence is a secret. He is the patient with no name,' said Darwin. He unlocked the padlock on the hatch.

When it opened, Julius coughed at the musky odour that emanated. Mr Flynn held a handkerchief to his nose.

'Mr Skinner,' said Darwin. 'Mr Skinner. I have water for you.'

Darwin filled a glass from a bottle on the floor. He clinked the bottle against the glass.

Julius stared through the hatch into the dark cell. Something large slithered along the floor. Then there was a low rustle, almost like a moan.

'Mr Skinner,' said Darwin. He tapped the bottle and glass together again.

Something hit the steel door on the other side. Julius jumped. He wanted to run away, but all the doors were locked. A stifled moan came though the hatch.

Julius felt Mr Flynn's hand tighten on his shoulder.

A man's face appeared at the hatch.

Julius jolted, falling back against Mr Flynn.

Wide bloodshot eyes stared out at them. Soulcatchers with flowers of pale orange and brown dry stems grew from the man's nose and mouth. They surrounded his face and entwined themselves in his long hair and beard. The man's fingers clasped the bottom edge of the hatch. His nails were black and cracked. Tendrils clasped at the sides of the hatch too, with languid movements.

Darwin held up the glass. The meagre gaslight shone through it. Skinner stared as if it was the elixir of life. His hand reached out and his fingers gently wrapped themselves around the glass. Then he carefully pulled it towards the hatch then stepped back and tilted his head. The water almost babbled as, with great care, he let it trickle into his mouth. He ignored the tendrils flicking about his face as if trying to lap up some of the water.

When he was finished, Skinner ran his tongue around his cracked lips and smiled, revealing his black teeth and bleeding gums. His eyes were still wide and staring as he reached out to return the glass.

'Thank you, Mr Skinner,' said Darwin.

'What's going on?' asked Mr Flynn. 'Why is this man locked away in the dark?' Julius could hear suppressed anger in his voice.

'I am trying to save his life,' said Darwin. 'And his mind.'

'How?' said Julius.

'All plants need light to survive,' said Mr Flynn. 'I hope to kill the soulcatcher by denying it that. It appears to be working.'

'And what of the poor wretch?' said Mr Flynn.

Darwin filled the glass again and gave it to Skinner.

'Mr Skinner is completely mad,' he said. 'It is the soulcatcher's doing. First the soulcatcher gives its host beautiful dreams, then the madness that you see before you. Finally—if what the Brazilian natives believe is correct—it will steal his soul.'

'How did Skinner come to be here?' said Julius.

Darwin stared at Skinner's face. Skinner was watching them as if they were the exhibit, not him.

'Six years ago Skinner tried to plant the soul-catcher's seeds into my blood. He meant to bring me back to England and make his fortune, with the most exotic orchid in the world.'

'What happened?' said Mr Flynn.

'The oddest thing,' said Darwin. 'Two native children came to my rescue. In the scuffle it was Skinner who was seeded. I banished him to the island where the soulcatchers grew. The deadly waters there make it a natural prison.'

'So he got away?' said Julius.

'Yes. A year or so later he was found floating along the river in a makeshift raft. The soulcatcher flowers had not begun to show, but he was already becoming unhinged. He was half dead from starvation and the blazing sun. The Missionary Society paid for his passage home and he was brought straight here. Then the orchids began to grow. I have been monitoring the soulcatcher's progress—and Skinner's—ever since.

'I think I've seen enough,' said Mr Flynn.

'You understand now?' asked Darwin.

'I'm sorry to say I do,' said Mr Flynn. 'We have to stop Tock before he does this to anyone else.'

Outside the gates of Bedlam the freezing fog nipped at their cheeks and noses. Julius, Darwin and Mr Flynn walked for a time, each in his own thoughts.

Julius breathed the cold air, like a newly released prisoner. When he thought of Skinner he felt ashamed of the relief he was feeling. The present was unchanged. Had he and Emily done the right thing after all? But still, he had to tell Mr Flynn what he had done.

'I was going to suggest that you lodge with me, sir,' said Mr Flynn. 'At least for this evening. Your own lodgings are less that inviting at present. It might be safer too.'

'That is most kind,' said Darwin.

They walked through the dark streets. Julius clutched the pocketwatch. How many more lies would he pile up around him before he confessed? Emily's blank face stared at Julius in his mind. She hated him now. Would she tell Mr Flynn about the time-jump before he summoned the courage to do it himself?

'You're very quiet,' said Mr Flynn.

'I'm tired,' said Julius.

Mr Flynn lingered, looking down at Julius while Darwin stood under a gaslight nearby, holding his coat tightly about himself.

'Is anything the matter?' he said, quietly.

'Me and Emily fell out. But she didn't get angry— it was as if she switched off something inside her. She stared at me as if she didn't care about anything.'

It was too dark to see Mr Flynn's eyes, but Julius knew he was looking at him.

'She's had a hard life, Julius. Harder than you or I could imagine.'

Julius hung his head. Mr Flynn's words were kindly meant but they stung him hard.

'Tell her you're sorry. And don't take long about it,' he said.

'Yes,' said Julius.

'Mr Darwin and I will check on Tock's lair first thing,' he said. 'We'll let you know how we fare.'

Julius waved across the street to Darwin and walked along Ironmonger Lane.

You can tell Mr Flynn everything tomorrow, Higgins.

He slipped through the bookshop door without letting it ring the bell. A crack of dim light under the curtain, told him that his grandfather was still up.

In the parlour, the fire was burning low. Mr Higgins was asleep in his chair with a book open across his chest. The clock on the mantel showed it was close to midnight.

Julius unbuttoned his coat and sat in his chair, suddenly realising how exhausted he was. He took the poker from the stand and dug it into the dying coals to coax out the last of their warmth.

'What, where…?' said Mr Higgins, jolting awake.

Julius slumped back in his chair.

'Ah, young Caesar,' he said. Then he remembered the terms of their parting earlier. He adjusted his glasses uneasily.

Julius kept his eyes on the fire.

Mr Higgins cleared his throat. 'Been out and about, young Caesar?' he said.

'Yes.'

Mr Higgins righted his book and pretended to read.

'I'm going to bed,' said Julius. 'Mr Flynn will be calling early. I'm going to spend the day with him.'

'As you wish.'

Julius rose. Mr Higgins cleared his throat again and turned a page with exaggerated care. Julius stopped at the foot of the stairs.

'You've seen her, I take it?' said his grandfather. 'Your mother, I mean.'

The stairs led up to darkness.

'Yes.'

Mr Higgins sniffed. 'How is she?'

'She works as a maid at Emily's school. She's fine.' Julius waited for his grandfather to speak again, though he did not know what he wanted to hear.

He realised he had forgotten to put some coals into the warming pan for his bed, but he could not bring himself to turn back to get them.

'Will you be seeing her again?' asked his grandfather, with the same disinterested tone, as if he was asking whether Julius would be combing his hair tomorrow.

'No,' he replied.

Another page turned. Julius waited for his grandfather to speak again, but he did not. He climbed the stairs and felt his way in the dark to his room. A little moonlight showed the black shapes of his bed and writing desk. Usually he would warm the bed with the warming pan and then undress and leap into it in a matter of seconds.

But now he stood, wrapped in the dark silence, wondering if it would tell him why his life was suddenly so confusing and sad.

He stood there for a long time, but no answer came.

☞

The next morning Julius sat at the top of the stairs, listening to his grandfather pottering about below. When hunger finally drove him down to the parlour he found his grandfather setting the breakfast table.

His jacket was crumpled. Julius suspected he had spent the night in his fireside chair.

'Porridge is pickling, young Caesar,' said Mr Higgins. It was the same joke every morning when porridge was on the menu. 'Sit down, sit down. You'll be needing a good breakfast if you're to be out with Mr Flynn.'

Mr Higgins disappeared into the kitchen. Julius heard sounds of porridge plopping into bowls and the grinding open of the range door as the bread rolls were taken out. Although Sunday breakfast was always more elaborate than other days, his grandfather had outdone himself this morning. Three preserve pots and a jar of honey stood next to the teapot and there was a plate of sliced ham next to the butter dish.

Julius sat down, and his grandfather placed a bowl containing more porridge than he could eat in front of him.

'Sleep well?' asked Mr Higgins.

'Yes, thank you. And you?' said Julius.

'Yes, very well.'

The stiff politeness made Julius cringe.

Mr Higgins poured tea for them both and sat down to his own bowl of porridge. Julius passed the honey, catching his grandfather's eye for a moment. His grandfather stirred his tea and clinked the spoon twice on the side making it ring like a bell.

'Put it behind you, that's my advice,' said Mr

Higgins. He spooned more honey onto his porridge, avoiding Julius's eyes.

Julius put a spoonful of porridge in his mouth. It felt like sawdust. His grandfather's guilty expression told him what he wanted to know. He knew what the secret was. He knew what his mother tried to hide from him.

'You told her to go, didn't you?' said Julius. 'You threw her out.' Julius felt rage welling up. He watched is grandfather's face, watched him weighing up his response—would it be contrition or righteous indignation.

His grandfather sipped his tea. 'What if I did?' he said. The cup clinked back into its saucer. 'Just you and me, young Caesar,' he said, without looking up. 'That's the best way. Just you and me.'

Julius stared at his porridge. He felt ashamed of the contempt he felt for his grandfather at that moment. After all, he had raised him—just as Clara had said.

A knock on the bookshop door interrupted his thoughts.

'I'm feeling a rather unwell,' said Mr Higgins. 'I might lie down for an hour.' He rose, avoiding Julius's eyes. 'Give my regards to Mr Flynn. Give him some tea.'

He went to the stairs.

Julius picked up his grandfather's porridge bowl and threw it in the sink. The bowl broke into three even pieces like slices of a cake, and the porridge oozed across the sink through yesterday's knives and forks.

The knocking came again.

When Julius, at last, unlocked and unbolted the door he found Mr Flynn and Darwin standing there impatiently. Darwin was pale and his eyes were red.

'Good morning, Julius,' said Mr Flynn. 'Growing deaf in your old age?'

'Sorry,' said Julius. 'I was in the privy.'

In the parlour Mr Flynn whistled at the fully laden breakfast table and the crackling fire.

'Help yourself, Mr Flynn, Mr Darwin,' said Julius.

He went to the cabinet and took out two extra sets of crockery and cutlery. Mr Flynn and Darwin sat at the table.

'There's good news and bad news,' said Mr Flynn, reaching for a warm roll. 'The good news is that I've pickled the soulcatcher in the jar—that's the end of that one. The bad news is that Tock's flown the coop. The house is as empty as a miser's pantry.'

Julius tried to eat his porridge.

'Gussy not around?' said Mr Flynn, referring to Mr Higgins.

'He's not feeling well. He's lying down.'

'Nothing serious I hope.'

'No,' said Julius blankly.

Mr Flynn stopped spreading his butter and looked

at Julius who had lowered his head over his porridge and pretended to eat hungrily.

'Mr Darwin was telling me about the clergyman who went to the Village of the Soulcatchers,' said Mr Flynn, between mouthfuls.

'He was a missionary,' said Darwin. 'Matthew Merrisham. He went to the Village of the Soulcatchers, much like other missionaries go to leper colonies. He intended to set up a school and a church. He ended up being seeded himself. It was he who told me most of what I know about the soulcatchers—when he was still sane enough to do so.'

'Tell Julius what you told me, sir. About how it all started,' said Mr Flynn.

Darwin ran his hand through his thinning hair while he gathered his thoughts. 'Years ago, one of the villagers woke to find a small red orchid by his bed. He did not know it at the time but he had been seeded by a soulcatcher,' said Darwin. 'He began to have the most delightful visions. He dreamt of a single raindrop falling on a leaf in the forest. The beauty of it made him weep with joy. The villagers listened to his tales as the soulcatcher took hold of his mind. They thought it was a blessing. They did not object when other small orchids crept up to them as they slept, and brushed their tendrils against their skin.'

Darwin stared at the empty teacup in front of him. He eyes were far away, in the Village of the

Soulcatchers. 'In the end, there was no one left. That is, no one except the youngest children. They were left to fend for themselves.'

Darwin looked up at Julius and Mr Flynn. He spoke like a witness on the stand.

'But even for them it was too late. The seeds were in their blood, too, waiting to grow.'

Julius ate his porridge slowly. He remembered the children staring blankly at him across the river. The soulcatcher seeds were growing inside them. Would they end up like their parents? Like Skinner?

'It's odd,' said Darwin, suddenly smiling at Julius. 'You put me in mind of the boy who leapt to my rescue when Skinner tried to seed me.'

Julius felt himself redden. He dropped the spoon in his porridge. Now was the time to tell Mr Flynn.

But before he could do that Mr Flynn pulled a sheet of paper from his pocket. 'Mr Darwin's drawn up a list of the less scrupulous orchid dealers and collectors,' he said. 'We're going to spend the day pretending to be orchid customers. We'll see if we can find out anything of Tock or his whereabouts.'

CHAPTER 17

Sunday 21st January 1838

4:53 PM

Julius, Darwin and Mr Flynn arrived tired and dispirited at the ticket office of the Surrey Zoological Gardens. It was rumoured that the gardeners in the Orchid House there did an under-the-counter trade in orchids, with no questions asked.

But after calling on crooked orchid dealers and growers all over London, they had learnt nothing. Although most of the dealers had heard of the strange Mr Tock, few had met him, and none knew where he could be found—or if they did they were not saying.

The gardens were situated in Kennington, in the parklands of Walworth House. High iron railings surrounded the fifteen acres of gardens, glasshouses, animal enclosures, teahouses and a lake on which ancient sea battles were re-enacted every afternoon at three o'clock.

It was dark when Julius, Mr Flynn and Darwin arrived. Mr Flynn placed three shilling pieces in front of the girl in the ticket booth.

'Three, please,' he said.

'We're packing up,' said the girl, barely awake. 'We close in 'arf an hour.'

She pointed to the clock behind her. It was coming up to five.

'We just want a quick stroll by the lake,' said Mr Flynn.

The girl shrugged. 'It's your money.'

She turned a brass handle three times and three tickets shot out of a slot in the counter.

In the gardens the Sunday crowd walked along the main thoroughfare, tightly wrapped in coats and scarves, determined to have a jolly time even though the clouds threatened rain.

Julius came to a crossroads and looked at the sign-post.

'Orchid House, this way,' said Mr Darwin.

They passed the Animal House—a vast, domed glasshouse lit by giant chandeliers. Caged lions and tigers snarled and paced back and forth, while families of monkeys swung through the trees overhead.

Young clerks and apprentices, in the brightest cravats and waistcoats, strutted or staggered with their ladies, depending on how much ale they had consumed. The ladies shrieked and cackled in their voluminous skirts and hats with more ribbon hanging from them than there was rigging on a warship. Julius, Mr Flynn and Darwin waded through the throng until they came to the Orchid House.

It was a large glass structure. Low privet hedges lined the pathways surrounding it and bordered the empty flowerbeds, where squealing children in their Sunday best ran and leapt with glee at the fireworks exploding overhead.

There was no lamplight within the Orchid House and the condensation on the glass walls made it difficult to see inside. A sign hanging on the door said: *Closed on Sundays.*

'Damn and blast,' said Mr Flynn. He rattled the door handle.

'What now?' said Darwin.

The whiz of a rocket made Julius look up. The firework exploded with a crack, sending out a circle of golden lights. Another exploded beside it, then another.

'Fireworks is bleeding ace don't you fink?' came a voice that Julius recognised.

In the bright flash of the fireworks Emily, Clara and Mrs Trevelyan were like actors making an entrance on an opera stage.

'Well, I'll be…' said Mr Flynn, when he saw Clara.

'Hello, Mr Flynn,' said Clara. 'It's been a long time.'

Mr Flynn raised his hat. 'It certainly has, Miss… er…' He suddenly became unsure of himself.

'It's all right, Mr Flynn,' said Emily. ''iggins knows who she is.'

She gave Julius a wot-you-looking-at stare until he turned away.

Clara looked as if she wanted disappear in a puff of smoke. Her eyes darted around, avoiding everyone's faces.

'Mr Flynn,' said Mrs Trevelyan. 'This is an unexpected pleasure.' She blushed and straightened her bonnet, which did not need straightening.

Mr Flynn cleared his throat. 'Mrs Trevelyan? Er…How do you do?'

Darwin raised his hat. 'Charles Darwin, at your service,' he said.

'Charmed,' said Mrs Trevelyan.

'How do you do?' said Clara. She bobbed an awkward curtsey in Darwin's direction.

They all stood for a few moments wondering what to say next. Then Mr Flynn laughed and slapped his side. 'It's blessed good to see you, Clara. Blessed good. It must be twenty years.'

'Seventeen, I think,' said Clara, and her face softened into a smile. 'Emily told me of all your kindness to her, Mr Flynn.'

'Oi, don't tell 'im that,' said Emily.

'Sorry,' said Clara. She smiled apologetically then cast a quick glance at Julius. 'Hello again, Julius,' she said.

Julius felt all eyes on him. He made himself smile.

Mrs Trevelyan shivered. 'Oh, the frigidity of it all,' she said. 'It makes me quite homesick for Scotland. Mr Flynn, would you see us safely to the gate? I hear there are wild animals about.'

Mr Flynn tipped his hat and held out his arm for her to take. Before Julius knew it, Clara was at his side.

'Perhaps I could take your arm, Julius?' she said. Her voice betrayed a hint of trepidation. But she slipped her arm through his before he could refuse. 'Emily,' she said. 'Take Julius's other arm to balance him out.'

'Don't fink so,' said Emily. She turned to Darwin and linked her arm in his. ''ello again,' she said. 'You'll do.'

'Have we met?' said Darwin. 'You look familiar.'

'Naaa,' said Emily. 'Don't fink so.'

'Julius, dear,' said Clara, as they all walked to the gate. 'Perhaps you'd like to stop by Walworth House to see my room? It's ever so nice.'

'Walworth House?' said Darwin. 'Lord Bloomingbury's residence. A splendid fellow? He has a fine orchid collection, I believe.'

'I haven't met His Lordship yet,' said Clara. 'He has a menagerie too, you know.'

'I carried Clara's bags up the stairs,' said Emily, to Darwin. 'We peeked frough a door and saw the queerest 'orse you've ever seen.'

'Just for a few minutes, Julius,' whispered Clara. 'It's not far.' Her voice was coaxing and her expression confident and kind. Her eyes stayed on his, waiting for an answer.

Before Julius could find an excuse, Mr Flynn thrust a few shillings into his hand. 'Here, take this. Get a hansom cab home.'

Julius stiffened and pulled away from Clara. Why was everyone trying to make him do things he didn't want to do? He felt Clara's arm tug on his.

'Come on, Julius. I'll show you the peculiar horse,' she said. 'Emily, why don't you come with us? Julius can see you home afterwards. You wouldn't mind if she's a bit late, would you, Mrs Trevelyan?'

'Not at all, Clara,' said Mrs Trevelyan. She still had a firm hold of Mr Flynn's arm.

'Don't worry, 'iggins,' said Emily. 'I won't let naffing eat you.'

Julius thought he saw a hint of a smile on her face.

CHAPTER 18

Sunday 21st January 1838
6:18 PM

Julius followed Emily and Clara across the park-land between the Surrey Zoological Gardens and Walworth House. The gravel scrunched under their feet when they arrived at the path leading to the stables and the trade entrance. The black shape of the mansion obscured most of the sky.

'It's a very large house for one old gentleman,' said Clara.

'Don't forget all the animals,' said Emily. 'Running all over the place like they own it.'

'Aren't they in cages?' said Julius.

'Cages?' said Emily. 'Cages is boring. When I grow up I'm 'aving an eagle.'

'We'll see,' said Clara.

They entered the stable yard and Clara led them down some steps into dark corridor lined with boots and coats on hooks. It opened into a sizeable kitchen—full of cooks and kitchen hands, all rushing about, busily stirring, peeling and chopping. It was as noisy as race day on Epsom Downs with the clash of pans and the hiss of the fires along with the oaths shouted at the poor kitchen maids. Clara leaned close to Julius. 'The kitchen is hot with jealousy. His Lordship's cook is in charge and she bullies the rest of them. There's a cook for the crocodiles. There's one for the all the monkeys, and twenty more for all the different animals, all the way down to the poor girl who sifts the bird seed for the fairy wrens.'

'You ain't seen naffing yet,' said Emily above the din. 'Come on.'

Clara and Emily took him up a flight of stairs. Clara opened the door at the top just a little. 'Strictly speaking we shouldn't be here but I wanted to show you,' she said.

She touched his hand as she spoke.

Despite himself, Julius was intrigued. He peered through the gap. Before him was a wide passage. After the cacophony of the kitchen it was eerily quiet. Gas jets shaped like long-necked birds lit the corridor, which was lined with wallpaper depicting exotic birds flying among branches that bore colourful fruits. Wooden panels below the wallpaper were carved to resemble climbing plants, and the carpet looked to be as thick as a mattress.

'Look up,' whispered Emily.

The ceiling was one long painting of a blue sky with wispy white clouds, interrupted by plaster mouldings, from which the chandeliers hung.

Julius heard a scrunching sound. There was movement further along the corridor.

''ere comes somefing,' said Emily. 'I 'ope it's good and peculiar.'

Julius, Emily and Clara watched in astonishment as a creature trotted along the carpet. It was as large as a badger but resembled an armoured rat. When it neared the door it stopped, pointed its long snout at them and sniffed.

'Off with you,' said Clara, nervously.

The creature lost interest and continued along the corridor.

'It's going to take me a while to get used to the wildlife,' said Clara. 'Follow me. I'll show you my room.'

They retraced their steps down the stairs. Clara took a spare oil lamp from a hook and led them to the back stairs and then up the four flights to the women's wing of the servants' quarters.

'They haven't put gas pipes up here yet,' said Clara. She stopped at one of the doors. 'Here we are. Home, sweet home.' She opened it and ushered

Julius and Emily inside.

'It's ace, ain't it?' said Emily. 'Mrs Trevelyan gave her all sorts of fings to make it nice.'

Julius looked around. A curtained window was set into the sloping ceiling and a narrow bed with a bedside table stood against the wall. A small fireplace with a dying coal still gave off a little warmth.

'You can see the dome of the Animal House from the window,' said Clara, as she unbuttoned her coat and removed her bonnet.

Julius pulled the curtain aside but all he could see was the black night. He remained there, looking out at nothing.

Emily sat on the edge of the bed and bounced. 'All you need is some pictures to 'ang and you'll be like royalty,' she said.

Julius felt Clara's eyes on him, he did not dare look around.

Clara stroked the bare wall with her fingers. 'Yes, a few pictures would be nice,' she said.

'We should be going,' said Julius. 'Grandfather will be wondering where I am.'

Clara fidgeted with the ribbons of her bonnet. 'Oh, yes, of course. Give Father my best wishes,' she said. 'Tell him I'm well.'

'Yes, I will,' said Julius. He realised that he meant it.

Emily jumped off the bed. 'I'll come back

tomorrow, Clara,' she said. 'If you find a small animal wot won't be missed, can you nick it for me? I'll bring a bag for it.'

'We'll see, dear,' said Clara, smiling to herself.

Julius took a last look around the room and at his mother. He hoped she would be happy there. 'I can get some prints for the walls,' he said. 'What sort of scenes do you like?'

Clara thought for a moment. 'Castles,' she said. She linked her arm with his to walk him out.

At the stairway, Julius heard a scraping sound. He moved closer to the stairs and saw the armoured-rat creature scrabbling up towards him.

'Good gracious,' said Clara.

Further down the staircase and around the corner came the sounds of many paws in pursuit.

The rat creature reached the top of the stairs and ran in an awkward hobbling motion along one of the corridors. A strange pack of terrier-sized dogs came into view at the turn in the staircase. They raced up the stairs as if on a hunt.

The rat creature, now too terrified to know where it was going, ran into a wall, then curled itself up into an armoured ball.

'Heel. Heel, damn you,' called out someone from below.

'Oi, pick on someone your own size,' said Emily, to the dogs snapping at the balled-up creature.

The dogs were not like any Julius had seen before. And they were not barking like dogs, but emitting high-pitched yelps. Their heads seemed too large for their bodies and their snouts too long for their heads. Black stripes ran across their sleek, brown backs, and their hind legs were disproportionately small. All in all, they looked like a child's drawing of a dog come to life.

A man appeared at the turn in the stairs. 'Heel,' he wheezed, and he grasped the banister and hauled himself to the top of the stairs.

Julius, Emily and Clara stared in disbelief. There were five or six tiny hummingbirds flitting around the man's head. Their feathers were a shimmering green and their wings were a buzzing blur as they took turns darting back and forth to dip their long beaks into the man's ears. The man paid them no attention.

'Heel, heel,' he called to the dogs.

The dogs left the curled-up creature and gathered around the old man's feet.

Clara bobbed a quick curtsey.

This must be Lord Bloomingbury, Higgins.

Julius reckoned His Lordship to be in his mid-seventies. His arms and legs were as thin as rake handles, but his belly was a dome over which his waistcoat buttons strained. His white hair was splendidly curled in the latest fashion and his side-whiskers were as bushy and white as clouds.

'Good Heavens,' he said, looking from Clara, to Emily and finally to Julius.

'Good evening, Your Lordship,' said Clara, a little flustered. She curtsied again.

The strange dogs sniffed around the man's feet, not able to be still for a moment.

'Who the devil are you?' he said.

'Clara Higgins, sir. I'm to start as under-house-keeper tomorrow morning, sir,' said Clara. 'I was just settling into my room, sir.'

Lord Bloomingbury's mouth opened wide to let out a long. 'Ahhh.' Then he continued. 'I comprehend, entirely. Welcome, welcome, my dear, to my humble abode.'

'Thank you, sir.'

'However…I thought my advertisement was clear, Miss Higgins—no family ties,' said Lord Bloomingbury. He glanced disapprovingly from Emily to Julius. 'I cannot have my servants' lives complicated by children and such like. I thought that was quite clear—no families.'

'Oh, it was, sir,' said Clara, curtseying again.

'We ain't family, gov,' said Emily. 'We're only visiting. We live next door, but one, from where Clara used to work. We just 'appened to bump into 'er in the Zoo Gardens. We got talking and we said we'd see 'er 'ome. Ain't that right, Julius?'

'Er, yes,' said Julius. He was impressed by what

214

a convincing liar Emily was. He almost believed her himself.

Lord Bloomingbury's disapproval turned into a concerned smile. 'So, my child, your parents do not know where you are?' he asked.

'Naaa. They don't 'ave the foggiest notion,' said Emily. 'Nobody does.'

'I'm terribly sorry, Your Lordship,' said Clara. 'They were just on their way out.'

Lord Bloomingbury did not appear to be listening. He tapped his chin. 'Interesting. Very interesting,' he said.

The armoured rat had unfurled itself and was trying to sneak away down the corridor. The dogs gave chase.

'Young man,' he said to Julius. 'Could I beg your assistance? Be so kind as to retrieve the creature yonder.'

Julius hesitated. He did not relish the idea of grappling with it.

'Do not fear, my boy. Armadillos are timid creatures,' said Lord Bloomingbury. 'I suggest you pick it up by its tail.'

Julius followed the escaping armadillo and grabbed its tail with both hands. It was surprisingly heavy, but, to Julius's great delight, it did not try to bite him—it curled up into a ball and hung upside down like a clock's pendulum.

'Splendid. You are a gifted animal handler,' said Lord Bloomingbury. 'Now, follow me and I shall show you a dodo.'

'A dodo, sir? said Julius. 'But, they're all gone aren't they? All dead for two hundred years.'

Lord Bloomingbury chuckled and shrugged his shoulders. 'What a clever young fellow you are,' he said. 'Perhaps you're correct. But what if you're not?'

''ow big is a dodo, sir?' said Emily. 'Would it fit in a sack, do you fink?'

'Probably,' said Lord Bloomingbury. 'Why do you ask?'

Clara put her arm around Emily's shoulder. 'I do apologise, Your Lordship,' she said. 'Shush now, Emily,' she whispered.

'Do you even know what a dodo is?' asked Julius.

'Yes, I bleeding I do,' said Emily.

Clara attempted a good-natured titter as she tried to edge Emily down the stairs.

'I'm most terribly sorry, Your Lordship,' she said. 'We really should be going.'

Lord Bloomingbury chuckled again. 'Think nothing of it, Miss Higgins,' he said. 'The child has spirit. What a specimen. I should like to add her to my collection.'

His shoulders shook as he laughed at his joke. 'Follow me,' he said, when he'd composed himself. 'Let's hunt down a dodo.'

He walked down the stairs, with the strange dogs scrambling after him

'Better do as His Lordship says,' whispered Clara. 'Emily, please don't speak again.'

'I'll try,' whispered Emily. 'But I ain't promising naffing.'

They followed Lord Bloomingbury through a door into another long and finely decorated corridor. Huge paintings of exotic animals and birds lined the walls. A horned creature walked gracefully by, ignoring everyone.

'That's my oryx,' said Lord Bloomingbury. 'It's rather aloof.'

'That's the peculiar 'orse wot we saw,' whispered Emily.

Lord Bloomingbury nearly tripped on the dogs many times as he wandered the corridors. They passed a herd of peccaries and a pair of sleeping warthog along the way—he stepped over them without comment.

'Here we are,' he said. They had come to a door with the word 'Library' painted on it.

Julius looked around for somewhere to put the armadillo. In the middle of the room stood round tables where volumes as large as cottage doors lay open to show exquisite paintings of birds, plants and animals. Some of the illustrations appeared to be stained with bird droppings. Looking up, Julius saw why—long-tailed parrots were perched on the chandeliers. He could make out at least one nest in the crystal pieces.

The thought of so many wonderful books being treated with such disrespect pained Julius. It would have made his grandfather weep.

'Put it anywhere,' said Lord Bloomingbury to Julius.

When Julius went to put the armadillo down the strange dogs leapt towards it.

'Oi,' said Emily. 'Them dogs, wot kind are they, gov? I ain't seen naffing like 'em in my life.'

'They're thylacines, from Van Diemen's Land,' Lord Bloomingbury said, as he shooed them out of the library and closed the door behind them. 'Still pups, though. I plan to breed them up. Soon every boy in England will have a pet thylacine, mark my words.'

Julius released the armadillo. It unfurled itself and ambled away to a corner where it hid under a globe mounted on a wooden stand.

'Your 'ouse is ace, gov,' said Emily. 'You must be the luckiest man in England?'

'Yes. I suppose I am,' he replied. 'I have creatures from all over the known world, and some of the *un*known, too. Come now. I promised to show you a dodo.'

With that, Lord Bloomingbury turned a doorhandle. Emily clapped her hands and pushed in front of Julius.

'Calm yourself, Emily,' whispered Clara.

The next room was a large sitting room with a fire roaring in a splendid fireplace. Lord Bloomingbury waved his hand at the portraits around the room—all finely attired gentlemen and ladies in regal poses. 'That's the family, all the way back to the Battle of Hastings,' he said.

Emily's eyes darted around the room looking for the dodo. All Julius could see were white streaks on the walls were the wallpaper had been pulled off. He noticed a faint odour and sniffed. It was like two-week-old meat.

A lizard, as long as a man, was sleeping on the couch. It flicked its tail, making Clara jump.

'There it is!' shouted Emily.

A bird like a large grey chicken tootled out from behind a chair. It pecked at the wallpaper with its oddly shaped beak and then pulled a strip off.

'This is the only remaining dodo in the entire world,' said Lord Bloomingbury, proudly.

'Pity you've only got the one, gov,' said Emily. She tried to corral the bird, but it hopped around her and ran along the wall squawking. 'I'd love to 'ave a dodo for myself.'

'I like to have things that no one else does,' said Lord Bloomingbury. 'I find it most invigorating. I'm always on the lookout for unique and extraordinary specimens. Which leads me to my next—'

'Per'aps I could borrow it?' said Emily. 'Or 'ave one of its eggs?' She had the dodo cornered and was trying to imitate the noises it made. 'I'll bring it back when I'm finished wiv it, honest.'

Julius looked at Clara. She appeared to be about to faint from mortification. 'Yes, well. Thank you, Emily, dear,' she said. 'I really think you ought to be getting home.'

Julius tried to give Emily a reproachful look but she did not see it. She had calmed the dodo and was cuddling it like a long lost favourite pet.

'Come on, Emily,' said Clara. 'Time to go home.' She took Emily's arm and quickly curtsied to Lord Bloomingbury. 'Thank you, sir,' she said. 'I'll see to the children. Thank you, ever so much.'

'Just a moment,' said Lord Bloomingbury. He tilted a book on a shelf and the whole bookshelf opened a few inches, like a door. The meaty odour Julius had noticed before wafted through the crack.

Clara coughed. Julius's eyes begin to water.

'You haven't seen anything yet,' said Lord Bloomingbury.

'Wot is it?' said Emily, gleefully.

Clara placed her handkerchief over her mouth and coughed again. She pulled on Emily's arm and led her back to the door they had come in through.

'But you really must see—' said Lord Bloomingbury.

'Thank you, sir,' cut in Clara. She spluttered into

her handkerchief. 'Come on children. Home with you.'

''ang on,' said Emily, as she was being pulled to the door.

'Good evening, sir,' said Julius. He opened the door for Clara who bustled Emily out.

'But you will miss the—'

'Thank you, Your Lordship,' said Clara. Cutting him off before he could say anything else to excite Emily. 'Thank you.'

Lord Bloomingbury stood at the bookshelf with a quizzical expression on his face. He was just about to say something when Julius quickly bowed and closed the door.

Clara coughed again but it quickly turned into the laughter of relief.

'Emily, you'll get me sacked before I even start,' she said. She gave Emily a playful push through the library door. 'I don't think anyone's ever spoken to His Lordship the way you did. I could have died.'

''e didn't mind,' said Emily. ''e was a nice old geeza.'

Out in the corridor the thylacine pups leapt around them, yipping and flicking their tails.

Clara tried to shoo them away. 'When you asked to borrow his dodo…I…I…' Clara burst into laughter again. 'Quick,' she said. 'Before he comes out.'

She took Julius and Emily by the hand and they ran along the corridor, with the thylacines bounding after them.

Through the hectic kitchen, they ran, and out the door. At the top of the steps they stood under the gas light, their laughter dying away. Emily sniffed at the cold.

'You've got your cab fare?' said Clara.

Julius nodded and jangled the coins in his pocket.

'Best go to Penton Place, there's a cab row there,' she said.

Julius hunched up his shoulders against the cold. Clara reached out and touched his arm as if to warm him.

'I'll bring some pictures of castles for you,' he said. 'When I come again.'

Clara looked happy and sad all at once. 'Safe home, now,' she mouthed when her voice failed her.

'And I'll speak to grandfather,' said Julius. 'I'll ask him to invite you to tea.'

'Oh, no,' said Clara. She held up her hands. 'No. It's better if—'

'I'll speak to him,' said Julius. 'It will be all right.'

Julius turned to Emily. 'I can see you back to the academy,' he said.

Emily shrugged. 'If you want. I ain't bothered.'

Julius felt the sting of the missing ''iggins' in her reply.

'Come on,' he said.

They walked across the stable yard and made their way across the parkland, towards the lights of

Penton Place. The air was still and the frozen mist burrowed into their bones. To Julius's surprise, Emily tucked her arm under his. He felt her lean into him as they walked in step.

'I saw Skinner,' he said. 'He's a patient in Bedlam. The soulcatchers are growing out of him. Darwin's working on a cure.'

'Ace,' said Emily. 'I told you we did it right.'

'Looks like it,' said Julius. 'Thanks for not telling Mr Flynn about, you know, the pocketwatch and the time-jump. 'I *am* going to tell him. I just need the right moment.'

Emily did not reply.

'I'm sorry for what I said,' he said.

He felt Emily's arm sliding out of his. It was as if his coat had suddenly disappeared. Coldness enveloped him.

Fine, be like that. See if I care.

'Did you hear me?' he asked, when it became clear that she was not going to respond.

'Come on. Let's run or the cold'll do for us.'

He followed her over the grass. The short cut to Penton Place took them past the Surrey Zoological Gardens. The spikes at the top of the fence could just be made out against the night sky. At the New Street gate Emily stopped. In the darkness she was an airy mixture of sounds and glimpsed movements.

'You missed seeing the Animal 'ouse. It was ace,'

she said. 'Not as good as 'is Lordship's, though.'

Julius followed her to the large wrought-iron gates. They put their faces through the bars.

'I'll 'ave all sorts of animals when 'ave my own gaff,' said Emily.

Julius wished she would call him 'iggins again.

'Look. Over there,' said Emily.

'I think that's the Orchid House. Someone's inside,' said Julius.

It appeared to be someone pushing a wheelbarrow piled high with birdcages.

'Bit late for gardening,' said Emily.

'Not Tock's kind of gardening,' said Julius.

CHAPTER 19

Sunday 21st January 1838

8:12 PM

Julius peered through the gate at the Orchid House. 'Did you see the cages, Emily?' he said. 'Tock keeps soulcatchers and rats in cages just like them.'

Emily rattled the gate. 'It's locked,' she said.

'We'll go and get Mr Flynn,' said Julius.

Emily snorted derisively. 'No we bleeding won't,' she said. 'Locks is always pickable. I don't know why people bother making 'em.'

Julius heard her rummage through her purse. 'It's in 'ere somewhere,' she said to herself.

'What are you doing?'

''ere, you 'old the light while I pick,' she said, handing him a box of Lucifers. 'The more we see, the more we can tell Mr Flynn when we fetch 'im.' She ran her hand along the wrought iron, feeling for the lock.

'Strike a light,' she said. 'I've got it.'

Julius lit a Lucifer while Emily rummaged through her purse again. She took out a two slim lengths of steel, like large pins with kinks at one end.

'You're in charge now then, are you?' said Julius.

Emily cast him a quick grin then inserted one of the pins. She jiggled it around to get a feel for tumblers inside the lock. Then she inserted the other pin at the bottom of the slot, and, six Lucifers later, the gate was open.

Julius and Emily moved silently through the gardens, guessing their progress by degrees of darkness. A large black block was a teahouse. Amorphous shapes were bushes. The grey lines before them were the pathways. Julius knew they had reached the domed Animal House from the growls and cries inside, as well as from the smell.

When they came to the Orchid House they hid themselves in the ivy growing up one corner of the building. Julius tried to see through the condensation dripping down the windows.

'I can't see naffing,' whispered Emily.

Julius edged along the front. Splinters of light escaped through the foliage inside, giving nothing away.

'Can you 'ear anyfing?' whispered Emily.

Julius shook his head. They crept towards the door where the closed sign still hung. Emily turned the handle but it did not give. She began to rummage through her purse again and took out her lock picks.

'Let's look round the back first,' Julius whispered. 'We might be able to see inside from there.'

Emily frowned. Julius turned away before she could object and made his way through the tangled ivy. At the next corner, he peeped around. More light spilled out through the glass at the back. It shone on an empty wheelbarrow.

Emily edged past him to see for herself. Muffled sounds came from inside, as if someone was throwing something around. Julius looked through the window and found a gap in the foliage. A brown-coated figure moved past. 'It's Baines,' he whispered. 'We've found them.'

'Ace,' whispered Emily.

'I can't see what he's doing,' whispered Julius.

'We might be able to see from up there.' Emily pointed to a ladder going up the side of the glass house. Ivy covered most of it. 'It probably leads to the roof. We can look down on 'em from there.' She already had her foot on the first rung. A loud noise inside the Orchid House made Julius turn back to the window. Baines was lifting a large steel trapdoor and throwing a birdcage down a hole.

He spun around to tell Emily and bumped into

something large. It smelled of dried sweat and bad breath.

Julius looked up. Edward Rapple leered down at him. His left cheekbone and eye were still swollen and bruised from the punch Mr Flynn had given him on the Bermondsey wasteground.

'Want to have a closer look?' he said.

'I…I…' stammered Julius.

Rapple stopped smiling. He grabbed Julius and dragged him to the back door of the glass house and opened it.

'Mr Baines,' said Rapple. 'We have a visitor.'

He picked Julius up by his lapels and pushed him backwards through the open door. Julius fell landed on his back. He looked up at the glass ceiling. Emily's face was looking down through a windowpane. He shook his head.

Don't come down, Emily.

Blue, white and yellow orchids surrounded him, entwining themselves around the wrought-iron posts holding up the glasshouse. The air was hot and moist, like in Brazil, but it stank with a rank odour that made Julius's eyes water.

Baines kicked him in his side, knocking the wind out of him. Julius rolled over and curled up into a ball. 'Where's Flynn hiding?' said Baines.

Julius did not have any breath to speak.

'There's no one else out there,' said Rapple.

'How do you know?' said Baines.

'I have eyes and ears, don't I?' said Rapple. 'It's as quiet as a dead fiddler out there.'

Julius clutched his stomach. Rapple and Baines leaned over him forming an ugly, rotten-toothed canopy.

'What's he up to?' said Baines to himself. He reached down and hauled Julius up to within an inch of his face. One of his eyes was still purple and swollen from when Mr Flynn had punched him too.

'What are you doing here?' he said. 'Who are you working for?'

Julius fought to breathe.

'I think the lad's shy, Mr Baines,' said Rapple.

'I think you're right, Mr Rapple,' said Baines. 'He's a touch on the delicate side.'

Julius gulped in some air at last but then retched at the smell of Baines's foul breath.

Baines chuckled. 'I wonder what Mr Tock will say, Mr Rapple?' he said.

'I wouldn't like to be in your skin when Tock finds out you've been spying again,' said Rapple.

'Still,' said Baines. 'You won't be keeping your skin for long.'

He threw Julius into a pile of empty birdcages.

'Careful, lad,' said Rapple. 'You'll pay for any breakages.'

Julius lay among the birdcages. He glanced up.

Emily's face was gone. He looked at the door. Perhaps he could make a run for it?

But before he could move Baines hauled him out from among the birdcages and towards the open trap door and pushed him down a spiral staircase.

Baines laughed. 'Down to Hades, we go.' With a firm grip on the back of Julius's neck, Baines pushed him further down the stairs. The sulphurous stench grew stronger with each step. Julius tried to get some air into his lungs and arrange his thoughts in his head. Soon, he saw light below. The spiralling stairs led down to an underground sewer.

Baines threw Julius down the last few steps. Julius managed to stop himself from falling into the river of putrid water. His eyes and nose strung from the stench.

'Mr Tock, sir,' said Baines. 'We found the boy lurking outside. It's the one from the bookshop.'

Tock was sitting on a stool on the bank of the sewer with a child's fishing net in his hand. They were in some sort of maintenance area. There were wide banks on each side of the sewer and three tunnels leading off. Oil lamps hung from nails on the brick walls, giving everything a sepia tint.

Abigail crouched behind Tock with two legs on each bank. Her claws were poised as if ready to attack. She almost filled the space, all the way to the vaulted ceiling. A hundred or more birdcages were stacked around the walls—all crammed with rats writhing around each other, screeching and flicking their tails through the bars.

Tock stared at Julius. His mouth was agape, but in a few seconds it stretched into a sinister smile.

'You have caught us fishing for blood and bone, young man,' he said. He swept the fishing net through the viscous brown river. 'What can be more restful than fishing?' said Tock. 'What? What?'

Abigail followed the progress of the net with her one eye.

The pole jolted. Tock lifted the net out and plunged his hand onto it. He pulled a squirming rat out by its tail. Then he thrust it onto a bucket of water, sloshed it around and then held it close for inspection.

'Hmm. A little sickly,' he said. 'We only use the finest specimens for our fertiliser. Only the finest.'

He swung the rat by its tail, dashing its head against the edge of the bank. On the third stroke the rat was dead. He tossed it onto a large pile of dead rats. Then Tock smiled up at Julius. 'You will tell me what you are doing here. You will. You will.'

Julius's stomach clenched. He leaned over the river of sewage. His stomach emptied itself in two full-bodied heaves. He wiped his mouth with his sleeve, and groaned.

'Oh dear,' said Tock. 'Was it something you ate? Was it? Was it?'

'I don't feel very well,' said Julius.

231

Rapple came down the stairs with his arms full of cages.

'That's nearly all of them,' he said to Tock.

'We'll need more,' said Tock. 'Lots more.'

Julius looked at the hundreds of caged rats.

How many soulcatchers does he have to feed, Higgins?

'Now, young man,' said Tock. 'Begin to talk and do not stop until I am satisfied. Or terrible things will happen.'

Julius tried to appear befuddled. 'I...I...er...'

Tock came face to face with him. His blue eyes held the cruel curiosity of a child who had found a butterfly stuck in a spider's web.

Julius's knees weakened. He tried to brace himself.

'I'm going to give you to Abigail,' said Tock. Abigail lifted her head at the sound of her name. 'Or, perhaps I'll give you to my soulcatchers.'

Julius's mind spun like the cogs of the pocketwatch, searching for something that would seem like truth.

'I spoke to Mr Darwin,' he said. It was the only thing he could think of.

Tock's eyes narrowed. 'Did you?'

'He...er, he said you had a plan to grow the soulcatchers in London.'

'What a nosy fellow Darwin is,' said Tock. 'He should have been the one seeded, you know. Not poor Mr Skinner.'

'Mr Darwin said you didn't have a soul,' said Julius.

Tock laughed. 'Darwin's correct,' he said. 'Would you like a surprise before you die? Would you? Would you?'

Julius stared at Tock. He had nothing to say.

'Watch this,' said Tock. He clasped his face in his hands and pulled it off.

Julius gasped and fell back.

The faceless Tock leaned over him. His glowing blue eyes were surrounded by clockwork. His false teeth were two lines of ivory beads set amongst the brasswork of his jaw. They moved as he spoke.

'I'm the finest in the shop,' he said. 'The very finest.'

Julius stared at the Tock's eyes in the clockwork skull. The wheels and pinions turned and brass rods shifted as his expression changed.

'You're…you're an automaton?' he said.

'What a clever fellow you are,' said Tock. 'Yes. I'm a good little machine.'

'So that's why you don't have a soul,' said Julius.

Julius thought he saw sadness in the clockwork expression—a slight dimming of the eyes. Then the wheels and pinions spun faster and the eyes glowed brighter. The small teeth ground together.

'I shall have all of your souls though,' he said. 'The soulcatchers shall trap them and I shall have them all forever.'

He belongs in Bedlam, Higgins. Even if he is a machine.

Julius looked at Rapple and Baines. They stood nearby, watching. Their faces were as blank as workhouse walls. He tried to recall what they'd said about a Pacific island.

'Are you going to let this happen?' he said to them.

'We'll be long gone,' said Baines. 'Living like kings.'

Tock gripped Julius by the collar and pulled him close. Julius could smell the watch oil and hear the soft tick of the wheels. 'Abigail can have you,' he said. 'She likes tearing things apart.'

'Oi!' shouted Emily. The sound rang through the sewer, echoing off the walls.

She glared at them all from the spiral stairs.

'Leave 'im alone,' she said.

Julius felt Tock's grip loosen as he turned and looked up at the intruder. Julius pushed him away. 'Run,' he shouted to Emily.

Julius leapt across the river of sewage and fell against the wall. Emily disappeared up the stairs. Rapple was already climbing after her.

'Get the boy, Abigail,' shouted Tock.

Julius ran into the nearest tunnel. Behind him the screech of iron rang out as Abigail squeezed her way through the tunnel after him. Julius held his left hand to the wall as he ran. Hopefully he could keep from plunging into the sewer. Abigail roared, making the tunnel quake.

The wall on Julius's left disappeared. He stopped and turned back to grope for it. *It must be a junction, Higgins.* He placed his palm firmly on the left wall and continued along the left fork.

Behind him, the sound of Abigail grinding against the sides of the tunnel stopped.

Can she see in the dark, Higgins?

Julius looked over his shoulder. The red eye shone, searching the different tunnels. It looked down Julius's tunnel, lighting it with a dim red glow. She advanced on him.

Yep, she can see in the dark.

Julius ran on, terror giving him speed. He came to another junction. *If you turn left again you'll be going a circle, Higgins.* Abigail was gaining.

He fumbled though his pockets for the watch and spun it in the air. He could barely see in the dark but he managed to tap its side and blue light shone out. Julius held his palm under the bobbing pocketwatch and kept running. The watch stayed above his hand as if it was tied to it.

Julius raced full pelt along the bank of the sewer. Behind him, Abigail scrabbled through the tunnel. Her back scraped the arched ceiling, sending out sparks like a grinding wheel in a foundry.

She was gaining on him. Even if Julius came to a ladder or a doorway he would only have a few seconds to use it—that was not enough time. He made a decision. He tapped the pocketwatch again. The top and bottom opened out.

It's working, Higgins.

Abigail was almost upon him. He only had seconds to do an emergency time-jump. But, where to? Did it matter? Anywhere was better than this.

Take me somewhere safe.

The ticking of the pocketwatch turned to a polyrhythm. The volume increased. Abigail was only yards behind. All the competing sounds combined in a deafening din.

Julius jumped to the other bank. Just as his foot touched down he felt a blow to his shoulder. He missed his footing and banged his shin against the sharp edge of the sewer bank, and he fell into the putrid water. The animal urge to live surged through him, and he hoisted himself out of the sludge. Pain shot through his body.

He rolled up onto the bank and looked up. 'No,' he cried.

Abigail's claw of forks closed around the spinning pocketwatch. Shafts of blue light shone out between the fork bars of the claw cage as she peered at it. Her hand of mirrors fanned and tilted to capture its movements. Julius imagined her tearing it apart.

'Wait,' he shouted. But the cacophony of the pocketwatch's cogs and wheels as it banged and rattled against the claws drowned him out.

He gritted his teeth against the excruciating pain in his shin and pulled himself up. He waved his arms to get Abigail's attention. Her eye turned to him and the claw of knives lifted and swept him away.

Julius fell back against the wall. One of the shillings Mr Flynn had given him for his cab fare fell out of his pocket.

He had an idea.

He grasped the handful of coins and fought to get to his feet, crying out in agony as he put his weight on his injured leg. Abigail rattled the spinning pocketwatch in her claw cage, appearing to grow impatient with it.

Julius shouted, trying to get her attention. He pushed forward, flinging the coins at her face. They bounced off her razor scales, breaking her concentration for an instant. Julius lunged for the pocketwatch. He slipped his hand through the gap between the fork-bars of Abigail's claw and tapped the edge of the spinning watch.

Julius tumbled uncontrollably, trying to gather his thoughts as he orbited the giant pocketwatch hurtling through time and space. Each tick of the watch resounded across the universe. He tried to see whether he had brought Abigail with him into the galaxies.

A fork flew past, just missing his ear, then another one. When he landed he would have to run as fast as he could, before Abigail re-assembled.

Julius felt himself falling. He hit hard ground. It felt like cobblestones. He flinched as he heard the jangle of cutlery falling around him. The pocket-watch spun an arm's length away. He reached out and it flew to him.

He leapt up. The time-jump had healed his injured leg and cleaned the sewage off him. He had landed in a street between rows of small, red-brick houses. A circle of forks lay on the cobblestones. He looked around. Everything was unnaturally quiet. Where was the rest of Abigail?

He picked up one of the forks.

Overhead, dark-grey clouds hung low in the sky. There was not a soul in sight. Not a child at play or a stray dog to be seen. Many of the windows of the houses were smashed and pieces of broken furniture lay on the street.

A sound made his ears prick up. What was it? Something was scrabbling over roof tiles—something small and metal. Julius looked up at the gutters of the houses.

Cripes!

A spider-like creature the size of a cat appeared over the edge of the gutter.

It was made of metal.

CHAPTER 20

Wednesday 23rd September 1846

3:53 PM

Julius backed away from the metal creature, trying not to make another sound. The creature felt along the edge of the gutter with its long, many-jointed legs and numerous antennae.

Julius kept his eyes on it as he took two more steps back. Its legs found the drainpipe. It scrambled over the edge and climbed down it. It was larger than a cat and even more agile.

Julius looked for somewhere to run. The door of one of the houses was open. He slipped inside and closed it. Before he could put his hand over his mouth the smell hit him. It was damp-rot and with something sickeningly sweet mixed in.

He looked up the stairs and down the passage

towards the kitchen. Something jangled outside. He bolted the door and peeped into the parlour. Cobwebs hung everywhere. A patina of mould grew up the walls and enveloped the chair by the fire. Julius heard the jangling sound again, then a grinding noise. He slipped into the parlour and edged along the wall until he came to the window overlooking the street. He peeped around the edge of the curtain.

The metal spider was examining Abigail's forks. Julius watched it run its appendages along the fork handles and between the prongs. It tested the forks' strength and malleability and tapped them against each other and on the cobbles. Julius realised that it could not see—it was exploring the forks by touch. He felt his shoulder relax a little. He turned to find a way out the back and knocked over a vase on a table. It smashed on the floorboards.

Julius froze. The sounds outside stopped—the creature could hear.

A second later, long thin copper legs appeared at the window. Julius tried to crawl behind the fireside chair. As long as he didn't make another sound he would be all right.

The metal legs felt their way along edges of the window and began to hit at the panes. The glass shattered and fell into the parlour. The spider-like thing sprang up onto the windowsill and stretched its legs and antennae between the shards of glass. It was close enough for Julius to see that it was made from thousands of washers and nuts all screwed together at odd angles.

Julius saw the poker by the fireplace. He picked it up, but as he readied himself to spring on the metal spider creature a loud hissing erupted.

Julius looked through the open door leading to the back parlour. Soulcatchers were growing up the wall and across the ceiling. He dropped the poker in horror. Hundreds of white tendrils reached towards him and the wall of soulcatchers quivered as if in anticipation.

The metal spider leapt through the window and landed on the floor. Julius backed away. The soulcatchers' tendrils flicked and slithered inches from his face as the spider examined the broken vase.

Julius looked into the gloom, trying to see where the soulcatchers were growing from. It was an old man. He was sitting in a chair with his head thrown back. Stems issued from his mouth, nose and eyes. One mummified hand lay on the arm of a chair, still holding a pipe.

The spider tossed the broken vase aside, scrabbled up to a cabinet and pulled open a drawer. It climbed inside and began to throw out cutlery, thimbles and keys.

Julius silently edged past it and out into the passage. He unbolted the front door and opened it a crack. There was no one about outside.

He walked along the street, looking through parlour windows at soulcatchers sitting by long-dead fires. He ran through Vine Yard and out onto Pickle Herring Street on the southern bank of the Thames. His chest heaved from his sprint as he stared across the river at the Tower of London. Down river, the dome of St Paul's Cathedral rose above the rooftops. A few seagulls glided on the breeze. The centre span of London Bridge had collapsed. He looked up and down the river. As far as his eyes could see, all the ships were gone. Only broken barrels and rotting planks floated past.

The grey sky was growing darker and a cool breeze blew across the river. Julius sniffed it. Something was missing. Then he realised. The stink of the Thames was gone. The water ran clear and clean. He shivered from the cold and looked at his clothes for the first time. He had a sturdy pair of workman's trousers, a waistcoat and a jacket. All were well worn and stained. A large handkerchief was tied around his neck and a flat cap was rolled up and stuffed into one pocket and a pair of thick leather gloves in the other. He put the cap and gloves on.

The light was fading rapidly. Where could he go? Were there soulcatchers in every house? Where was safe? Julius wandered around until he came to New Street. Large grey blocks of stone lay on the road—an ornamental turret had fallen from the roof of

St Thomas' Hospital. Julius noticed that one of the hospital's doors was open. He took a last look up and down the street and went inside.

He found himself in a wide corridor. There were long scratches in the dull green paint as if a giant claw had scraped the walls. Bloodstained rags and smashed teacups lay across the floor. Julius listened. There were no sounds.

He went through the nearest door. Five or six small metal creatures scurried over a cabinet and table containing an assortment of medical implements. There were oddly shaped scissors and knives, as well as drill bits of various sizes and a small hammer. The metal creatures were blindly examining them with their antennae. A creature resembling a large ant but with many more legs pushed aside a smaller creature and snatched away the scissors it was trying to pull apart. The smaller creature wrestled to retrieve its prize, but the larger one turned on it and savagely tore it to bits. The pieces tinkled when they hit the floor and the other creatures scrambled down and began to pick through the disassembled corpse.

Julius backed away. He opened another door and gasped. Lined up along both sides of the ward were hospital beds. Each one contained a mummified patient with a soulcatcher growing from it. The plants stretched across the walls and spread out along the ceiling. Small metal creatures clambered across the tangled sheets and blankets and through the orchid tendrils like ants at an abandoned picnic.

Julius left the ward. He ran along the corridor, looking for a broom cupboard or a laundry room he could hide in for the night.

A loud crashing sound made him halt, and a sharp chill ran up his spine when he heard the scrape of metal against stone. He knew that sound. Suddenly the claw marks on the walls made sense.

Julius looked back the way he had come. The entrance was too far away. The scraping sound rattled through the corridor, like giant nails on a huge blackboard. He had to keep going—away from the sound.

Around a corner Julius tried a door. It was locked. The next door he came to had been pulled from its hinges. The scraping sound was growing louder, sending vibrations through the floor. Julius ran and pushed a set of double doors. They opened into another ward—it was full of soulcatchers. He let the doors close back on him. Perhaps he could climb out a window.

Around the next corner he came to a flight of stairs. He ran up, trying not to make a sound. At the first landing his path was blocked by a scramble of chairs as if someone had made a hasty barricade.

He cursed and searched in the scant light for a way through. He swung his leg over the banister and climbed his way past the chairs but accidentally tapped one of the chair legs. The barricade fell crashing and tumbling down the stairs. Julius gripped the banister, squeezing his eyes shut as the avalanche resounded through the hospital.

Julius ran up the stairs. At the top he turned for an instant to see Abigail's red eye looking up at him from the foot of the stairs. She had added to herself since he had last seen her, and she had a new claw to replace the fork one she had lost. She scrambled up the stairs. At the turn she became entangled in the fallen chairs and she flailed her limbs in rage, bashing them to pieces.

Julius ran. Would she remember him from the sewer? Would she be angry about her missing claw?

He came to a long empty corridor and sprinted along it. Abigail roared, rattling his skull and making the walls quake.

If he had a few seconds to prepare, he could time-jump to escape.

Julius's mind raced. Where could he go? Tock had released soulcatchers all over London. It seemed he had captured all the souls, just like he said he would. What had happened to Emily and Mr Flynn? What about his mother and grandfather? Were they sitting in armchairs somewhere with soulcatchers spewing from their mouths?

Abigail was coming up the stairs.

Julius ran through a door and collided with a

trolley, knocking it over. Surgical knives and saws clattered around him. A torture rack stood in the centre of the room. Julius shuddered. Then he realised it was an operating table. Thick leather straps with sturdy brass buckles hung from it. There was no way out but through the windows or back the way he had come in. In the near dark he scrabbled amongst the operating tools to find the biggest knife.

'Aaagh,' he cried out, when a blade cut through his glove and into palm of his hand. Blood oozed through the gash and down his arm.

Abigail scraped along the corridor outside. Julius sprang up and slammed the door. It was made of thick oak with brass bolts top and bottom. He closed the top bolt just as Abigail collided with the door. It shuddered with the impact. Julius closed the bottom bolt as another blow came. *Boom*. It made the knives and saws rattle.

Julius pulled the leather straps out of their brackets on the operating table. He fumbled to thread the four belts through each other to make one long one. Abigail roared and hit the door again. It split down the centre.

Julius slid the top buckle behind a water pipe close to the window to anchor it and threw the end of the belt through the window. He looked out to find out what was below, but it was too dark to see. Above, the clouds were thinning and the ghost of near-full moon could be seen through them.

Abigail pounded the door with faster and harder blows. The bolts rattled and the screws holding them began to loosen.

Julius cried out with exertion as he heaved the operating table against it.

Boom. Abigail hit the door again. This time the top half of the door came away, narrowly missing Julius's head, and he saw what she had replaced her fork-claw with—scalpels twisted like corkscrews. The claw raked through what was left of the door, shredding it. Julius jumped up to the windowsill and grabbed the leather belt.

Abigail filled the doorway, grinding and screeching her way through. She pushed the operating table aside.

Julius slid off the windowsill and gripped the belt. He screamed in agony, as his injured hand tightened on the leather, but the bloodied glove made his hand slip. Abigail's snout came through the window. Her red eye glared at Julius as he dangled from the belt. She opened her razor-toothed mouth and roared. Julius's hand slipped again. He let go.

That's the last thing you'll see or hear, Higgins.

Julius fell. He wondered how long it would be before he was safely dead and would not have worry about anything ever again. He wondered if he had a soul. He hadn't given it much thought until now. He wondered where it would go.

Julius's back crashed through something. Above him he saw a circle of broken glass surrounded by thousands of tiny spinning shards, all twinkling in the moonlight as he continued to fall. It reminded him of the galaxies he had passed through to get here. He wondered if he was dead yet.

Then he landed on a table. Two of the legs collapsed, spilling Julius onto the hard floor. A second later the galaxy of glass rained down on him. He curled into a tight ball, shielding his face as much as he could.

When the shower ended, Julius lay still for a few seconds. He could not feel anything except his blood surging through his body and surprise and relief that he was still alive.

Abigail roared somewhere above him, comfortingly far away. Julius staggered to his feet. Pain shot through every part of his body at once. He clutched his cut hand and looked up through the hole in the glass roof. He could see Abigail's head two storeys above. She appeared to be trying to force her way through the hospital window.

When Julius took a step, his right leg nearly gave way. He leant against the remains of the table to steady himself. Dead and dried plants in cracked pots littered the floor. He was in a conservatory of some kind.

He began to tremble uncontrollably, but he managed to stumble against the glass wall searching for a door. His hand found a handle and pushed down. He fell out onto gravel, scraping his knees. When he rolled over for a moment to collect himself he saw Abigail poised on the windowsill ready to jump.

Julius was too exhausted and in too much pain to be afraid anymore.

Why can't this be like cricket, Higgins? You get a tea break after a good innings.

Abigail's red eyes stared down at him. Then her nose dropped and she dived.

Julius did not wait to see any more. He staggered away, ducking down a side street as the metallic crash of Abigail landing in the conservatory rang out.

Julius kept going until he arrived back at the bank of the Thames. The moon came out and shone down on the surface of the water. Across the river the craggy black skyline of the city could be seen against the night. The only sound was the distant metallic grinding sounds of Abigail trying to disentangle herself from the conservatory.

Julius rested against the embankment wall and laid his head on his arms. His shoulder throbbed, but not as much as his wounded hand. His back ached, his face was covered in tiny cuts and his clothes were strewn with glass shards

But he was alive. It felt so good he would have

laughed if he'd had the energy.

He tried to think. Abigail would free herself soon and come looking for him.

He ran along the embankment wall until he came to the stone stairs leading down to the river. He climbed down and stood on the muddy riverbank. Stars peeped through gaps in the clouds.

Somehow, Tock had made this happen.

You didn't stop him, Higgins. You failed.

From where Julius stood he could see that the middle of Southwark Bridge was demolished too. Someone was blowing up bridges. Was it to keep Abigail away? The dome of St Paul's rose above the rooftops, beckoning him across. He wanted to go home to Ironmonger Lane and sit in his fireside chair and think things through.

Driftwood and pieces of rope lay along the muddy shore. Julius dragged planks of wood and laid them out like a raft. He had to walk hundreds of yards each way to find enough rope to lash it all together.

To Julius's surprise the raft floated when he pushed it out. He kept pushing until he was up to his knees in the water, all the time hugging his wounded hand to his chest.

When he sat back on the raft his corner sank below the water so he rolled to the centre to try to spread his weight more evenly. The tide took the raft and carried it up river, under London Bridge and through to the other side. Julius lay on his back, trying to summon the energy to sit up and paddle. All he had to do was to use the plank to part-paddle, part-stir it to the other side.

He managed to sit up without disturbing the raft too much and braced the plank under the arm of his injured hand so he could grip it with his good hand. He wedged it between two of the raft's struts and tried to stir a course for Cheapside.

The river became rougher the further he got out into the middle. Most of the time the raft was bobbing just below the surface and by now Julius was wet through. He prayed the raft would hold.

The river was only a hundred yards across, but the other side seemed like the other side of the world. He had drifted under Southwark Bridge and Blackfriars Bridge. Both had been demolished in the centre.

The muddy shore was only yards away when the raft began to fall apart.

Julius sloshed through the mud and crawled to the shore. The tide was high, leaving only a couple of yards of riverbank. He staggered along the embankment wall until he found another set of steps and sat exhausted on the second one.

☛

Julius woke with jolt. He sat up shivering and looked at the expanse of river before him. Every cell in his body was cold and aching, and he was hungry enough to eat a plate of Brussels sprouts.

The cloudless sky was a deep blue with a streak of lighter blue along the rooftops on the far bank. He pulled himself to his feet and climbed the steps, his sodden boots sloshing all the way. At the top he sat again. He ached to hear the raucous sounds of London. But none came. There were no horses' hooves clopping on the cobbles, no costermongers calling their wares, no ships' bells or the slamming of doors and windows.

The streets were strewn with scraps of newspaper and broken furniture, but there were fewer broken windows and damaged roofs than he had seen on the southern shore.

Julius walked along Water Lane—that would take him past St Paul's on his way to Ironmonger Lane. Flame-red soulcatchers stretched through open windows and rippled in the morning breeze

St Paul's loomed overhead. Julius walked across the churchyard. He stopped beside the statue of Queen Anne and looked up the steps to the grand columns. St Paul's seemed even more magnificent than he remembered it. It was if the cathedral was still as proud of itself as it was when people were teeming inside to marvel at it. Nothing would lessen its splendour.

Julius felt a little lighter in himself. Maybe there were some survivors?

He walked up the steps and stood among the columns. It was like he was in the cathedral's embrace, imbibing some of its eternal presence. When he touched the cold stone he felt as if the cathedral acknowledged him in some way. He felt a stone-like strength flow through him, a strength that would see him through anything.

The door was slightly ajar.

He looked inside. The early morning light shone through the cathedral's high windows and onto the soulcatchers inside.

People sat facing the Grand Organ, dotted among the rows of chairs. Their heads were thrown back with soulcatchers issuing from them. The stems and flowers spread out along the chairs, up and around the columns and up the walls.

Nothing moved.

Julius went inside. The thin, cool air held a faint perfume. He stepped quietly, almost afraid of disturbing the terrible beauty of the scene. He walked along the central aisle until he stood in a shaft of light. The hint of warmth tickled his face. He closed his eyes and felt the light on his eyelids.

A soulcatcher nearby rippled. The pale tendrils flicked out as if sniffing the air. He stepped closer to it.

The host was a woman. Her mouth stretched wide in a silent scream. Her eyes were slits from which the stems grew. Her small hands rested among the flowers on her lap, as if she was holding a bouquet. He recognised the dress, and what was left of her face.

It was his mother.

Julius felt as if the floor had given way beneath him. He ran out the door and collided with a man standing between the columns.

CHAPTER 21

Thursday 24th September 1846

8:05 AM

Julius fell back and looked up at the tall silhouette standing before him.

'I saw you go in,' said Mr Flynn. He leaned over and offered his hand. His face was thinner and his hair longer than the last time Julius had seen him.

'What happened?' said Julius.

'Come with me,' said Mr Flynn. 'We'll talk at the top.' His expression gave nothing away as he walked into the cathedral.

Julius followed him past the soulcatchers and up the wide spiral stairs leading to the balustrade around the dome. The cool air up so high made Julius blink. Far below, the roofs of London stretched out and the Thames snaked past.

Mr Flynn kept his back to Julius. He looked out across the river. 'I knew you'd come one day,' he said. 'Emily told me you stole the pocketwatch. I knew you'd have used it to escape from Abigail.'

Julius clutched it in his pocket.

'I've waited eight years for you to come,' said Mr Flynn. 'I wanted to tell you so many things.' He sighed and lowered his head. 'None of them seem important now.'

'What happened?' said Julius.

'It doesn't matter,' said Mr Flynn. 'Tock won. He did what his planned to do. That's all you need to know.'

'Emily?' said Julius. He voice cracked.

Mr Flynn raised his shoulders as if he was drawing a long slow breath.

'Is she here?' said Julius.

Mr Flynn turned to face him. 'There is one thing I'll tell you,' he said. 'She wanted to keep it a secret, but it doesn't matter now.'

'What do you mean?'

'Emily thought the world of you. You didn't know that, did you?' The trace of a smile escaped from Mr Flynn's lips. 'She'd be furious if she knew I was telling you this. Right at the beginning, she took Darwin's diary to the bookshop because she wanted to see you again.'

'No...I didn't know,' said Julius. 'So why did she

run away when she saw me.'

'Because she was afraid,' said Mr Flynn.

'Of what?'

'Afraid of happiness, and all that guff,' said Mr Flynn. 'She didn't trust happiness, let alone those who promised it.'

'So she took fright,' said Julius. 'She thought I'd end up hurting her.'

'Yes.'

'And I did,' said Julius. 'I told her she wasn't wanted. I didn't mean it.'

'I know that,' said Mr Flynn. 'But she didn't. She pretended she didn't care, but she was lost.'

'I tried to tell her I was sorry,' said Julius. 'But she wouldn't listen.'

'Of course not,' said Mr Flynn. 'Words meant nothing. You should have shown her when you had the chance.'

'Shown her what?'

'That you loved her, too,' said Mr Flynn. 'That you were on her side. No matter what.'

'But I did. I was,' said Julius. 'She never knew?'

Mr Flynn walked around the balustrade and stopped at the door.

'She knew, Julius,' said Mr Flynn. 'It just took her a long time to realise it.' Mr Flynn turned the door handle. 'Use that pocketwatch of yours. Find yourself a new time or realm. Leave this Godforsaken place and never come back.'

'But there must be something we—'

'There's nothing,' said Mr Flynn.

'Where's Emily?'

Mr Flynn turned away. 'Go now,' he said. 'There's nothing here for you.'

He went through the door and down the stairs.

'Mr Flynn,' called Julius, but he was gone.

Julius stared across the Thames. The chill made his eyes water. He felt empty, like a hollowed-out tree trunk, with only the wind whistling through him. How could he run away? How could he go away and forget all this. He stood for an hour, hardly moving. Why wouldn't Mr Flynn answer him about Emily? Was she now a soulcatcher host, like his mother?' The thought was too sad to bear, but Julius felt a murmur of gladness that Emily had forgiven him in the end.

☛

Julius walked down the steps of St Paul's. He was going home. It was the only place he could imagine figuring out what to do next. As he walked, he tried not to look at the soulcatchers growing out through the windows. He tried not to see the dolls' houses in the toyshop window, or the trays of buttons scattered in the haberdasher's. Before he knew it he was in Ironmonger Lane.

The windows of the bookshop were broken and the door was open. Julius paused. Would he find his grandfather sitting by the fire with a soulcatcher growing from his mouth? He stepped over the threshold and into the musty odour of mould. He held the handkerchief around his neck up to his mouth. The bookshop was dank and dark. Green mould was growing on the books on the shelves. The curtain over the parlour door had fallen from its rings. He stepped over it and went through.

His grandfather's chair was empty.

Maybe he got away, Higgins.

The carpet under his boots squelched with damp. He sat in his mouldy chair and looked to where his grandfather would have sat. The fireplace was cold and water dripped from the chimney. The dark, dank parlour was a miserable parody of his home. Julius stood and walked around the table, trying to rekindle old feelings. None came. He took the glove off his good hand and when he tried to take the other one off he found the blood had glued it to his wound. He left it on. He did not want to see the gash in any case.

His eyes fell on the wall by the fireplace. That was where he and Emily had gone in search of Tock. He felt a sting inside when her name ran through is mind.

He touched the wall with his fingertips. They hadn't found Tock's realm. Instead they had found a beautiful seaside resort full of beautiful, happy people. Perhaps he could go there? He could walk among them and think things through.

Julius stopped. *Did* they go to the wrong realm? Tock was an automaton. Why hadn't he thought of it before?

Julius took the pocketwatch out and in a surge of excitement he spun it in the air. Blue light shone when he tapped it with his finger. The pocketwatch bobbed above his open palm. Gradually the blue light grew in intensity, forming an expanding sphere that made his skin tingle.

Soon, Julius was surrounded by a dome of light. Through the wall, he saw the promenade and the beach. He could smell the sea salt and he looked up through the dome to see a cloudy sky. The lack of sunshine had taken the colour from everything. The turquoise sea was now a dull green where choppy waves jostled one another. The beach showed the scars of storm tides. Seagulls pecked along the line of debris at the high-tide mark.

Julius walked along the empty promenade.

Where is everyone, Higgins?

Then he saw the soulcatchers. They were growing through broken windows and across the walls of the houses.

Julius touched the side of the pocketwatch with his finger. Instantly the watch stopped spinning. He felt the vibration run down his finger and spread through his body. Then the watch closed up and tumbled into his hand.

Julius was dressed as he was on his previous visit, in a pale-green summer suit, but there was something different. His clothes were soiled and creased. He looked at his injured hand to find the pocketwatch had healed it. He brushed his cheek to find his cuts had been healed too.

The sound of thousands of soulcatcher petals fluttering in the wind cut through the roar of the waves like an infernal whispering.

Julius came to Papa Putching's workshop. The painted sign was peeling and faded. The door was padlocked, so Julius peered through the window. A small automaton lay, dismantled, its parts scattered across the workbench. He could just make out the lines of shelves, and the edge of the woodstove.

A stooped figure was coming up the promenade. He stumbled against the wind, clutching a bundle to his chest. His head was down so he did not see Julius. It was the old man who had given his grandfather a cup of tea. Julius was sure of it.

The old man approached gripping his package under one arm. He fumbled through his pocket and took out a large key ring with a single key.

Julius stepped out from under the eaves. 'Do you remember me?' he said.

The old man did not hear. He was trying to fit the

key into the padlock.

'Do you remember me?' said Julius, louder.

The old man let out a cry and jumped back, dropping his package.

'I'm sorry,' said Julius, 'I didn't mean to startle you.' He stooped and picked up the package. It was a sack tied up with string. The old man was reluctant to accept it. 'Where are you from?' he said.

'London,' said Julius.

'London? Where is that?'

'Far away.'

'And…is it the same there?'

Julius nodded.

The old man's expression softened as if he was too weary to be afraid for long. 'You'd better come inside,' he said.

When the door was closed behind them the roar of the sea faded into the background, but the whisper of the soulcatchers' fluttering petals still found its way in. The old man took the sack from Julius and placed it by his stool. He untied the string and took out a bottle of water, a few vegetables and candle stubs and put them on the workbench.

Then he balanced his spectacles on his nose and strained his eyes to see his visitor. The workshop was not as tidy as Julius remembered it. A layer of fine sand lay over everything and it scrunched under his feet. He noticed a makeshift bed under the shelves in the far corner. The smell of creosote and wood shavings had been replaced by old-man smells, similar to the ones his grandfather left around the bookshop.

Papa Putching sat on his stool and leaned one elbow on the workbench.

'What happened?' said Julius.

The old man's eyes wandered the shelves as if he was trying to remember where he was.

'The flowers growing? When did that happen?' said Julius.

'Long ago. Years…I think.' He turned to the grimy window and looked out at the sea.

'They climbed out of the earth,' he said. 'It all happened in one night. Flowers attacking people. Who could have imagined it?'

'Who planted them?' said Julius.

'Mr Tock did.' Papa Putching's expression fell like a viscous liquid. It was as if the sound of Tock's name had taken something vital from him.

'Mr Tock?' said Julius. 'How? I mean…?

'He said he found the flowers on his travels,' said Papa Putching. 'He offered to plant them in all the gardens. He said he wanted to show everyone what a good little machine he was. Of course, everyone was delighted. Everyone loves flowers.'

'So you knew Tock?' said Julius.

'Knew him? Yes. I made him,' said Papa Putching. *Of course, Higgins.*

263

'Mr Tock was my finest creation,' he said. 'It took me seven years to make the multiple gearing alone—gyroscopes within gyroscopes, all spinning independently, all tilting with gravity, sensitive to the minutest touch. It gave the illusion of life. Each move Mr Tock made could lead to any combination of movements, even to his toes. His fingers were capable of the finest precision.'

Papa Putching's expression changed, as if he remembered something. He made a pretence of tidying the workbench.

'What happened?' said Julius.

The old man carefully picked up one tiny cog after another, returning each one to its correct slot in a tray of watch parts.

Julius clenched his fists, forcing himself to be patient.

'Mr Tock asked me once, what would happen to his soul if I forgot to wind him,' said the old man. 'I laughed. "But you don't have a soul, Mr Tock," I said. "You are good little machine." I could tell straightaway that I had hurt his feelings. I tried to make amends. "Don't worry, I'll always be here to wind you," I said. But he was never the same after that.'

Papa Putching looked through the dusty window again. 'He would go away for days on end, only coming back when he needed me to wind him. He'd look at me and smile, but he wasn't smiling, not really.

I tried to talk to him, like we used to, but…'

'How long ago was that?' said Julius.

'Years. I was a young man—well, young from where I sit today.'

A shadow crossed the old man's face.

'He asked for the key once. I was winding him at the time. I stopped in surprise. Mr Tock's smile stayed frozen on his face. "No, Mr Tock," I said. "An automaton must never have his own key." "Why not, Papa?" he asked. I finished winding him and locked the key in my safe. "Off you go, Mr Tock," I said. I could not look him in the eye. I think that saddened him even more than not having a soul.'

'Why?' asked Julius.

Papa Putching continued to sort the tiny cogs. 'Because he realised that his own Papa was afraid of him. I think that's when he gave up being good. He never did anything bad when he was here. But there was always the threat in his eyes. I was glad when he was gone for days at a time…I did not dare ask him what he got up to.'

'But you kept winding him?' said Julius.

'Yes. Of course. He was my finest creation,' said the old man. 'And when he brought the red flowers I thought he was going to be a good little machine again. But he wasn't. It was all a trick. The night after the flowers attacked, Mr Tock came along the promenade and asked politely for his key. I was too afraid to refuse him. He winds himself now.'

Julius felt anger rising. He wanted to shout at the befuddled old man. He wanted to tell him what his creation had done. He went to the window and looked out to the sea to calm himself.

Papa Putching took a soiled handkerchief from his pocket and blew his nose. 'Where is Tock now?' asked Julius.

'He's mad, you know,' said the old man. 'It's the gyroscopes in his head, they're out of balance. He comes along the promenade to call on me, but I lock the door. He taps on the window and I hide under the bench until he's gone.'

'Why does he come?' asked Julius.

'He's lonely, now that everyone's gone,' said Papa Putching. 'He has no one to talk to. He asked me to make a friend for him.'

'Did you?'

'No,' said the old man. 'I do not want to make another Tock. I've lost the skill anyway. So he tries to make his own *friends* to talk to. But he hasn't the skill either—he makes abominations instead.' The toymaker stared at the tiny cogs scattered across his worktop as if bored with the task of tidying them.

'Where can I find him?' said Julius.

'You shouldn't try,' said Papa Putching.

'But I must speak to him.'

The old man did not reply. Julius could not contain

himself. He grabbed Papa Putching's shoulder and spun him around. 'Where is he, you old fool?'

The old man cowered. His face contorted in fear.

'Where is he?' said Julius.

'He has a workshop on the hill,' said the old man. 'You'll find him there.'

Julius let go of the toymaker's shoulder as gently as he could. 'You shouldn't have kept winding him,' he said quietly.

'I know,' said the old man. He began to cry. 'I know.'

Julius walked up the hill. The narrow streets blocked the wind. Soulcatchers were growing through windows and across the walls. Julius went along street after street avoiding the tendrils reaching out to him as he passed. He stopped at a shop where all the windowpanes were intact. He looked inside at strange contraptions made of twisted spoons, washers, door hinges and bent nails, all cobbled together into haphazard shapes. They flailed around like blind things, writhing and twitching as if lost and in pain.

A sign on the door said 'Open'. Julius pushed the door a crack. The shop bell tinkled. He waited, but no one came. He pushed the door a little more and went inside.

There was an empty wooden counter and empty

shelves around the walls. Julius stood there like a customer and listened. Quiet, indistinct sounds came from behind a curtain. He went around the counter and peeped through.

Tock was sitting at a workbench. Julius couldn't see what he was doing. An oil lamp burned low beside him. A clock on the wall ticked, but too slowly, and there were no hands on its face.

Julius watched Tock at work.

He seemed as harmless as Papa Putching now, passing his time trying to make things that would talk to him. Julius's skin tingled as he felt anger rising up. Millions of people had been devoured by the soul-catchers because of Tock. Julius wanted to crush his clockwork skull. But he couldn't, at least not yet.

He walked into the workshop and let the curtain fall behind him. Tock turned around on his stool.

Julius tensed.

Tock's face lit up with a smile. 'Welcome,' he said. 'Take your time. Look around.' His face was frayed at the edges and parchment-like creases distorted his mouth. It looked as if he has scrunched his face up into a ball and then flattened it out before putting it back on again. Tock's eyes glowed faintly, as if Julius was a long-lost friend.

Julius did not move or speak. Tock tilted his head. His eyes dimmed a little. He studied Julius as if he recognised him but was not sure from where. His face crackled when his smile fell away. 'Can't you speak?' he said.

'You don't remember me?' said Julius, trying to control the tremor of anger in his voice.

Tock's face lit up again. 'Remember you? Are we old friends?'

Julius shook his head. 'We met long ago,' he said. 'Before the soulcatchers destroyed everything.'

'Did we?' said Tock. 'Do you want your soul back? Do you? Do you?'

'No,' said Julius. 'You didn't get mine.'

Tock studied at Julius. He was like an old man whose memory was failing.

'Are you sure?' he said, with kindly condescension. 'I have all the souls, you know. All of them.'

Julius clenched his fists to stop himself flying at Tock. 'How did you do it?' he said. 'Where did you hide all the soulcatchers?'

Tock looked quizzically at Julius. 'Did I *hide* them?'

'You propagated them in secret somewhere in London,' said Julius. 'Then you released them and, and…'

Tock smiled again. 'London?' he said. 'I remember London. I should like to visit. But I can't remember how to make the mixture.'

He took a small wooden box from his pocket and opened it. It was empty. 'All gone,' he said. He closed the box and put it back.

'Where did you grow the soulcatchers?' said Julius.

Tock rested his elbow on the workbench like Papa Putching had done. He looked as if he was trying to think.

'In the house of animals,' he said. He looked gleefully at Julius as if he expected a prize for remembering. 'No one looked.' Tock's shoulders shook when he chuckled. 'They looked everywhere, but not among the animals,' he said. 'We fed the soulcatchers on blood and bone, made from rats, you know, gallons of it. It made them strong and eager to hunt for souls.'

Julius lunged at Tock knocking him onto the floor. The contraption he was working on fell off the workbench and squirmed and twitched on top of Tock. He pulled it away, ripping the lower half of his face off with it.

Julius snatched the lamp and held it over Tock.

'I should burn this whole place down,' he said. 'With you in it.'

'I'm a good little machine,' said Tock. There was no fear in his voice, just a childlike curiosity about what was going to happen next.

Julius lifted the lamp higher, preparing to smash it over Tock but something held him back. He had the answer he wanted. Tock could stay in his self-made hell forever for all he cared.

'You don't deserve to be set free,' he said.

Julius put the lamp down and left the workshop. His whole body was trembling. He did not dare to hope that he had found a way. As he rushed past the counter he noticed a book lying on an otherwise empty shelf. It stopped him instantly. It was Darwin's diary. He placed it carefully on the counter. He knew what he wanted to see but did not have the courage to look. Like an automaton, he forced himself to turn the pages until he came to the portraits Darwin drew. He ran his finger across Emily's smile. He knew that Tock was propagating the soulcatchers in the Animal House. Could he go back and save Emily and Clara? Could he save everyone?

Julius closed the book and took out the pocket-watch. He spun it in the air as he walked out of the shop. In his mind he imagined the Animal House in the Surrey Zoological Gardens. He had to land there soon after he had left.

CHAPTER 22

Sunday 24th January 1838

11:34 PM

The next thing Julius knew he was tumbling through space in the orbit of the pocketwatch. The stars flashed by as thin white streaks, while the spinning pocketwatch shot through time and space. He tried to hold the image of the Animal House in his mind, but he kept returning to the confession he had to make to Mr Flynn. He would tell him everything. Everything.

Julius felt himself falling and hitting soft ground. The pocketwatch flew to him and he clasped it tight.

He had landed in freezing darkness. Clouds obscured the moon. He listened—low growls rumbled in the air. The Animal House was nearby.

He made a bowl of his hands and blew into them. It seemed like a lifetime ago that he and Emily had walked past here on their way to the Orchid House. Had he come back to the right time? He took out the pocketwatch. A faint glow on its face showed him it was twenty-five minutes to midnight. He pressed his face to the glass dome of the Animal House. Vague, dark shapes moved inside, giving off a continuous chorus of growls and calls.

Julius felt his way to the door. His hands found the padlock. How would he get inside without Emily to pick it for him? He groped in the undergrowth until he found a good-sized rock and smashed it against the padlock. The animals roared. The rock split. He found another one and continued to pound it against the padlock until, finally, it broke.

Inside, the air was warm and pungent. Julius found his way back to the door and felt along the interior, looking for the gas taps. His boots sank into the soft earth as he pushed aside large waxy leaves, feeling along the damp glass. Eventually he found the taps. His fingers fumbled in the dark as he turned on one after the other.

The chandeliers all around the Animal House hissed as they came to life. The dome lit up like a quick sunrise. The animals' cries rose to a deafening pitch. Julius pushed through the dense undergrowth and emerged on the gravel path. He stared in wonder.

Lions, tigers, hyenas, and baboons roared and howled in their compounds and jumped at the bars. Large monkeys swung, whooping, through the branches. Vultures flicked their open wings and pecked at one another.

Julius ran to the tigers' compound. They bounded around, crazy with excitement at the unexpected dawn and the juicy little visitor staring at them through the bars. Julius looked at the thick foliage and expanse of rich soil inside the enclosure.

He imagined Tock picking the locks and fearlessly doing his gardening at night, with the wild animals looking on. He was not made of meat. He was like the bars and the gas pipes. He was not prey; he was a machine. He could grow the soulcatchers and harvest them without anyone knowing.

'Oi,' said Emily's voice above the din.

Julius turned to see her standing at the doorway.

'Emily,' he shouted, unable to disguise his delight.

Mr Flynn and Darwin joined her a second later, then Abberline and a handful of constables. They all stared at Julius.

'I know where Tock's hiding the soulcatchers,' he shouted and began to laugh.

'How did you get away?' said Mr Flynn.

Julius stopped laughing. There was so much to tell. So much to confess. He took the pocketwatch out and showed it to Mr Flynn.

Mr Flynn glanced at it lying on Julius's open palm then at Julius's face.

'Please excuse us for a moment, gentlemen,' he said.

He grabbed Julius by his shoulder and practically carried him to a far corner of the Animal House. Emily followed.

'What's going on?' said Mr Flynn. 'This had better be good.' His face was like a granite carving of a wrathful demon.

Julius had practised his speech a hundred times during the time-jump.

'I stole the pocketwatch,' said Julius, above the animal calls all around him. 'I pretended to put it back, but I didn't. But it's worse than that. I found out that I had made a time-loop six years before. It had already happened so I had to go back in time to do what I'd already done.'

'What are you talking about?' said Mr Flynn.

'There's a drawing in Darwin's diary of Emily and me as natives. It's from when we went back it time and stopped Skinner from making a soulcatcher seed Mr Darwin.' He paused to let Mr Flynn speak.

'You took Emily with you?' Mr Flynn said.

'Yeah,' said Emily. 'I 'elped 'im, Mr Flynn. 'e'd 'ave been in right strife if I 'adn't…'

Mr Flynn's glare silenced her. 'Go on,' he said to Julius.

'I did a time-jump to escape Abigail, just now,' said Julius. 'I went eight years into the future to a

London overrun with soulcatchers…possibly a whole world overrun.'

'And…' said Mr Flynn.

'I know how to stop it from happening.'

''ow's that then?' said Emily.

Mr Flynn glared at her. 'Do not speak again,' he said.

Emily reddened.

'Go on, Julius,' said Mr Flynn.

'I found out where Tock is secretly propagating the soulcatchers. Somehow he'll let them loose all over London. But if we know where he's growing them we can stop him.'

'So where's that, then?' said Emily.

'I met Tock in the future,' said Julius. 'He's an automaton and he's mad. He told me he grew the soulcatchers here, in the Animal House.'

'In the—?' said Mr Flynn.

'It's perfect,' said Julius. 'It's a hothouse. It's as warm as Brazil. The soulcatchers Tock gave us and Darwin needed to warm up before they attacked. No one would think of searching here. Look around, there loads of hiding places among the undergrowth, and there's lions and tigers to guard them.'

Mr Flynn straightened his back and looked up at the domed ceiling, then at the pacing tiger on the other side of the bars. Julius watched Mr Flynn gradually putting it all together in his mind.

'And they've been planted already?' said Mr Flynn.

'I'm not sure. If they haven't, they soon will be,' said Julius. 'If we don't find them we could put a watch on the—'

'Yes, yes,' said Mr Flynn, still thinking.

Julius waited. He cast a quick glance at Emily, but she was looking up at the vulture on a branch above them.

'Good work, Julius,' said Mr Flynn. 'Emily said Tock was in the sewer under the Orchid House.'

'Yes,' said Julius. 'He might still be there. He was fishing for rats for his fertiliser.'

Julius felt a weight of nervous tension slide off him, leaving only happy exhaustion. Tock would be stopped. The future London full of soulcatchers would fade away to become nothing more than a potential timeline.

Mr Flynn held out his hand. 'I'll take the pocket-watch,' he said. His expression was kind but resolute.

Julius reached into his pocket and took it out. He didn't look at it as he handed it over, but he could feel its absence as soon as it landed in Mr Flynn's hand.

'You two go home,' said Mr Flynn. 'Do you still have the cab fare I gave you?'

'No,' said Julius. 'I lost it.'

'But we can 'elp,' said Emily. 'If Tock's still in the sewer I can—'

'Emily,' said Mr Flynn, almost grinding her name between his teeth. 'You will do as you are told.'

☛

Julius and Emily sat in their hansom cab with the cabbie's blanket across their laps as they made their way home through the black streets. They had not spoken since climbing in.

The cold and the rocking of the cab was lulling Julius to sleep. Emily's head fell against his shoulder. He put his arm around her.

'Emily, are you awake?' asked Julius.

'Yeah. Wot?' said Emily, when Julius did not speak.

'Nothing.'

Emily showed her annoyance by burrowing deeper into his side.

'Wot 'appened?' said Emily.

'When?'

'In the future.'

'Er, there was no one left,' he said. 'Only the soul-catchers.'

'No one left at all?'

'Only Tock,' said Julius, 'and the toymaker who made him.'

'So 'e's an automaton,' said Emily. 'I always knew there was somefing wrong about 'im.'

'Yes, well, the future Tock's getting the punishment

he deserves,' said Julius. 'He winds himself with his own key, and he's stuck in that workshop making his odd friends for eternity.'

'Wot you talking about?'

'That wooden box of his, with the vials in it,' said Julius. 'It's empty now and he can't remember how to make the mixture that lets him go through the walls.'

'Good,' said Emily. 'But here, in our time, Tock's still lurking about. I'm going back there tomorrow in case Mr Flynn needs me.'

'I think we should let him calm down a bit before—'

Emily began to snore. Julius held her gently as the cab clattered through the streets.

At Mrs Trevelyan's Academy, he nudged her awake. 'Emily, we're home.'

She groaned and clambered down from the hansom cab. Julius followed her to the back door, where she retrieved the key from under the mat. She opened the door slowly in case it creaked.

'I thought you'd prefer to pick the lock,' said Julius.

Emily smirked. His joke had not worked as well he thought it would.

'Thank for coming to my rescue,' he said. 'Abigail would have got me if it wasn't for you.'

'It weren't naffing,' she said. She crept inside and was just about to close the door.

'Emily,' said Julius.

'Can't stop,' she said. 'Got to be up early to 'elp Mr Flynn.'

'I'm sorry for what I said. You know I didn't mean it.'

Julius heard the swish of her cape as she walked away. He stared into the dark corridor.

'Emily.'

But she was gone.

CHAPTER 23

Monday 22nd January 1838

8:02 AM

Julius woke with a start. *Where are you, Higgins?*

Everything was soft and warm. What was that sound? He looked up at his bedroom ceiling then slumped back onto his pillow and sighed. The cold at the tip of his nose, along with the warmth under his many blankets, was the usual winter's morning greeting, as were the sounds of his grandfather clattering around downstairs.

Julius suspected his grandfather made the noise out of spite—if he had to get up to light the fire and make the porridge every morning, then Julius would hear every sound of it. Julius made a mental note to offer to share the morning duties in future.

Outside, someone ran down the street—a boy, off

to the bakers for warm rolls, no doubt. He could hear the scrunch of snow beneath the boy's feet. Julius closed his eyes again. The memories of last night and the time-jump had the quality of a dream. Impossible events made of mist and shadows. The thought of Clara caught in that silent scream in St Paul's now seemed too fantastic to have ever been real. Maybe it was a dream?

Suddenly, he wanted to see Clara again more than anything else.

He leapt out of his warm bed. With the expertise of a circus contortionist, he dressed in seconds, before frostbite took hold, and then ran down the stairs, surprising his grandfather.

'Good morning, young Caesar,' Mr Higgins said as he set the table. 'Eager to be at school, I see.'

'School?'

'Yes, you remember. The place of elucidation you go to every Monday.'

'It's Monday?'

'Are you quite well, my boy? Been up to mischief with Mr Flynn? I didn't hear you come in last night. You've not been drinking, I hope.'

'No.'

Mr Higgins went to the kitchen. Julius heard the porridge being stirred. His mother would be sitting at breakfast in the servants' hall at Walworth House at this very moment. Emily would be sneaking out of the back door of Mrs Trevelyan's and marching to the Animal House to offer Mr Flynn her assistance.

When Mr Higgins came back with the porridge he found Julius pacing in front of the fire.

'Sit down, young Caesar,' he said as he placed the steaming bowl on the table.

'Grandfather?' said Julius.

'Yes,' said Mr Higgins, as he poured the regulation amount of milk over his porridge. It seemed to take all his concentration.

'I saw Mama again,' said Julius.

Mr Higgins stopped pouring. He put down the milk jug with great deliberation and slowly poured himself a cup of tea.

'I see,' he said.

'I think we should invite her to tea.'

Julius waited for his grandfather's reply, listening to the tea trickle into the cup.

His grandfather reserved this behaviour to express his displeasure—the slow, deliberate dealing with the everyday things of life. He poured the milk and stirred the tea. Then tapped the side of the cup twice to make it ring.

The muscles in Julius's shoulders tensed—he hated that sound.

Mr Higgins sipped his tea and returned the cup to the saucer. 'I thought we had agreed, young Caesar,' he said. 'Just you and me.' He began to spoon the honey into his porridge.

'I know, but…'

He looked up when Julius stopped. 'We will not speak of this again. I don't understand why you insist on trying to mend the past.'

Suddenly it was as if every cell in Julius's body burst apart.

'Because I don't want to end up a bitter old man, like you,' he shouted.

Mr Higgins jumped, dropping his spoon. He glared across the table at Julius.

Julius glared back, startled by his own outburst.

'Bad blood. I knew it,' said Mr Higgins. He pushed his chair back and made for the stairs.

'Where are you going?' said Julius. The rage had escaped; it would not be easily put back.

'To lie down,' said his grandfather.

'Don't do this, Grandfather.'

Mr Higgins spun round in anger. 'Do what, pray tell?'

'Walk away. You always do that.'

'I will return when you are capable of rational debate.'

'I'm going to invite her.'

'No, you are not.'

Julius felt his rage boiling under his skin. He wanted to smash everything in the parlour, just to see the look on his grandfather's face.

But he knew he would not do it. He slumped back into his chair.

'I just want a proper family.' He had not known it until he said it. The solid truth of it calmed him. He stared at the carpet. 'I just want to have my mother home for tea,' he said, almost in a whisper.

'Are you and I not a family?' said his grandfather.

Julius kept his eyes on the carpet, following the swirling lines of its pattern.

'Mama said you brought me up when you didn't have to. She said I should never forget that.'

'Did she?'

'She knows she broke your heart. She's sorry.' Julius waited for his grandfather to speak. But he did not. 'I know what it's like to be angry with someone you love,' said Julius. 'To tell them to go away. Later, you're sorry, but by then it's too late to mend it—but you still have to try.'

Julius heard his grandfather sit down in his fireside chair.

'She shouldn't be sorry, Julius,' he said. 'She brought you into the world.'

Julius was not sure he heard his grandfather correctly. He looked at the back of his head.

'Can she come to tea?' he said.

His grandfather kept his face turned away, staring into the fire. 'Very well,' he said, quietly.

'I'll go and tell her.'

'Now?'

'Yes. I have to be at the Surrey Zoological Gardens this morning. It's just next door.'

'Surrey Zoo…what the devil are you going there for?'

'I'm meeting Mr Flynn,' said Julius.

'But it's a school day?'

'You can write a note for me. Say I've caught a chill.'

Julius ran out to the shop and snatched a sheet of his grandfather's personalised stationery. He plonked it down with the inkpot and quill on his grandfather's reading table.

Mr Higgins's hand hung poised over the blank page. It was all Julius could do to stop himself from grabbing the old man's hand and writing the words for him. Just then Julius noticed Harrison's diary still tucked down the side of his chair.

'Get some cake on the way back,' said Mr Higgins, rummaging through his coin purse. 'Any kind. And some sugared apricots.

'Pardon?' said Julius. He was looking at the diary, trying to think.

'Sugared apricots.'

'Er, yes. We'll have to tidy up a bit,' said Julius.

'Tidy up?

'It's all right, I'll do it when I get back.'

In one movement he plucked the diary up,

snatched the note from his grandfather's hand and
ran for the curtain. In the bookshop he slid Harrison's
diary back into its in-full-view hiding place.

He looked at its spine for a moment longer, and
then pushed it into its place.

*You have to tell Mr Flynn you have the diary, Higgins. Tell
him the moment you see him.*

☛

Julius ran along Ironmonger Lane clutching the letter.
He wondered if Mr Flynn and the constables had
found any sign of Tock. He would know very soon.
Snow fell, carpeting the cobblestones in white. He
took a shortcut through an alleyway to King Street,
then to Laurence Street. In Honey Lane he saw one
of the younger boys from school.

'Hey, you,' he called out.

After handing over a sixpence and a quick instruc-
tion to slip the letter under the headmaster's door,
Julius raced to Blackfriars Bridge.

The sleet turned to an icy drizzle as he ran. Every
hansom cab was occupied. At Albion Place he saw a
young clerk springing out of one. And before the clerk
could reach up to pay the driver Julius had leapt into
the seat.

'Walworth House, please,' he called out.

He did not have a cane to knock on the roof so he

stamped his foot instead. He pulled the blanket over his knees and waited for the driver to whip the horse into action. Nothing happened.

'Walworth House, quickly, please.'

'Show me your money first,' came the reply from the roof. 'I've been done by young whippersnappers like you before.'

This is bloody marvellous, Higgins.

Julius fought the coins out of his pocket then leaned out to show the handful of shillings his grandfather had given him.

'There,' he said.

'Very good,' said the driver. 'Get on,' he called to the horse and whisked the whip across her rump.

Julius sat back as the hansom cab lurched forward.

Half an hour and you'll be there, Higgins.

Three quarters of an hour later the hansom cab passed the Surrey Zoological Gardens. The gates were closed, but Julius leaned out to see if he Mr Flynn was still there. He caught a glimpse of a police constable standing guard just inside the gate but nothing else.

You'll be back there in ten minutes, Higgins. Just give the invitation to Clara and run back to see what's happening.

At the back of Walworth House Julius leapt out of the hansom cab and paid the driver. Snow lay across the grounds and on the trees and windowsills of the mansion. Julius ran to the stable yard and down the stairs. He knocked on the door. No one came, no matter how loudly he knocked. Then he remembered the long corridor and the chaos in the kitchen. If he fired a cannon at the back door no one would hear.

Gingerly he turned the doorknob. It gave way. He opened the door a little.

'Hello,' he said. 'Hello.'

No reply came, only the sounds of kitchen bustle at the end of the corridor. He went in. The kitchen was as he remembered it—mayhem and commotion. No one paid him any mind.

Everything was being chopped, hacked, pummelled, pulled, whisked and burned by a frantic army of small children and fat women.

'Wot you doing here?' called out a cook with sweat pouring down her face.

'I'm looking for Clara Higgins, the new under-housekeeper.'

'Under-wot?'

'Housekeeper.'

'Don't know nothing about that. Housekeeping's above stairs,' she said, with a disapproving sniff, and then returned to her work of hacking meat from a large bone.

Julius ran to the door leading up to the main house. At the top of the stairs he opened the door just a slit. The corridor was silent. He opened it a little more and peered up and down.

He recognised the odour of wild animals but

there were none to be seen. He hurried along the corridor, wondering what the punishment would be if he went before the magistrate for trespassing in a lord's house. At a door, he stopped and listened. There was someone inside. Could it be a servant perhaps? Could it be Clara?

He poked his head inside.

The walls of the sitting room were lined with landscapes, and overstuffed chairs and couches filled the floor space. Sitting on the chairs was a family of orangutans. They all turned to look at Julius with bored stares.

'Sorry,' said Julius, and closed the door.

He had an idea. He could leave a note in Clara's room inviting her to tea. Julius tried to recall how he and Emily had got there the last time he visited.

It was up some stairs, Higgins. Back stairs. It was dark. Mama carried a lamp.

He went back to the corridor outside the kitchen. From there he retraced their route up the backstairs he had climbed with Clara and Emily.

At the attic corridor he looked at the doors on each wall. Clara's was the third one along, he was sure of it. He turned the handle and it creaked open. The room was empty but for a steel bed frame without a mattress.

He walked to the window and looked out at the snow-capped Animal House. Where was Clara?

Out in the corridor a floorboard groaned. Julius started.

A flock of hummingbirds flew in, followed by Lord Bloomingbury. He stared at Julius in astonishment.

'I thought I saw someone skulking about up here,' he said. Then he squinted a little. 'You're that boy— the armadillo handler.'

'Yes, sir.'

'What are you doing here?' said Lord Bloomingbury.

'I…that is…er…I have an important message for Miss Higgins.'

'Miss Higgins? I thought you barely knew the woman,' said Lord Bloomingbury. 'And now I find you running messages for her. What are you up to, sneaking around my house?'

'Nothing, sir,' said Julius. 'I really need to speak to her. I have to tell her something.' Julius looked at the bed frame. 'Where did she go?'

Lord Bloomingbury looked at the bed too.

'Go?' he said. 'I haven't the foggiest notion. I'm not in the habit of charting the movements of my servants.'

'No, of course not, sir,' said Julius. 'It's…it's just that I must get a message to her.'

'Perhaps she left?' said Lord Bloomingbury. 'Perhaps she didn't take to my pets?'

Julius looked at Lord Bloomingbury. There was

something wrong in his tone. He was not as good a liar as Emily—no one was as good as her. But why was he lying? He had been so accommodating the night before.

Julius tried to disguise his concern with a mask of befuddlement.

Lord Bloomingbury had been rather vexed when he thought Clara had a family. But then he was so pleased to hear Emily's lie about them just being neighbours. And he believed Emily when she said no one knew where they were. Julius remembered His Lordship's smile when she said it. Something had changed. He had made a joke about adding Emily to his collection, and there was something else—something about collecting unique specimens.

Did he want to collect you, Higgins? For what?

Julius looked out the window at the Animal House, trying to look simple-minded.

He pictured Lord Bloomingbury opening that secret door and the rank odour coming through. His Lordship had wanted to get them down there. Why? It was only the stench and Clara's embarrassment at Emily's behaviour that had stopped them. Julius remembered the disappointment in Lord Bloomingbury's face before he said goodbye. His quarry had gotten away.

What was on the other side of the door?

Julius smiled and shrugged his shoulders. 'Perhaps

you're right, sir,' he said. 'It is rather odd having so many animals. We just have a cat.' He edged past Lord Bloomingbury. 'Oh, well. I'd best be off to school. Goodbye, sir.'

Julius walked towards the stairs, with an attempt at a carefree stride. How many footmen could His Lordship call down on him if he raised the alarm?

'Just a moment,' said Lord Bloomingbury.

Julius turned.

'What was the message?' he asked. 'If I see her I could pass it on.'

'It's nothing, sir. It wasn't important,' said Julius.

Julius and Lord Bloomingbury looked at one another. Each knew the other was lying, but neither knew why.

Suddenly Julius was not afraid anymore. What was one old man after all he had been through? Even if he was a lord?

'If you've harmed Clara you'll be sorry,' said Julius.

Lord Bloomingbury's expression shifted. The kindly mask of confusion was gone, and in its place was a stare cold enough to freeze fire.

'I have never been sorry in my life,' he said. 'But you will be. You shall hang for that remark.' He came closer. His eyes fixed on Julius as if was about to strike.

Julius realised he had made a terrible mistake.

CHAPTER 24

Monday 22nd January 1838

10:34 AM

Julius ran down the stairs and fell into the corridor outside the kitchen tumbling across the floor and out the door. He sprinted out of the stable yard and only stopped in the parklands, when he was sure he was not being chased. Everything was white and still and silent. The snow began to fall, cascading dots of white, matching the white mist from his heavy breaths.

He had got it all wrong.

Tock said the 'house of animals', Higgins. Not the 'Animal House'.

Lord Bloomingbury was hiding Tock in his vast house of animals. Was Tock going to give him a soulcatcher in exchange? Was Clara going to be the host—a servant with no family?

Julius ran to the Surrey Zoological Gardens. At the ticket booth he paid his shilling and bolted to the Animal House. There was a chain across the door with a sign saying 'Closed for maintenance'. Julius ducked under it and burst through the door. It was full of constables.

'It's not the Animal House,' he blurted out. 'It's the "house of animals"—Tock's hiding in Lord Bloomingbury's house.'

'What are you talking about?' said Abberline.

'I went there to invite my mother home for tea,' said Julius. 'But she wasn't there. Lord Bloomingbury's kidnapped her. He's going let a soulcatcher seed her, if he hasn't already.'

'Julius, slow down,' said a steady voice.

Julius spun around to see Mr Flynn and Darwin. 'Tock's hiding at in Walworth House,' he said. 'He has Clara.'

'That's impossible,' said Darwin. 'His Lordship knows how dangerous the soulcatcher is. I've discussed my theories with him a dozen times. He's seen what the soulcatcher did to Skinner.'

'Bloomingbury's the Governor of Bedlam. He could have been the one who got the soulcatcher cuttings from Skinner and gave them to Tock,' said Julius.

'It can't be,' said Darwin. 'The man's beyond reproach. He's President of the Royal Society and countless other boards and charities, for goodness sake. He's the confidential advisor to the Queen and—'

'That's just it,' said Julius. 'No one would suspect him. No one would search his house.'

'You're right about that,' said Abberline. 'If anyone's above the law it's Lord "High and Mighty" Bloomingbury.'

'But Mama's somewhere in Walworth House,' said Julius. 'You could search his house on suspicion of—'

'There's certain people a constable knows not to interfere with,' said Abberline. He hung his head. 'And His Lordship is top of the list.'

'It's the boy's mother, we're talking about, Abberline,' said Mr Flynn.

'I'm sorry. There's nothing I can do,' he said.

Julius turned to Darwin. There was no time to argue with Abberline. 'You and Mrs Trevelyan will call on Bloomingbury.'

'Why would we do that?' said Darwin.

'To keep him occupied,' said Julius. 'While Mr Flynn and I search the house.'

'Good idea,' said Mr Flynn. 'I'll send a cabbie to the academy with a note for her.'

A hansom cab came to a halt at the end of Kennington Road and Mrs Trevelyan climbed out waving her umbrella in greeting. The snow had stopped but the crispness of the air made her cheeks glow.

'Mrs Trevelyan,' said Mr Flynn.

'Mr Flynn,' she replied, as Emily climbed out behind her.

'Thank you for coming,' said Mr Flynn.

'Say nothing of it, Mr Flynn,' she said. Her white teeth sparkled as she smiled. 'If poor Clara is in difficulties I will play my part. You can be sure of that.'

'I'm 'ere too, Mr Flynn,' said Emily.

'No, Emily, we'll take care of this,' said Mr Flynn. 'Go back to the academy and wait for us.'

'But I—'

'Now, Emily,' said Mr Flynn. 'Do as I say. Take the cab home. That's my final word on the matter.'

Emily's chin quivered with indignation.

'Let her come, Mr Flynn,' said Julius. 'She loves Clara.'

Mr Flynn peered down at Julius. He was by met by something unshakable in Julius's eyes.

'Er…hmm…very well,' said Mr Flynn. 'Don't make me regret it, Emily.'

'You won't, Mr Flynn,' she said.

But he and Darwin were already striding for the cover of some fir trees. Mrs Trevelyan picked up her skirts and followed.

Julius waited for Emily to thank him.

'I suppose you fink we're even now?' she said.

'I'm sorry, Emily,' said Julius. 'I didn't mean what I said last night.'

Emily let out an exaggerated sigh and marched away through the snow, treading in Mrs Trevelyan's footprints.

'All right, all right,' she said. 'Don't go all soppy, 'iggins. It weren't naffing to begin wiv.'

Julius ran after her. He wished he could give her a hug.

Mrs Trevelyan nestled close to Mr Flynn in the cold as he pointed to the grand entrance of Walworth House and explained the plan.

'Call at the front door,' he said. 'Ask for His Lordship and don't take any refusals. Demand to speak to him if you have to. Keep him talking while we search the house.'

'I'll tell him I wish to take my girls to see his menagerie,' she said. 'Mr Darwin can introduce me to him.' She pecked a kiss on Mr Flynn's cheek, and took Darwin's arm. 'Come, noble knight. Lead us into battle,' she said.

'Yes, indeed,' said Darwin, and they scrunched through the snow to the front door.

Julius, Emily and Mr Flynn went in through the back door and up the stairs.

The corridor was empty.

Julius, Emily and Mr Flynn listened. Far away, wings flapped and something squawked. Emily flicked her head to the side and stepped out onto the thick carpet. She put her ear to the first door. Julius did the same. There were sounds from within. Emily opened the door a crack. A scratchy chattering noise seeped out.

'It's upside-down fings,' whispered Emily.

Julius looked around the door. The room was full of bats the size of cats. They were hanging from the chandelier and the tops of the picture frames. Every so often one of them twitched or wiggled as if dreaming bat dreams. The furniture and carpet was covered in guano.

Each of the rooms they looked in contained at least one species of mammal, bird or reptile. At one of the doors near the grand entrance Emily listened longer than usual.

'Mrs Trevelyan's in there,' she whispered. 'She's talking up a storm.'

'Is Bloomingbury there too?' whispered Julius.

'Yeah. She's asking 'im all about animals and fair flirting the ears off the old geeza.'

Julius, Emily and Mr Flynn climbed the central staircase where squirrel-sized monkeys played nervously while a python watched.

At the library, they stopped. 'There's someone moving around in there,' Emily whispered.

'Clara?' said Julius.

'I don't know,' said Emily. 'It sounds like pages of a book crackling when they're being turned.'

Julius reached out to turn the handle.

'Wait,' whispered Mr Flynn. 'I'll go first.'

He straightened his top hat and opened the door.

Julius rushed in after him but stopped when he saw Edward Rapple sitting on a chair, trying to prise the armadillo out of its ball. Benjamin Baines was standing at the table, examining the large books with a magnifying glass. Parrots squawked from the chandelier above. Both men stared at Mr Flynn, their still-bruised and swollen faces frozen in astonishment.

'I didn't know that you were interested in flora and fauna,' said Mr Flynn.

'Always keen to expand my horizons, Mr Flynn,' said Baines, trying to disguise his surprise. 'We are planning a little trip, as it happens.'

Rapple pushed the armadillo off his lap. It bounced across the carpet, still in a ball, and Rapple's hand casually rose to the opening in his brown overcoat.

'Let's cut through the preliminaries, gentlemen,' said Mr Flynn.

'I'm not sure I follow,' said Baines. His hand hovered over his side pocket.

'You can tell us where Tock is,' said Mr Flynn. 'Or I can throw you both out the window. I'd prefer not to exert myself, if it's all the same to you.'

'And we wouldn't wish you to, would we, Mr Rapple.' said Baines.

'No. We wouldn't want it on our conscience, would we, Mr Baines.' said Rapple. 'I have enough trouble sleeping as it is.'

Rapple's fingers disappeared into the folds of his overcoat as a door opened.

Mr Tock walked in. 'Nearly ready for—' He stopped and his broad smile turned into a gape when he saw Mr Flynn, Julius and Emily. He hastily closed the door behind him.

It took him barely half a second to collect himself.

'Why, it's our young friends…and Charlie,' he said. 'Is it? Is it?'

Mr Flynn flicked a warning look at Rapple whose hand stopped halfway into his coat.

'You are full of surprises. You are. You are,' said Tock to Julius. 'You must tell me what you did with Abigail's claw. We can't find it anywhere.'

'Shut up and listen, Tock,' said Mr Flynn. 'We've come for Clara Higgins. Hand her over now, or I'll pull your head off and throw it out the window.'

'Dear me,' said Tock. 'You're a forthright fellow, aren't you? Aren't you?' He turned to Rapple and Baines, his smile closing into a stern slit. 'Mr Rapple. Mr Baines. Get rid of these people once and for all,' he said. 'All of them.'

'Yes, Mr Tock, sir,' said Baines. 'Right away, sir.'

Mr Tock pushed the door and was gone, slamming it shut behind him.

A machete wheeled through the air, missing Mr Flynn's nose by a quarter of an inch. It embedded itself in the spine of a book on the bookshelf.

Rapple pulled another machete from his coat. Julius reached for the nearest bookshelf and pulled out a large volume.

'Mr Flynn,' he called out and flung the book to him.

Mr Flynn held the book up in front of him like a shield. The second machete stuck firmly in its cover.

Baines pulled out a meat cleaver and came at Mr Flynn's flank.

Emily plucked a porcelain figurine from a bookshelf and threw it. The ornament smashed against Baines's elbow, giving Mr Flynn a second to pull the machete from the book. He kicked over a table, sending large volumes cascading over Baines. Then he threw the shield book at Rapple.

It hit him squarely on his nose, making him cry out in pain. In two steps, Mr Flynn was within striking distance. He punched Rapple, sending him tumbling backwards, crying out oaths as he went.

Julius saw Baines rise up with a meat cleaver like an angry phoenix. Emily threw a book at him but he knocked it aside and made for her.

'Not so fast,' said Mr Flynn.

Baines turned to see the machete flying towards him. He ducked and swung the cleaver at Mr Flynn's head. But the champion boxer was too quick. He dodged the blade and it cut into the edge of the table, sticking there. Mr Flynn drove his fist into Baines's jaw. Julius heard the bone crack.

Baines wailed like a wounded bloodhound and staggered back. He slammed against the window, shattering the glass, and fell through it.

'Mr Baines,' called out Rapple.

'Quick,' said Julius, pushing open the door Tock had gone through. 'We have to find Clara.'

Julius took one last look at the library before following Emily and Mr Flynn after Tock. All that could be seen of Baines was his bloody hand clasping the window frame and Rapple leaning across the glass-strewn windowsill clutching his friend's collar to stop him from falling two storeys down to the snow.

Julius slammed the door behind him. Tock was gone.

'What's that smell?' said Mr Flynn.

Emily was already at the bookcase, prodding and pressing the books. 'The secret door's frough 'ere somewhere,' she said.

Julius remembered which book it was. He tilted back a small green volume and felt a click under his fingers.

The bookcase opened like a door. The stench of open graves flooded over them.

Emily put her hand over her nose. 'Smells like 'e's collecting whale offal,' she said.

Julius looked at a stone stairway, winding down into the gloom. 'Bloomingbury wanted us to go down here,' he said.

'Let's not disappoint him, then,' said Mr Flynn.

Julius, Emily and Mr Flynn climbed down. The air grew warmer the further they went.

The stairway stopped at a wooden door. 'There's water sloshing around,' said Julius. 'It's like something very large is having a bath.'

He opened the door far enough for one eye to peek through.

'What is it?' whispered Mr Flynn.

'It seems we've found where His Lordship keeps the crocodiles.'

CHAPTER 25

Monday 22nd January 1838

12:42 PM

Julius, Emily and Mr Flynn looked through the gap in the door at a pool of dark sloshing water enclosed by rusty, wrought-iron railings. The sloshing was caused by an indeterminate number of very large crocodiles. One of them raised its jaws above the water and snapped at another, which lifted its gaping jaws to snap back. A third crocodile thrashed at them with its tail. The spectacle gave the impression of a single, many-limbed and many-jawed leviathan in an ill mood.

Julius opened the door wider. They were in a large hothouse where long-armed monkeys and exotic birds whooped and squawked in branches wedged into the decorative ironwork under the glass ceiling.

Three rows of planting boxes with wire mesh covers stretched across the marble floor.

The rank odour of blood-and-bone fertiliser stung Julius's nostrils as he hurried around the crocodile enclosure. He looked at the neat lines of red buds poking through the dark soil.

'There's bleeding 'undreds of the fings,' said Emily.

'And that's what they'll grow into,' said Mr Flynn. He pointed to an aviary in the corner of the hot-house. Instead of birds it contained twenty or more soulcatchers. They flicked their tendrils through the bars when they sensed Julius coming near.

'Tock must have used cuttings from these to prop-agate the buds,' said Julius. 'We have to destroy every last one of them.'

Before anyone could reply a set of double doors opened on the right side of the crocodile enclosure. Lord Bloomingbury walked in with the humming birds flitting around him.

'And here are my favourite pets,' he said. 'It's nearly their feeding time so they're quite ravenous. I'd advise you not to lean over the railing.'

'What an interesting odour,' said Mrs Trevelyan, stepping into the hothouse behind him, 'And so warm.' She held a handkerchief to her nose. Darwin followed close behind.

'Yes, quite pungent.' said His Lordship. 'But not unpleasant.'

He held his arm out to invite her to the railing, but then he saw Julius. He took a moment more to glance at Emily and then at Mr Flynn.

'You again,' he said to Julius. 'You are trespassing in my home, and you shall hang for that as well as for your insolence.'

'Your Lordship,' said Mr Flynn. 'We came to warn you about Mr Tock. He's—'

'Silence, whoever you are,' said Lord Bloomingbury. 'How dare you address me before you are spoken to. You will warn me about nothing. You shall hang too.'

'If I may, Your Lordship,' said Mrs Trevelyan. 'I'm sure the fellow meant no offence.'

Lord Bloomingbury patted Mrs Trevelyan's hand reassuringly. 'Do not distress yourself, my dear lady,' he said. 'Let me show you my komodo dragons. I have a breeding pair, if I might be so bold.'

Mrs Trevelyan pretended to simper. 'Oh, Your Lordship,' she said, and blushed.

Lord Bloomingbury smiled rakishly and held out an arm to lead her and Darwin back through the door.

'Oi, Bloomin-bod. Wot 'ave you done wiv Clara 'iggins?' said Emily.

Lord Bloomingbury glared. 'Ah, the guttersnipe speaks,' he said. 'I advise you to hold your tongue… while you still have it.'

'You 'old yours, you poxy old git,' said Emily. 'You

wanted to feed us to the crocodiles last night, didn't you?'

'No. I had something far more imaginative in mind.'

'You were going to let the soulcatcher seed us,' said Julius. 'Along with my mother. You thought no one would know.'

'So the Higgins woman *is* your mother? I thought as much.' Lord Bloomingbury smiled briefly but then scowled. 'She lied. She told me she had no family. And now I find a gaggle of her brats whining about my ankles.'

'Your Lordship,' said Mrs Trevelyan. 'Is something amiss?'

'No, my dear lady,' he said. 'Just a minor irritation with the servants.'

'I'll give you a bleeding irritation,' said Emily.

Mr Flynn advanced towards Lord Bloomingbury, but a loud metallic screech made everyone stop.

Tock stood at the door Lord Bloomingbury had come through. He held Clara's arm with one hand and a single soulcatcher in a birdcage with the other. Clara's hands were tied in front of her and tears were streaming down her cheeks. Abigail loomed over both of them from behind.

'Your Lordship, I—' said Clara, but Tock shook her into silence.

'What are you doing here?' said Tock to Lord

Bloomingbury. 'We're not seeding until after dinner.'

'Ah, Tock,' said Lord Bloomingbury. 'Just the fellow. I was going to show Mrs Trevelyan and Mr Darwin the komodo dragons. Would you be so kind as to have your metallic friend entertain the brats and the bruiser while we're gone.'

Lord Bloomingbury smiled graciously at Mrs Trevelyan and held out his arm for her to take. 'So good of you to call,' he said to Emily over his shoulder.

Mrs Trevelyan did not take his arm. She stood to attention as if on a parade ground. 'Your Lordship,' she said, with her regiment-commanding voice. 'Kindly explain what is happening. I will not move until I receive a satisfactory explanation.'

Lord Bloomingbury was affronted for just a moment. He turned to Darwin.

'Now I see it all, Mr Darwin,' he said. 'This was no social visit, was it?'

'No, Your Lordship, I'm afraid it wasn't,' said Darwin. 'We know Tock means to seed that poor woman as a special exhibit for your bizarre collection in exchange for you hiding him and the soulcatchers. But what you don't know is that Tock intends to release hundreds of them to seed everyone in London.'

Lord Bloomingbury chuckled. 'Mr Darwin, my good fellow. What a feverish imagination you have.'

'I speak the truth, sir,' said Darwin.

'Only half of it, actually,' said Lord Bloomingbury.

'We're going to sell the soulcatchers for ten thousand pounds apiece. It will be the new fashion. Lords and Ladies of distinction will have these magnificent orchids in their parlours—the serving class will provide the hosts.'

Lord Bloomingbury appeared to grow bored with Darwin. He turned to Tock. 'Tock, my good fellow,' he said. 'Have your contrivance dispose of them all.'

He made for the door but Mrs Trevelyan gabbed his arm and pulled him back.

'I think not, Your Lordship,' she said. 'I haven't finished with you.'

'But I have finished with you, my dear lady,' said Lord Bloomingbury. 'Tock, you stupid little man, unleash the monster and have done with the lot of them. But keep the Higgins woman.'

Everything happened in a matter of seconds.

Abigail clambered towards Mrs Trevelyan.

Lord Bloomingbury lifted his arm to break her grasp. Instead he got Mrs Trevelyan's elbow square in his face.

'Aaagh,' he yelled as he fell back. His head and shoulders fell across the railing and a pair of gaping jaws rose up and snapped shut around his head. The crocodile heaved Lord Bloomingbury over the side and into the water.

Darwin pulled Mrs Trevelyan aside, just missing being bowled over by one of Abigail's claws as she slammed into the railing. Her knife claw plunged into the water after Lord Bloomingbury as another crocodile rose up and bit down on her shoulder trying to pull her in.

Mr Flynn ran forward, and with a Herculean effort, he lifted Abigail's hind legs the next couple of inches needed to tilt her over the railing. The crocodile did the rest and she disappeared in the murky water.

Julius looked around for Tock. He had pushed Darwin away and dragged Clara around to the far side of the crocodile enclosure.

'Tock,' said Darwin. 'I implore you, stop this madness now. Let the woman go.'

Abigail rose up, sending gallons of black water into the air. It cascaded over everyone like a storm wave, sweeping Mrs Trevelyan and Darwin against the wall, knocking Julius's feet from under him and sweeping Emily across the marble floor.

Two crocodiles emerged. One of them snapped its jaws around Abigail's leg and the other around her head. When she twisted to break away bolts shot from the joints on her neck. She fell against the railing, smashing it.

The combined din of the monkeys and birds calling out in alarm made the hothouse vibrate.

Emily got up and ran past Darwin and Mrs Trevelyan on one side of the enclosure and Julius tried to scramble to his feet on the other.

Tock's teeth ground together in rage as he hauled Clara up off the floor where the wave had deposited them. They were both soaked through. He jiggled the cage, violently shaking the water off the soulcatcher and held it up to Clara's face. Its dripping tendrils reached through the bars, almost touching her cheek.

'Stay back,' said Tock. His words were barely audible above the cacophony of all the animals and Abigail's thrashing to free herself from the water.

'Let Clara go,' said Julius.

Abigail was pulled below the surface again, sending another torrent across the floor.

'Let her go?' said Tock. 'I don't think so.'

Emily edged closer to Tock.

Just then one of the crocodiles rose up with Abigail's head between its jaws. Two more bolts flew out, her neck snapped and her severed head spun through the air. Everyone looked up as it crashed through the ceiling of the hothouse, sending down a shower of glass and branches. It landed on one of the planting boxes, shattering it and toppling the others beside it, sending soil and soulcatcher buds across the floor.

The birds and monkeys flew and leapt through the gaping hole in the roof and an icy wind swept in. Snow fell onto Abigail's disembodied head as it lay in the mud of the black water and scattered soil.

'Let Clara go, Tock,' said Mr Flynn. 'Just drop the cage and you can leave.'

'Can I? Can I?' said Tock. 'How kind you are. How kind.' He looked across the hothouse at the muddy heap where his buds had been growing and laughed. 'Come out my friends,' he said. 'It's time to play catch the souls.'

Julius looked behind him. A large branch had fallen against the aviary and one of the soulcatchers was trying to force its way out through the twisted bars. The others were jostling behind it in a frenzy, flicking their tendrils and trying to prise the bars apart.

Mr Flynn ran towards them, but slipped in the mud. The first soulcatcher broke through the bars and another leapt out behind it.

Julius turned to see Emily kick the caged soul-catcher from Tock's hand.

'Get back, you brat,' shouted Tock.

Clara tried to pull her arm away, but Tock gripped her tight. He clutched a clump of Emily's hair with his other hand and held her face up to his.

'I shall have your soul first,' he said. 'I shall. I shall.'

'Oh, yeah?' said Emily.

As Julius rushed to them he saw Emily's hand slip inside Tock's coat. Mrs Trevelyan and Darwin edged towards Tock as one of the crocodiles lurched out of the water and fell against the railing on the other side, flattening it completely.

Tock faltered for an instant. He looked at Emily's face closely.

'Recognise me do you?' she said. 'That's right. I'm the one in Darwin's diary.' Her hand came out from Tock's coat and she tossed the box of vials over her shoulder. Julius ran to catch it.

'Noooo,' shouted Tock, loosening his grip on Clara.

Mrs Trevelyan pulled Clara away. Darwin went to snatch Emily, but Tock pulled her out of his reach and held her over the railing.

'Get back, Darwin,' he said, and he shook Emily over the choppy black water as if she were a rag doll.

Emily punched him on the chin, dislodging his face slightly.

'Wait, wait,' said Julius. A mass of soulcatchers fanned out and scrambled towards them over Abigail's severed head and the muddy wreckage of the planting boxes.

Mr Flynn picked up a fallen branch and brandished it like a sword.

The crocodile clambered over the flattened railing and raised its long snout towards Mr Flynn.

Julius opened the wooden box. There were four vials inside. He held them up.

'Look, Tock,' he said. 'I'll swap you. Give me

Emily for these. You can escape through the wall. We'll never be able to follow you.'

'I'll have them anyway,' said Tock, 'when my friends have finished with you.'

Julius looked around. His knees went weak with desperation. Mr Flynn was trying to hold off the advancing soulcatchers on one side and a hungry crocodile on the other with just a piece of wood. In a few more seconds either the soulcatchers or the crocodile would have him.

A severed hand, which must have belonged to Lord Bloomingbury, bobbed to the surface of the water, and a crocodile's jaws snapped shut around it. Emily lashed out at Tock. He fought to keep her teetering over the edge.

Julius looked at the four delicate glass vials in his hand. Clear, green liquid bubbled like champagne inside them. There was nothing he could do. Tock had won. This was the moment before everything would fall apart. This was the moment before the soulcatchers would begin their spread across London, seeding everyone. He knew what would happen—he had seen it all. He had seen the desolation the soul-catchers would cause. The only difference was that this time Tock was going to kill Emily himself, rather than let a soulcatcher slowly steal her soul.

In his rage Julius wanted to crush the vials in his hand. He wished it could make Tock and the soulcatchers disappear and have done with it.

Then he had an idea.

'Tock,' he yelled. 'Watch this.'

He turned to the advancing soulcatchers. 'Mr Flynn, stand back,' he said.

And he threw the vials at Abigail's severed head.

It took less than a second, but to Julius it all unfolded with an unhurried beauty. The vials tumbled through the falling snow and smashed against Abigail's razor-scaled jaws. There were four tiny explosions of glass and the green liquid splashed out. As soon as it touched the wet metal it began to fizz and steam. Then, as quick as fire racing across spilt oil, it spread into a circle of hissing vapour that enveloped the mounds of mud and the advancing soulcatchers.

Mr Flynn hit the crocodile on the snout with his stick and leapt over it as if it was a stile. In the next moment the hissing vapour began to bubble and then everything dissolved and disappeared.

Julius teetered at the edge of the void looking down on a turquoise sea, far below. The planting boxes, Abigail's head, the soulcatcher, all the buds and the crocodile gracefully plummeted into it. There was just enough time to see the splashes as they hit the water before the hole closed up and all that was left was a clean marble floor with a few ribbons of vapour rising up.

Julius spun round. Tock still held Emily over the

railing. One of the crocodiles was moving towards her.

'That's it, Tock,' he said. 'It's all over.'

'No it's not,' said Tock. 'I still have one little friend left.'

Julius saw the remaining soulcatcher. The cage was on its side. The orchid looked beaten and bedraggled, but it was still alive.

Tock made to push Emily over the edge.

'No,' screamed Julius.

'You've forgotten one bleeding fing, Tock,' shouted Emily.

'Oh, yes,' said Tock. 'What is that? What? What?'

'Who'll wind you now?' said Julius. 'You're stuck here in this realm and you've haven't got a key.'

Tock loosened his grip on Emily. She slipped her hand inside his coat again. His dislodged face took on an almost comical expression of childlike indignation.

'But I don't want to wind down,' he said. 'I don't. I don't.'

Darwin lunged at Tock. He threw him aside and lifted Emily off the railing just as a crocodile surged up and snapped the air where her head had been.

Clara looped her still-tied arms around Emily's neck and held her tight. Julius's knees gave way and he knelt on the marble floor.

Tock fell against the wall and stared around him as if he could not quite believe what was happening.

'But I don't want to wind down,' he said.

Julius picked up the cage holding the last soul-catcher. Its damp tendrils flicked half-heartedly at him.

He flung it into the crocodile enclosure and watched it disappear below the black water.

Tock's expression changed into one of simmering hatred. His blue eyes glowered at Julius. He tried to straighten his face but lost his patience with it and tore it off to reveal his clockwork innards. The cogs turned as his two rows of small teeth ground against each other.

'You'll be sorry for that,' he said to Julius. 'I'll come back and make you sorry. I will. I will.' He pushed Darwin aside and looked at each of them in turn. 'You'll be sorry,' he said. Then he walked through the door and was gone.

Mr Flynn made to follow, but Julius stopped him.

'Let him go,' he said. 'He's winding down. No one can punish him more than he's being punished right now.'

'But he has my diary,' said Darwin. 'I must have it back.'

'No 'e don't,' said Emily. 'I nicked it back for you.'

She slipped out from Clara's arms and held out the dripping diary to Darwin.

Julius felt Clara's wet arms wrap around him. She held him tight as if he might try to escape. He didn't. The hummingbirds flew down and flitted around them.

'I came to ask you to tea,' said Julius, when she let him go, at last.

Clara laughed.

'Will you come home, Mama?'

'For tea?'

'No…forever.'

Clara cradled his face in her bound hands.

'That would be very nice,' she said.

CHAPTER 26

Monday 5th February 1838

2:34 PM

Two weeks later, Julius sat in a corner of the King's Library in the British Museum. He had just finished telling his story to Professor Fox and the other ten members of the Guild of Watchmakers. He told them everything, from his stealing the pocketwatch, to the time-loop he had made and his time-jump into the future.

The professor sat in an old armchair. He weighed the pocketwatch in his hand while he considered Julius's tale.

'Thank you, Julius,' he said. 'Be so kind as to fetch Mr Flynn and Emily.'

Julius found them seated at a table at the far end of the library leafing through books about orchids.

''ow did it go, 'iggins?' said Emily.

'Not very well, I don't think,' said Julius. 'They asked me to get you both.'

When Julius returned the Watchmakers ceased their whispered discussion and waited while Mr Flynn and Emily sat down.

'Well, well, well,' said Professor Fox. His steel-grey eyes moved from Julius to Emily. 'Quite an adventure. You and Emily showed great courage and ingenuity. You saved our timeline from the soulcatchers and for that we, the Guild of Watchmakers, thank you.'

'Hear, hear,' said the other Watchmakers, quietly so as not to disturb the readers in the library.

'But'—the professor's eyes rested sadly on Julius again—'you stole the pocketwatch. That cannot be forgotten. Added to that, you altered the past in this timeline, and so you have altered its present and its future—who knows what the consequences might be? The question is, can we still offer you a place with us? A Watchmaker must have the trust of his brothers. Can we trust you, Julius?'

Julius swallowed. He felt Emily's hand squeeze his.

Beneath his coat Julius clutched Harrison's diary. He had brought it with him to tell the truth about that too—that he'd had it all along.

If you tell them you stole Harrison's diary now they'll never make you a Watchmaker, Higgins

He said nothing.

The professor sighed. 'Perhaps I was too hasty in choosing you,' he said. 'You showed such promise.'

Julius felt his cheeks burn with shame.

The professor's face softened. 'The Guild of Watchmakers will consider the matter.' His reluctant tone didn't give Julius much confidence.

The professor shifted in his chair. He looked very tired, but he was trying not to show it. 'Thank you, Julius…truly,' he said. 'Whatever our decision, you have our gratitude, and our friendship.'

☙

Julius, Emily and Mr Flynn walked through the vast entrance hall of the British Museum. No one had spoken since leaving the library.

Julius felt Mr Flynn's hand on his shoulder. It lifted his spirits a little. But he felt like half a person without the pocketwatch. The thought of never holding it again left him with a feeling of loneliness he felt would stay with him for the rest of his life.

But he knew he didn't deserve to be a Watchmaker, not if he couldn't tell the truth to his friends. Harrison's diary burned his side but, still, he held it secretly to him.

He tried to turn his mind back to the bookshop. His mother and grandfather were continuing with their excruciatingly awkward politeness towards one another. Julius was partly amused by it but wondered whether it would end and they could be at ease with each other.

Mr Flynn and Mrs Trevelyan were coming to tea. Julius hoped they would help to hasten the thaw in the parlour. Clara had sent an invitation to Darwin too, but he had not replied. None of them had seen him since they had all walked out of the hothouse and across the snowy parkland to tell Abberline that Lord Bloomingbury had been eaten by his favourite pet.

'Come on, 'iggins,' said Emily. 'Let's say 'ello to Mr Tock.'

A group of boys crowded around a statue on plinth. As Julius, Emily and Mr Flynn drew nearer they could read the sign pinned up nearby.

Automaton found in Shorditch. Could the owner please make himself known to Museum staff. If not claimed within one month this automaton will become the property of the British Museum and may be auctioned to fund further building works.

Julius had read it on his way in but had been too nervous about his meeting with Professor Fox to give it much thought.

'They say there was loads of keys in 'is pockets,' said one of the boys. 'And more scattered on the ground when they found 'im.'

''e was probably trying to find a key to wind 'imself wiv,' said Emily.

The boys laughed.

Julius looked into the automaton's dead eyes. Tock's hand was reaching out as if he was about to implore a stranger for help. Even now that he could never move again he still made Julius's pulse quicken.

'Oddest thing, don't you think,' said someone. 'No one would believe us if we told them the truth about Tock. They'd haul us off to Bedlam.'

Julius turned to see Mr Darwin.

'I just did, and I got laughed at,' said Emily.

Beside Darwin stood another man. He was wearing a beekeeper's hat and veil.

Darwin glanced at the group of boys surrounding Tock. 'Let's talk outside,' he said.

Julius, Emily and Mr Flynn followed Darwin out onto the steps of the museum.

'Can't be too careful,' he said, when they gathered around him.

Julius looked at the man beside Darwin. The veil was too thick for him to discern anything under the brim of the hat.

Darwin smiled at his confusion.

'You don't recognise our old friend?' he said.

'Mr Skinner?' said Julius.

Darwin patted Skinner's shoulder. 'The very one,' he said. 'The veil is to avoid any unpleasantness. People wouldn't understand.'

'Understand wot?' said Emily.

Darwin glanced around to make sure no one was

looking. He rolled up the veil. Julius saw Skinner's gaunt face. There were dark circles around his dead, staring eyes. Withered soulcatcher stems and dried flowers hung from his mouth and tangled in his beard. It was if he was wearing a garland of dead weeds.

'His mind is completely gone, poor fellow,' said Darwin. 'But my experiment was successful. Complete, unrelenting darkness killed the soulcatcher, as I predicted it would.'

Darwin smiled uncomfortably at his companions. 'I'm glad I ran into you, as a matter of fact,' he said to Mr Flynn. 'When we parted on that dreadful day I was determined to put something else right. I've been working on my plans night and day ever since.' Darwin patted Skinner's arm. 'Mr Skinner caused quite a sensation with the museum's funding committee. I've just come from my final meeting with them: they have agreed to pay the cost of my return expedition to the Village of the Soulcatchers.'

'Why are you going back there?' said Emily.

'*We're* going back—Skinner and I,' said Darwin. 'I mean to use the darkness cure on the village children. If the soulcatchers are not too advanced in their life cycle, I am confident I can save the children—and their minds. I mean to take them away from the village to somewhere they can have new lives.'

Darwin dropped the veil and stirred up some forced jollity. 'At least that is my hope,' he said. 'Well.

We must be off. Lots to do. Lots to organise, aye, Skinner? Please give my apologies to you mother, Julius—I won't be able to come to tea.'

Darwin was about to leave when Julius stepped forward.

'Mr Darwin?' he said.

'Yes.'

'I wonder? Could I ask…'

'Yes?'

'The picture you drew of those two native children?'

'Yes?'

'Could I have it?' said Julius.

Darwin recoiled as little as if he had been struck.

Julius looked down to cover his embarrassment, but looked up again immediately.

'I know it means a lot to you, sir,' he said. 'They did save your life after all. But, you see, I'd like to have a keepsake of our adventure.'

Darwin's hand went protectively to the diary. His expression showed a battle between his reluctance to part with it on one hand and his gratitude to Julius and his friends on the other.

He pulled the diary from his pocket. It had been dried out but it still looked very tatty after all it had been through. The spine creaked when he opened it at the picture. Carefully, he tore it out. 'Here. It's yours, Julius,' he said.

When he held it up he saw the portrait and Julius both at once for the first time. Before he could look too closely, Julius reached out. He took the picture and held it to his chest.

'Thank you,' he said.

Darwin stared at Julius for a moment and then dismissed all the fanciful ideas that were forming in his mind. The similarity between the boys' faces was purely a coincidence. What other possible explanation could there be for a rational person?

He nodded a goodbye to Julius, tipped his hat to Emily and Mr Flynn, then guided Skinner down the steps.

Julius watched until they reached the bottom and were lost in the Sunday crowd. Then he held the page out to Emily. She looked at the drawing of the pretty, smiling girl and the anxious but handsome boy. The edges were crinkled and a little stained from the black water that had drenched Tock.

'Keep it,' said Julius. 'So even when you're old and grey you won't forget that once upon a time, you and I went time-travelling together.'

'Don't you worry, 'iggins,' said Emily. 'I won't never forget.'

There really was a policeman named Fredrick Abberline. He lived some years after this story takes place. He investigated the infamous Whitechapel murders in 1888.

Lord Bloomingbury is based on a Victorian eccentric named William Buckland, who kept an extensive menagerie in his house and regularly fed specimens from it to his dinner guests.

The phenomenon *orchidmania* was rampant in Victorian England. Fortunes were won and lost and unspeakable crimes committed, all in pursuit of the rarest and most exquisite orchids.

New Bethlem Hospital was a lunatic asylum, known as Bedlam for short. Consequently, the word 'bedlam' became synonymous with chaos and confusion.

Luckily, Charles Darwin's diary was not really stolen. He wrote a book based on it called *The Voyage of the Beagle*. It was published in 1839 and is still in print today.

There was an orchid hunter called George Skinner, although he collected his orchids in Guatemala, not Brazil.

Surrey Zoological Gardens was as it is described

in this book and would have been a wonder to see. There really were thylacines in captivity in London at this time.

Rapple and Baines are loosely based on the Resurrectionists Bourke and Hare. In Edinburgh, in 1828, they murdered people to sell to their bodies to medical schools for dissection—it was easier than digging up corpses.

And finally, Tock. There was an expectation among philosophers, at the time, that as machines grew more and more complex, consciousness would arise within them. The most famous example of a supposedly *conscious* automaton was the Turk, who travelled Europe and the Americas playing chess against baffled opponents including Napoleon Bonaparte. They could not understand how a machine made of cogs and wires could win every game. What they did not know was that there was a chess master hiding inside, who operated the automaton's arms.